MW01153722

A Mystery by

VICTOR METHOS

Man is the cruelest animal.

— Friedrich Nietzsche

1

Tommy Hatcher's guts tightened as he stepped out of the police cruiser. Something wasn't right. The spruce-lined field in front of him didn't look any different from the thousand other times he'd been out to McCabe's property. But something was off—a smell in the air.

Blood had a particular scent. He hadn't known that before he joined the department. He thought it was odorless. The thing it smelled most like was wet copper. Even that didn't describe it, though. The odor of human blood was unique.

He shut the door and took a few steps through the tall grass. This part of Laramie County had more cows than people. There was no one and nothing within thirty miles of where he stood, and he suddenly felt stupid for his bravado in not calling for another deputy.

A breeze blew, and the scent was unmistakable now. Like human blood, a dead human body had a distinct smell, too—nothing else like it. Animal carcasses didn't even come close. When someone smelled a dead body, they knew it was a dead body.

He pulled out his firearm, a .38, and held it low. Dispatch said a hiker who didn't want to be identified had called it in. Sometimes kids liked to pull pranks on the cops. They'd call in an injured hiker or something similar and then hide in the bushes, trying not to laugh as the deputies ran around. Tommy couldn't guess why someone would find that funny. But kids nowadays were far different from when he'd been growing up.

"Hello?" he shouted. "Anybody here? Sheriff's Department."

The breeze rustled the spruce and grass. The sky above was a deep blue with a few scattered white clouds. Perfect weather for hunting. Tommy wondered if he could knock off after this and go up to Fiddler's Gorge. Two years ago, he and his brother-in-law had landed a ten-point buck at seventy yards.

The familiarity of the memory calmed him. This was a prank. It had to be. His nose was playing tricks on him. Nothing ever happened up here besides teenagers getting drunk and having sex. McCabe was a cranky old fart and liked to call up the sheriff's department and complain about the kids. But the kids never really did much.

Tommy strolled through the grass into the trees, confident he wouldn't find anything worth looking at.

He was about to pass some spruce trees when he heard it: branches cracking and breaking. He froze. His heart raced as he scanned the line of trees. The breeze kept everything in motion, making it difficult to discern what should and shouldn't be moving. He gripped his .38 with both hands and cautiously stepped farther into the thicket of trees. He kept his eyes up, constantly scanning around him. The fear was crowding everything else out of his mind. Right on the periphery, though, he could pick up something: the odor of decay was getting stronger.

A branch snapped to his right. He spun toward it, the weapon in front of him. A shadow moved away from him, close to the ground.

"Sheriff's Department, hold it! Hold it!"

The shadow ran. Tommy knew he should run back and call it in. He shouldn't be out here in the woods chasing people down by himself.

The adrenaline was too much. He ran into the trees.

The branches whipped his face, dropping itchy needles down his collar. He braced his hand in front of him as though he were a receiver with the ball, and the linemen were closing in. His heart pounded so hard he could only hear his pulse in his ears.

He came out of the trees into a small clearing and saw the shadow. Four legs and fur. A coyote.

Tommy replaced his weapon and put his hands on his knees, hunched over, and breathed deeply, feeling as he had when he was forced to run the mile in gym class. The sweat dripped down his forehead and stung his eyes, and his legs felt on fire. But damn, if that wasn't a rush.

As he stood up, the sun in his eyes, another shadow came into view. Something larger.

He saw her.

Nausea gripped him as he stared at the body. His stomach churned and bubbled, and before he could stop it, vomit burst from his mouth.

He fell to his knees and retched onto the grass.

2

Interrogation room two was soft beige from the carpet and chairs to the elongated tabletop. Kyle Dixon sat across from the young woman and ran his finger along the edge of the table. Silence was sometimes more powerful than words. He stayed silent a long time.

The woman stared down at the table, her eyes glistening with tears. She looked like a kindergarten teacher, not a murderer. But appearance never counted for much in Dixon's estimation. What lay in the soul mattered, and this woman's soul was diseased.

"You loved your baby, didn't you, Danielle?"

She nodded. "Yes," she whispered.

"No one questions that. I got a baby, too. Four months old. Little boy. Tyson was about four months when he passed, wasn't he?"

"Thirteen weeks."

"Thirteen weeks," he said with a smile, pulling out a package of gum from his breast pocket. He unwrapped a piece and shoved it into his mouth before offering the pack to her. She took it but didn't unwrap it. "Thirteen weeks... and you loved him. I get that. I get that you didn't want him to suffer. That's why you did what you did, ain't it? You loved him so much, the thought of that little boy growin' up in this world was unbearable to a mother who loved him as much as you did."

"This world is filled with nothing but pain," she said quietly. "Darkness and pain."

"That's right. And you spared Tyson that. You didn't give darkness a chance to sink itself into him. For that, I have to commend you. It takes guts to do something like that." He paused a beat. "But how'd you do it? Did you drown him? 'Cause we found him in the bathtub."

She shook her head. Her hands were trembling, but a slight smile came over her lips. "No. He was asleep, and I took a pillow and… he never even woke up." The tears came down her cheeks. "My angel's in heaven now, and he never even woke up. I washed him after."

Dixon shifted in his seat. "Have you ever done this before? Anyone else you sent to heaven?"

She shook her head.

"I believe you," Dixon said.

"Can I go now? My girls will be coming home from school soon."

Few things surprised Dixon anymore. He felt as if after six years in homicide, he'd seen just about everything on God's green earth. But what she'd just said made him sit in stunned silence for a few moments before he could answer. "No, you can't go home just yet, Danielle." He rose, glancing at the video recorder set into the ceiling, and left the room.

Next door in the observation room, his captain Bill Jessop stood with his arms folded, staring through the one-way glass.

"Nice job," Jessop said.

"Thanks."

"Sick bitch doesn't even know she just confessed her way to a life sentence."

Dixon watched her through the glass. She had leaned back in her seat and wiped the tears away with her fingers. He couldn't shake the feeling that what she looked like on the outside was nothing like what she looked like on the inside.

"How long you been without a partner?" Jessop said.

"Three months, twelve days."

"You been keepin' count?"

Dixon shook his head, his eyes still on Danielle. "Nope."

Jessop grinned. "New hire'll be here today. Transplant from LAPD. I'm pairing you two."

"LAPD? What the hell's he doin' out here?"

Jessop shrugged. "Who cares? He's a warm body."

As Jessop left, Dixon kept his attention on Danielle. She looked calmer now, almost peaceful. The other inmates would not be kind to her. Even in a place filled with murderers and thieves, the sin of hurting a child was not forgiven lightly. Danielle's life would be one long, living nightmare from now on.

He turned away from the glass and left the room, going down the corridor to the bullpen. The bullpen was nothing more than desks pushed together based on partnerships. Dixon had sat across from an empty chair for the past three months.

The Cheyenne Police Department had a detective division, but unlike larger cities, they weren't split up into subgroups like property crimes and robbery-homicide. The detectives had all developed certain specialties over the years, and it was understood that some were homicide, some sex crimes, some property or white collar, but that any of them at any time could catch something outside their specialty. It'd never bothered Dixon much to go from a homicide to a broken car window. Cheyenne didn't have that many murders to begin with, and he liked to stay busy.

After an hour of typing up his report on Danielle and preparing a screening packet for the District Attorney's Office, he saw someone on the periphery: a man wearing a black jacket, carrying a box.

Dixon looked over. The man had jet-black hair, and sunglasses hung from his collar. The jacket was leather, and he wore jeans. The receptionist pointed the man at Dixon.

"Ethan Baudin," he said, placing the box down on the empty desk opposite. He held out his hand. Dixon shook it.

"Kyle Dixon."

Baudin sat down with a sigh and leaned back. "Looks like we're paired."

Dixon kept typing. "Looks like it."

Silence fell, and Baudin began taking things out of the box. A pen holder, folders, books that he stacked on his desk, and a photograph of a young girl and a woman. Dixon kept typing but glanced at the books. He didn't recognize any, but one was *From Freud to Jung: A Comparative Study of the Psychology of the Unconscious.* Another was *120 Days of Sodom* by the Marquis De Sade.

"So how long you been with the CPD?" Baudin said.

"Ten years. Six years homicide."

"No shit? I was told there weren't any divisions—that they might have us writing parking tickets."

"I haven't written one in eight years, so I doubt it."

Baudin rocked lightly in his chair, scanning the bullpen. "Everyone I've met has been nice so far."

"It's a good group."

Dixon finished the report and saved it. He rose, stretched his back, and took his suit coat off his chair.

"You leaving?" Baudin said, still arranging his desk.

"Yeah."

"Where you going?"

"Excuse me?"

Baudin looked up. "Sorry. Didn't mean to pry. It's only four. I thought you and me could get a beer or something."

"Can't right now. I volunteer at my parish serving food. They need me from four-thirty to six."

"Well, I'll come with ya. I could use some charity work."

Baudin rose. Dixon began walking out, and Baudin fell into step. When they reached the door, Dixon turned and said, "Listen, you seem like a nice guy, but I got my space, ya know? We'll do all the bonding, male-hugging bullshit later, but I like my space."

Baudin held up his hands as though in surrender. "I understand. Just being friendly."

"I appreciate that. But give it a little time."

Dixon was almost through the door when he heard Baudin say, "Asshole."

"Excuse me?" he said, turning around. "You say somethin' to me?"

Baudin took a step forward, staring him in the eyes. "I said you're an asshole."

A beat of silence passed.

"You got somethin' you wanna say to me?" Dixon said.

"I'm just trying to be friendly to my new partner, and he's treating me like some punk. It's fine. I get it. You're the big bad wolf, and you work alone. Me too."

Dixon chuckled. "I don't know what kind of horseshit you pulled in LAPD to land your ass in the middle of farm country, but 'round here we respect our seniors. I've been here ten years. You've been here one day. You got a problem with that, then you get your ass in Bill's office and ask for a transfer."

Dixon turned and left without waiting for a reply. He'd never been good at the partner thing, but this had to be some kind of record for getting into a pissing contest. Dixon was angry with Baudin, but he was angry with himself, too. Something about Baudin rubbed him wrong. Maybe his swagger, the fact that he was big-city homicide and probably thought nothing of these yokels he was forced to work with… could've even been his jacket. Whatever it was, Dixon thought he could've handled it better than he did.

Once out the double doors of the precinct and into the warm Wyoming air, he stopped and put his hands on his hips, glancing back at the building. Maybe an apology was in order? *No*, he thought. Partners got shuffled around all the time. They probably wouldn't be together long enough for it to matter, anyway.

He got into his black Ford truck and drove to his church.

3

When Ethan Baudin had first walked into the Cheyenne Police Department, he thought the building looked like an ugly box. Two stories with a blue and black sign that read Police Department on the south end of the building, it looked like something built fifty years ago that just hadn't decayed quite enough to be torn down.

He marched up the steps and found the detectives' division on the second floor. In Los Angeles, everything was compartmentalized into subdivisions, units, and cells. People developed specialties over years, and that brought a certain something—instinct, maybe. But the detectives also lost the freshness the rookies had. Hardened homicide detectives with a decade of murder under their belts tended to see the world a specific way, and it was almost impossible for them to see it any other.

CPD, though—this would be something new. The days, at least Baudin hoped, would be varied and interesting. No two days alike.

After Dixon had stormed out, Baudin went back to his desk and sat down. He looked at the murder board up on the far wall. A white SMART board had the names of victims written in columns with updates on the case in various cells across the board. CPD had exactly two open homicides right now. When he had left the homicide table in West Hollywood, they had had seventy-six.

"Don't be too hard on him," Jessop said as he sauntered over and leaned against Baudin's desk.

"I'm good. We all have bad days."

"His last partner, the man you replaced, was shot and killed on duty."

He was silent a moment. "Oh. I wasn't told that."

Jessop nodded, looking down at his shoes. "Why'd you come out here, Ethan? No one from LAPD applies to come out here."

"I have a daughter. Just didn't want her raised in LA. I wanted someplace quiet where everyone knows everyone else."

He grinned. "Careful what you wish for."

The first day in most new jobs consisted of meetings to go over sexual harassment policies, vacation time, retirement, and the myriad other things the department felt it needed to cover. That was all given to Baudin in a single packet, and he was told to consult the packet should he have any questions. He was also told he probably wouldn't be catching any cases today. He was put into the rotation but would have to wait until his name was called.

So he spent his entire first afternoon online reading about Cheyenne and its history. He'd done research back home, a lot of research, and spoken to a cousin who lived here. Everything seemed to indicate that it was a quiet city where not much at all happened— exactly what he'd been looking for.

When six o'clock rolled around, Baudin headed to the parking lot and found the Mustang he'd had for almost ten years. When he pulled out of the lot, a few detectives were milling around in front of the building. He waved hello, but they didn't wave back.

The cost of living was cheap enough that Baudin could afford a rambler with a fence for him and his daughter, and enough yard for a dog. He parked in the driveway and stared at the home for a minute. He'd lived in condos and apartments so long that he hadn't been sure he'd ever get into his own house. But there it was.

Baudin got out and sat on the porch for a while, staring at the cars passing by. Children played at one of the houses, and their squeals echoed around the neighborhood. A neighbor across the street, a woman in flood pants and a tank top, waved to him, and he smiled and waved back.

The bus dropped his daughter off a few minutes later not half a block from his house. She stared at the sidewalk as she walked, her black hair falling forward, and danced with the motion of her awkward teenage gait.

"How was the first day?" he said.

"Fine," she mumbled and went inside.

For a moment, he didn't move. He looked over at the school bus and watched as it pulled away before he rose and went inside.

The house was clean. He considered himself a minimalist and tried not to have clutter because he thought the external world a person saw every day influenced the internal. Messy homes would lead to messy thinking.

"Did you make any friends, Heather?" he said as he sat at the dining table.

She pulled out a half gallon of almond milk and poured a glass before searching the cupboards for snacks. "Not really. The kids here are weird."

"How?"

"I don't know. They all know each other from church or something."

"You wanna go to church?" he said, taking out a package of cigarettes and lighting one.

"No."

"Let me tell you something, Heather, if someone tells you they know the secrets of the universe and all it takes is sacrifice, you run the other way. 'Cause you can bet your ass that sacrifice will be yours, not theirs."

She found some Oreos and put a few on a plate. Carefully, she took out each cookie and spread them on the plate evenly. Seeing her like this, in the kitchen, felt like a weight bearing down on Baudin's chest. An ache he neither acknowledged nor denied.

"Molly's coming over to babysit tonight," he said, pulling an ashtray close.

"Who's Molly?"

"My cousin. You've met her. You were just young."

"Why's she coming to babysit?"

He tapped the ash off his cigarette and took only one more drag, knowing how much it annoyed Heather when he smoked in front of her. "I have to go out for a minute. Won't be long." He rose and kissed her forehead. "I love you, baby."

As he was leaving, she said, "Dad?"

"Yeah?"

"I don't like it here. Are we ever gonna go back home?"

He hesitated. "This is our home now, baby. For better or worse."

When night had fallen, Baudin dressed in jeans and a tank top, exposing the myriad tattoos that sleeved his arms. He tucked his badge away in his pocket and put on the ankle holster with its Smith & Wesson before pulling the jeans over.

Molly pulled up just then and limped across the yard to the front door. He answered before she rang the doorbell.

"What's wrong?" Baudin asked.

"Damn gout," she said, brushing past him and sitting down on the couch. "They call it rich man's disease, but I got it without the riches."

"You sure you okay to do this?"

She waved him off. "Fine. Just get me the clicker."

He handed her the remote to the television. "She's watching TV in her room. I shouldn't be more than a couple of hours. Make sure she does her homework."

"Where you goin'?"

"To make some friends."

She guffawed. "Shit. Since when do you need friends?"

"Since I moved to a new city and the only person I know is my crippled-ass cousin."

She cackled and looked at him. "Stay outta trouble, Ethan. This ain't LA. The people in charge here ain't scared of the common folk like over there."

"I will. Thanks for doing this."

The night air was warm and stuck to the skin. He pulled out his cigarettes again and lit a fresh one, letting it dangle in his mouth as he got into his Mustang and pulled away.

The city was small but spread out to make it appear larger than it was. Like any other city, night was when the real inhabitants came out. The ones who were all smiles and goodness when the sun was out but who changed when darkness came.

Some of the research he'd done at the precinct was related to the prostitutes in Cheyenne. Going on to some local forums, he had discovered that the best place to find them was a Motel 6 intersection in the heart of the city.

Up until the 1960s, prostitution had been legal in Cheyenne. The locals were long-haul truckers, ranchers, miners, and laborers, with few women residing there back then. The powers that be had decided the men needed their release, and prostitutes from all over had flooded the city only to find the population was, by and large, broke. Slowly, the prostitutes left, and eventually the practice was technically outlawed, though Baudin doubted the law was ever enforced.

Back in Los Angeles, he'd had a network of contacts. The three most valuable types were crime reporters, drug dealers, and prostitutes. The prostitutes were the best of the three. They were always on the streets with their ears to the ground, always knew what was going on in their neighborhoods.

The Motel 6 looked shabby and rundown. Up the street was a group of half a dozen women. A few were wearing little more than lingerie. He put his hands in his pockets and approached them.

"You lookin' for company?" one of them said as he walked by.

He stopped and looked them over. Some were grizzled veterans with vacant eyes, and some were fresh out of the box, looking as though they'd just woken up in a dream but didn't know they were dreaming. A girl in white clothing leaned against a lamppost, her long blond hair past her shoulders, her arms folded. A little gold purse dangled from her fingers.

Baudin brushed past the others and went to her. She watched him with blue eyes, a blue he could clearly see in the dim light of the street lamp.

"Hi," he said.

"Hi."

"Can I buy you a drink?"

She stared at him a moment. "Whether we're fuckin' or drinkin', it'll cost you the same."

He grinned. "There someplace close we can go?"

She hesitated before looking over at someone, a woman sitting in a car. "Down here."

They strolled along the sidewalk to a bar with a neon sign out front. She didn't speak a word to him until they were inside and sitting down.

The bar was barely lit, and the bang of pool balls echoed behind them. Baudin ordered two beers, and the bartender set them down over napkins. He took an ice-cold sip that made his teeth hurt.

"So you just looking for a party?" she asked.

He lit a cigarette, offered her one, and lit that as well. "No, not exactly. I'm a cop. I'm surprised you didn't make me."

"Everyone's odd here, honey. That don't mean nothin'." She exhaled a puff of smoke through her nostrils. "I ain't broke no laws."

"Even if you had, that's not what I'm interested in."

"What you interested in, then?"

He inhaled the smoke softly, letting the tobacco flavor whirl around in his mouth. He'd been trying to quit for the better part of six months, but when he moved out here, he'd quietly started again and didn't know why. "Information, from time to time."

"What kind?"

"Nothin' that'll get you in trouble. There'll be cases where I'll need to know what's being said on the street."

"The street, huh?" she said with a grin. "You talk like you on a TV show. You don't talk like no cop from around here. And I know all the cops around here. They my best customers."

"I bet." He took a long drink of beer then went back to his cigarette. "I'm from LA."

"California?"

"Yeah."

"I been tryin' to get to California for a long time. Leave this place and just go somewhere where the sun don't stop shinin'."

"Whatever problems you got here, they'll follow you there, too. Movin' don't solve 'em."

"Then why'd you move?"

"This ain't about me. You interested?"

"I don't know. What do I get for what's bein' said on the street?"

"I'll help you out whenever you call me. Nothing too serious. You get busted dealing dope, you're on your own. But solicitation, possessing pot, DUIs, violent johns, things like that, you call me."

She nodded, holding the cigarette up and staring at the tip. "Had this trick once that burned me with these. Burned me all up and down my back. He was just laughin' like it weren't nothin'."

"Now that's exactly the type of thing you call me for. I'll make sure he never does something like that again. What's your name?"

"Candi."

"Your real name."

"That is my real name. Candi-Jean Carlson."

"Candi-Jean. I like that." He held out his hand, leaving the cigarette between his lips. "Ethan Baudin. Pleasure."

She shook, a smile on her face. "No, you definitely ain't like the cops out here."

"No, I definitely am not."

4

The church had nearly emptied. Kyle Dixon chatted with a few other volunteers. After serving the food, he'd decided to stay and help them clean up. The homeless in Cheyenne weren't numerous, but they were needy. The city had no shelters since the Comea House closed, or food kitchens, so the local churches were the only way they got fed.

Dixon took off his apron and walked back to the altar. He knelt, made the sign of the cross, and prayed for his family and friends and the homeless who froze in the winter and starved in the summer. When he was through, he rose and left the church without looking back.

About halfway to his neighborhood he had to flip on his headlights. His home sat in the middle of a partially finished development. The developer had run out of money and was in bankruptcy proceedings.

He parked in the garage and got out. A child's bike, still in the box, leaned against the wall. He'd bought it last Christmas. His wife, Hillary, had told him they shouldn't buy anything for the baby at only four months, but he couldn't help it. The bike spoke to him when he saw it.

Inside, he was met by the smell of cooking meat. He kicked off his shoes and threw his jacket over the back of one of the chairs at the dining table. Hillary had a pot and two pans going on the stove. He quietly came up behind her and slipped his arms around her waist. Her neck smelled like lotion, something fruity, and he kissed it and nibbled on her ear.

"Oh, mister, please stop. My husband will be home soon."

"Well, he's got a fight on his hands then, 'cause I ain't lettin' go."

She turned, wrapping her arms around his neck. "How was work?"

"Good, I guess," he said, kissing her then pulling away and going to the fridge. "Got a new partner."

She turned back to the food. "Yeah? Who?"

"Ethan something. He used to be LAPD, and now he's out here."

"Oh, that sounds interesting. You two hit it off?"

He popped the top on an apple juice and took a long pull. "More or less. Where is he?"

"He's sleeping. Don't wake him up."

"I just wanna see him."

Dixon rounded a corner and crossed the hallway. He came to a bedroom and poked his head in. His son, Randy, was wrapped up tight and lying on his back in a crib. Dixon had built the crib from scratch. It had taken him three months to do it because he didn't want any imperfections. He enjoyed the fact that his boy slept in something made with his own two hands.

He crossed the room and peered down at his boy, with his cherubic face—chubby cheeks and little nose. Dixon kissed his own finger and then placed it on the boy's forehead before leaving the room.

Hillary was setting the table when he got back to the kitchen. He leaned against the wall and watched her. She hadn't changed much since college. Same figure, similar clothes, but her hairstyle had completely changed. He watched her until she noticed and smiled.

"Dinner's ready."

He kissed her again and sat down at the table. As he sat, he caught a reflection of himself in the balcony's sliding glass doors. Though she looked the same, he looked older and tired. She sat across from him and served the food.

"Ain't we forgettin' something?" he said.

"What?"

"Grace."

"Oh," she said with a grin. "Yeah."

They both bowed their heads, and Dixon said a quick prayer thanking the Lord for the food. He then took up his fork and dug into the Salisbury steak with mashed potatoes.

"What'd you do today?" he said.

"Nothing much. Went shopping with Brianne, cleaned the house… nothing worth talking about. Do you have any new cases?"

He shook his head and lifted a piece of steak to his lips. "Not really. Been slow the past couple of weeks."

"That must be nice."

He chewed a moment before saying, "Well, it has—"

The home phone cut him off. He looked over at it, waiting to see if it would ring again. When it did, he laid his silverware and napkin on the table and rose. The phone—which they only had because their alarm system, installed by the only company that served the area, required a home phone—never rang. He answered.

"Hello?"

Silence on the other end.

Dixon waited a moment. "I can hear you breathing. Just tell me what you want... hello? Hello? I can hear your damn breathing."

The line clicked. He pushed star six nine, but the digital voice said that the last incoming call was a blocked number.

"Third time this week," he said.

Hillary was staring down at her plate. He sat back down and watched her a moment.

"You okay?" he said.

"Yeah. Yeah, it's just weird."

"Just some pervert hoping you'll answer. If we could get any other alarm company out here, I'd toss that damn phone. Maybe just don't answer it anymore. No one we wanna talk to calls on that line anyway."

She nodded, sipping her water, not meeting his eyes.

5

In the morning, Dixon rolled over and put his arm around his wife. She was wearing a see-through nightie, and her breasts were plump with pink nipples. He placed his hand over one and kissed her neck. She smiled but kept her eyes closed. He pushed his hips against her backside and ground into her... and the baby started crying.

His head drooped against her shoulder, and he said, "Any way we can ignore that for, like, five minutes?"

"Not a chance," she said, throwing off the covers.

He pulled away and rolled onto his back. "Didn't think so."

A painting of Christ on the cross hung on the wall over their bed. He didn't remember where he'd got it, a garage sale or swap meet, something like that, but he remembered thinking that Christ's face looked... it wasn't pained, not really; it was more apathetic. As though he'd accepted that this was his fate.

Dixon swung his feet over the bed and rose to shower. Cold showers prevented him from lingering when he was in a hurry. When he was finished, he dressed in slacks and a sports coat and polished his wedding ring with a handkerchief before slipping it back on.

Breakfast was toast and coffee and a quick kiss for Hillary and Randy. He got all the way to the door before he turned back and picked up his boy. He held the infant against his chest and rocked him, laying kisses on his bald head. He handed him back to Hillary and then reluctantly left the house.

His house was his castle, his refuge from the world and the job. He'd seen a lot of cops eaten up by the job, and he guessed it was because they didn't have a place like this where the outside world couldn't penetrate. People needed a place to feel as if the rest of the world didn't exist.

The drive to the precinct was quick, and he only got to listen to a few songs. He parked in the officer parking in back and stepped out. A few uniforms lingered by the door, eating bagels and sipping coffee out of Styrofoam cups. He nodded hello and went inside.

Rhonda, the receptionist for the detective's division, was eating a slice of pie and reading a trashy celebrity gossip website.

"When's the next barbeque?" she asked without looking up.

"Any time you and the boys want to come over, just ask. Give Hillary a call and set it up. Oh, hey, did Jonathan Fillion call? He's that DV case, said his wife beat him up."

"Nope."

"If he calls for me, just set up a time for him to come in. He refused to fill out a witness statement last time, and I want him recorded."

"Will do."

Dixon crossed the bullpen to his own desk. Baudin was already seated across from him, his face buried in a book. Dixon took off his sports coat and slung it on the back of his chair before sitting down. He hit the power button on his computer. It would take another five minutes to boot up.

The five minutes passed without a word between them. The only sound Baudin made was flipping pages, and Dixon tried not to look at him but couldn't help it. He had this intense look of concentration on his face, and it didn't seem that he'd even notice if Dixon spoke directly to him.

Dixon rose. "Coffee?"

"No, thank you," Baudin said softly.

The coffee maker was in the break room, and getting coffee gave Dixon a chance to be alone. He poured a cup, leaned against the fridge, and took a couple of sips before going back to his desk. Baudin still had his face buried in the book. Dixon glanced at the title: *The Poetry of Baudelaire*.

"Kyle, Ethan, get your asses in my office," Jessop bellowed through his open door.

The men glanced at each other and stood.

Jessop's bland and windowless office didn't have any photos up anywhere, and the only decoration was a fake plant in the corner. Jessop sat behind the old gray desk, and a man in a gray suit with cowboy boots sat on the couch against the wall, a white Stetson on the cushion next to him. He seemed preoccupied with a toothpick that was darting in and out of his mouth.

"You two caught a case the sheriff's handing off to us. I want you to get out there. We got forensics and the sheriff's people on the scene. They haven't removed the body yet."

"What is it?" Dixon said, sitting down.

"Young female, about twenty or so. Cut up pretty bad. That's all I know."

Dixon looked at Baudin, who seemed focused on a large nick on Jessop's desk.

"I want this handled delicately," Jessop said. "Work it straight and clean. The chief himself offered to take this from the sheriff's office. They don't have the experience with homicides that we do. So don't shit all over it."

Dixon was quiet a moment. Jessop had never called him into the office to hand him a case. This was a show for the man on the couch. Dixon looked at him. The toothpick was now hanging from his lip as he stared at the two detectives.

Dixon rose. "Where's the body?"

The long drive took them through vacant desert. Baudin drove, and Dixon relaxed in the leather seat. Hanging from the rearview mirror was a colorful snake, wood with red, white, green and black paint.

"What's that?" Dixon asked.

"Spirit snake. The Navajo think we all have a snake in the spirit world, and if we connect to it, it's good luck."

"You believe that?"

"No. No such thing as luck."

A long silence followed. Baudin didn't turn on the stereo, and Dixon didn't attempt to, either. He kept his eyes out the passenger window, on the mounds of dry dirt and tumbleweeds, the bushes and trees that looked as if they'd survived a fire.

"Who do you think that guy was in Jessop's office?" Baudin said.

"I don't know. Maybe someone from the sheriff's office."

"He ever done that before? Bring in a stranger and handed a sheriff's case to you?"

Dixon shook his head. "Not really. The sheriff sends us the more complex cases 'cause we got better resources, but I ain't never seen that guy before." He looked at Baudin, who had the same gaze of concentration he'd had in Jessop's office. "I ask you somethin'? Why here? Why'd you move from LA to Cheyenne?"

"I thought you needed your space and didn't want to get to know me."

Dixon was silent. "Yeah, well, who says I do? I'm just curious."

Baudin grinned. "Maybe I just like how nice and welcoming everybody is."

They didn't speak again until they got to a fence. Dixon got out and pushed the call button for the intercom on the gate. A surly male voice said, "Who is it?"

"This is Detective Kyle Dixon with the Cheyenne PD."

The man sighed. "There ain't enough of you up here already? You gotta bring more?"

"The quicker we get in, the quicker we get out, sir."

The man paused. "Fine."

The gate clicked open with a groan of metal. Dixon pushed it open all the way, allowing Baudin to pull the car through. The property was at least an hour's drive from the nearest gas station and forty minutes from any other houses. This wasn't a place people moved to when they wanted strangers wandering on their land.

Dixon got back in the car, and they took a paved road up a winding hill. At the top of the hill stood a ranch house and a barn, and several fences penned in dogs and livestock. A man in a black Navy cap stood with a bloodhound by his legs. His clothes were dirty, as was the beard that came down past his neck.

"You Brett McCabe?" Dixon asked.

"Your friends are down that trail about fifteen minutes. Then you take the first dirt road you see to the end. You'll have to walk up a ways. Ain't no roads past that."

"We'll be fine. Thank you for your help."

The man grunted and turned around, the dog following.

The dirt trail looped around the property. Massive trees and fields of golden weeds dotted the landscape. A green shed, probably a watershed, stood out from the fields like paint on canvas. Just past that was another dirt road.

"Always wanted me a place like this," Dixon said. "Place to raise a family and have the rest of the world leave you the hell alone."

"It'll always find you, even in the boonies. That's why we're here."

The road ended after a quarter of a mile, and on a far hill they saw two sheriff's cruisers and a van with a logo Dixon couldn't make out on the side. He glanced at Baudin, who tapped the snake on the rearview as he got out of the car.

6

The house was spotless. Hillary Dixon took a lot of things out on housecleaning. Whenever she felt stressed and anxious, cleaning was what she turned to.

Randy had slept most of the morning, only waking up once to feed and then lying quietly in his crib, staring at his mobile. He wasn't a fussy child and didn't require the effort Hillary had seen other children need.

After a shower, she leaned against the counter in the kitchen and sipped chamomile tea, staring blankly at the clean linoleum floors. The only thing on the agenda for the day was to pick up formula and batteries for the remote. Though they lived on only one income, in a place like Cheyenne, a steady paycheck and government health insurance was enough, and they didn't worry about making ends meet. Every other year they got to take a real vacation, and once a week they got to eat out at a decent restaurant. It was more than Hillary had had growing up.

The teacup was at her lips when she heard a knock at the door. She put the cup down on the counter and crossed the kitchen to the front room. Looking out the peephole, her heart dropped. She didn't move for a moment and then pulled away and put her back against the door, losing her breath to the panic that grabbed her.

"I know you're home," a male voice said through the door. "I saw your car in the garage."

She closed her eyes, trying to steady her heartbeat. In a flash of resolute anger, she turned and opened the door.

The man was lean and handsome, with sandy hair. He smiled.

"It's good to see you," he said.

"I told you never to come here. And you can't call and hang up anymore," Hillary said, the door held in front of her like a shield.

"You don't answer your cell when I call. You don't have to see me if you don't want to. It's a free country. But he's my son. I have rights."

"We agreed that—"

"We didn't agree on anything," he interrupted. "You told me how it was gonna be, and I said yes to make you happy." He gently pushed open the door and stepped inside far enough to lean against the doorframe. "Are you happy?"

"Yes."

"Bullshit. You look me in the eyes and tell me you love him. You look at me right now and tell me that, and I'll leave and never come back."

"I love him," she blurted out but couldn't meet his eyes.

"I call bullshit again."

She sighed and looked down, noticing for the first time that her hands were trembling. "What do you want from me, Chris?"

"I want to spend time with you. With him. I don't want him growing up not knowing who his real father is." A car passed by on the street, and he looked back at it. "I know I probably can't be with you. But I can be close to you."

Her eyes widened. "What are you talking about?"

"I rented an apartment in the duplex across the street."

She shook her head. "You couldn't be that stupid."

"Why am I stupid? Because I want to see my only child and the love of my life?"

"He'll kill us both."

"Fuck him. You told me yourself he doesn't talk to you anymore, that it feels like you guys are roommates. Just leave him."

"Get out."

"Hillary, please. I just want—"

"I said get out," she hissed.

He hesitated, running his tongue along his lower lip, and then stepped out. She shut the door, leaned against it, and slid to the floor, the warmth of tears flowing down her cheeks as she wept.

7

Dixon opened the sunglasses case he carried in his breast pocket and slipped on his crimson-tinted glasses. Baudin squinted from the morning sun, his hands on his hips as he watched the scene in front of the two sheriff's office's cars.

"Shit," Dixon said. "You seein' what I'm seein'?"

"I am," Baudin said.

"Shit."

The grass was soft underfoot, but the heat was pronounced. Dixon knew that if he was out in the sun for more than ten minutes, he'd be sweating, and he hated sweating in a suit. He took off the coat and tossed it onto the passenger seat before loosening his tie. His Cheyenne PD detective's badge was clipped to his belt, and he noticed that Baudin wore his on a thin chain around his neck—not a lanyard but an actual chain.

Dixon was five or six paces ahead when he noticed Baudin hadn't moved.

"You comin'?"

Baudin exhaled and set off through the grass. Dixon was just ahead of him, his eyes on the scene up the hill.

The climb was grueling in the heat, and within a minute Dixon felt a trickle of sweat on his head. The drop that rolled down his scalp and over his neck gave him a dull, sick feeling.

When they reached the top of the hill, they saw that the squad cars had taken a dirt trail on the other side of the hill that wasn't visible from where they were. Dixon swore silently at himself. He should have insisted they drive around first and find how the sheriffs had driven up the hill.

Two sheriff's deputies and a forensic tech stood in the shadow of the thing they were analyzing. Between and a little behind them was a light tan wooden cross. Eight feet high and probably six feet across, a young woman hung from it with massive nails sticking out of her hands and feet.

"Ho-leey shit," Dixon mumbled.

The woman was nude, her flesh already a putrefied off-green. Her eyes had sunk back into her head, which leaned to the side as if the neck were nothing more than melted rubber.

Her stomach had been cut open, and part of her intestines hung down, swaying lightly in the breeze. The rest was flopped on the ground in front of her. Dixon could see the vacant stare of her green eyes from where he stood, as if she weren't dead but hadn't noticed the men around her.

She'd been wounded several times—vicious attacks that took flesh with them. Her breasts were completely gone, leaving ragged, gaping wounds in their place. Several fingers and toes were missing, as were her ears. Hanging out of the wound in her belly was a blackened organ he didn't recognize. Dixon wondered whether that was how organs really looked, or if rotting exposed to the air made organs look like that.

A sheriff's deputy walked up, tipping his hat back with his thumb. "Detective."

"What is this, Caleb?"

He looked up at the body. "Hell if I know. But she been out here a while. You see 'em things in her wounds? In the breasts and such? Them's mushrooms. She been out here so long mushrooms is growin' all inside her body."

Baudin went to stand within a foot of the body and stood gazing at it.

"Who called it in?" Dixon said.

"Anonymous. Some hitchhiker who said he didn't want no part of testifyin' or any of that. Just said there was a body up here and to come have a look-see."

Dixon and the deputy slowly walked up to the cross. Dixon had a vision of his Savior just then, hanging dead on a cross in Golgotha. He pushed the thought away, instead focusing on Baudin, who stood at the body's feet, staring up at her privates.

"The genitals are missing," Baudin said.

The forensic tech, a man in a blue jumpsuit and plastic gloves, crouching down over the organs, said, "Might be in this here," pointing with his chin to the mound of organ and tissue oozing at the foot of the cross.

"What else is missing?" Baudin asked.

"Won't know that until the autopsy." The tech rose and mopped the sweat off his brow with the back of his arm. "Body out in the elements for even a day compromises the evidence. This thing been out here for weeks. Don't think I can pull much from it."

"It's not a *thing*," Baudin said softly.

The tech didn't reply. He turned to the deputy and said, "That's it for me. Ben was already out here and took all the measurements and photos. We'll have everything processed and ready in a day or so, Deputy."

"Don't tell me. This is Cheyenne PD now."

Dixon said, "What you know about that, Caleb? Why they bring us in? You got murder people, same as us."

"Beyond my pay grade, Detective." He looked up once more at the body. "But I sure as shit am glad they did." He turned. "Coroner's people will be out shortly."

Dixon stood a long time. The body no longer looked human, as if it had never been human. His uncle had told him something once about skinning and cleaning a deer, and the line kept running through his head: *Turn her inside out.*

Baudin snapped some photos of his own on an iPhone. Then he walked back about ten paces, taking in the entire scene.

"He's an amateur," Baudin said.

"What makes you say that?"

"Look at the hands. The body's weight is making the nails rip through the palms, and the hands are almost loose. You don't crucify people by nailing their hands. You have to nail into the wrists. If he'd done it more than once, he'd know that. Some of the paintings of Jesus show him crucified through the hands. If he was a real person who was crucified, they would've showed wounds in the wrists."

"Christ was a real person."

"You there to see him?"

The two men glared at each other a moment before Baudin looked back at the body. "But he's learning. The next one'll be much cleaner."

Dixon ran his eyes over the mutilated body. Now that it'd been pointed out to him, he could clearly see the gaping red hole where her genitals should have been.

"You ever seen anything like this?" Dixon said.

Baudin was quiet before saying, "No."

8

Several hours passed before the crime scene was fully processed. The forensic techs had done a decent job, but Baudin insisted he and Dixon process as much as they could themselves. They walked the perimeter, analyzed blood trajectory based on droplets on the ground, and searched the surrounding area for any additional evidence. The one thing they could say for certain was that she was alive before she was crucified. The hands and feet had large bruises in the centers where the nails had gone through. She had to have been alive for bruising to occur. Someone wanted her to suffer before she died.

Dixon had pit stains and a ring of sweat around his collar. He wished he'd brought a bottle of water with him.

The coroner's people didn't get there until after lunchtime. By then, Baudin and Dixon were sitting in the car with the air conditioner running. Not a single word was exchanged, not until Baudin rolled his window down to smoke.

"That's a disgusting habit," Dixon said.

"We all got 'em."

"My dad died of lung cancer. Fifty-eight years old. Them last few years he was coughing up blood every fifteen minutes."

"Did he stop smoking?"

Dixon sat quietly. "No."

Two assistants and the coroner himself were going to take care of the body. The coroner, a man named Gil Rothfield, had just pulled up. He walked over and knocked on Dixon's window.

"Dude creeps me out," Dixon said.

"Why?"

"Wait 'til you meet him."

They got out of the car, which they'd driven up the hill to where the deputies had parked, and followed the coroner.

Gil whistled through his teeth when he saw the body. "Hot damn. They did a number on her, didn't they?"

Baudin said, "Anything similar to this come through the past few years? Cutting off the breasts and genitals specifically?"

He shook his head and spit a glob of green and brown on the grass. "No, I'd remember somethin' like this. Most of the killin's we get are suicides. Shotguns under the chin, mostly. Had this one where the damn fool put it to the side of his head and blew half his face off but lived. And he got to walk around lookin' like hamburger meat. Then he finished it off with pills."

Baudin watched while Gil ordered his two assistants around. "You a pathologist?" Baudin asked.

"Nope. I was a family doc. Elected coroner in 1989 and ain't lost an election since."

The assistants brought out a ladder from the back of their van. Dixon thought it'd be better to lay the cross down, as the body could fall apart, but Gil did as he pleased. One of the men climbed the ladder and looked the body over. The other assistant grabbed the body's legs as the one on the ladder pulled the hands off the nails.

They lowered the body, rigid as plaster, into a black zippered bag lying on a plastic board. They tucked the feet in first and then pulled the rest of the body inside. Dixon watched them pull the zipper all the way to the top, and the girl wasn't visible anymore.

"How long for the autopsy results?" Baudin asked.

"Six weeks, mostly."

"You're shitting me."

"You want me to work faster, get me a faster lab. Otherwise you gots to wait six weeks."

Dixon could see Baudin's face flushing red, so he stepped in and said, "How 'bout just a preliminary report, Gil?"

"Oh, that won't be no trouble. Two days, tops."

"Can you get one of the dentists in there today so we can ID her?"

"Will do."

Dixon glanced at Baudin, who looked away, back at the cross that was casting a shadow across the black bag.

The drive back felt longer than the drive out. Dixon stared at the emptiness of the passing landscape and decided it could've been any desolate planet. Maybe Mars—wouldn't have looked any different: only rock and dirt for as far as he could see.

"You hungry?" Baudin asked.

"I could eat."

There was a diner at the next exit, a dirty-looking place Dixon had never been to but had seen several times while driving by. Baudin pulled in and parked up front. They got out, and Dixon opened the diner's door for him.

The hostess was an older woman and the only person in the place other than the cook. Soft country music was playing. They sat at a table by the window. Dixon looked at a menu, which consisted of sandwiches and grilled meats, and decided the safest bet would be a turkey sandwich with fries. There was no way to screw that up.

He looked at Baudin, who only glanced at the menu and then set it down. He was staring out at the freeway, rubbing his hands together. Dixon ran his eyes down the tattoos on Baudin's arms. One was of a samurai with a skeleton face. Another was an American soldier bent in prayer, empty boots next to him.

"Were you in the service?" Dixon asked.

He nodded. "Infantry in the second Iraq war."

"Iraqi Freedom, right?"

He scoffed. "That war didn't have anything to do with freedom."

"Sure it did. We were attacked."

"Not by Iraq. Besides, we knew about it."

"About what?"

The waitress, who was also the hostess, came by and asked for drink orders. Baudin ordered a coffee, and Dixon asked for a Sprite.

"September eleventh," Baudin said when the waitress left. "We knew about it."

Dixon was quiet. "Shit on me, you are a damn truther, aren't you?"

"Call it what you want," he said, pulling out a package of cigarettes. He set one between his lips without lighting it. "Just before the eleventh, there was an enormous amount of put options placed on American and United Airlines stocks. The put option gives the owner the ability to sell at a predetermined price. Prices fall after an attack like that, then the owner sells for the much higher price they got before the attacks. Traders knew it was going to happen. Even *The Journal of Business* said the volume was so high and unusual that the only conclusion is that traders had knowledge of the attacks before they happened. And not just the airlines—the insurance companies and banks in the World Trade Center all had jumps in put options."

"That don't prove the government had anything to do with it."

He leaned back in his seat. "When the attacks happened, what's the first thing our government did?"

"I don't know. Close down the airports?"

Baudin shook his head, replacing the cigarette in the package. "No, man. They rounded up the Bin Laden family and gave them passage back to Saudi Arabia on military planes."

"So you're telling me our government killed thousands of people, committed one of the worst atrocities in history, protected the people that did it, and nobody knows about it?"

"I wouldn't go so far as to say our government did it. But clearly they knew about it, and a lot of people in the investment banks made a lot of money from it." He turned the package in his hand. "Covered up, man. That's what they do best."

"There's a flaw in your logic, though," Dixon said, pointing his finger. "The government is so inept that they can't keep it a secret that the president got a blow job in the middle of the night. No way they could hide something this big."

"Maybe, maybe not."

Dixon shook his head. "You were a soldier. You're supposed to defend this country, not accuse us of being terrorists."

"We're all terrorists, Kyle. Some people just hide it better than others."

The waitress came back with the drinks and set them down hard enough that some spilled onto the table. She took a green notepad from her apron and said, "What'll y'all have?"

Dixon ordered the turkey sandwich with fries, and Baudin ordered a salad.

When the waitress left, Dixon debated not saying anything. He thought maybe he wouldn't work this case with Baudin. He could ask Jessop for a new partner. He felt that he had enough credibility to get his request granted.

"She was put up there for us," Baudin said, his eyes gazing out the window. "She was put up there to die for us."

"How do you figure?"

"That was a show. The whole thing. It was meant to shock us."

He nodded, taking a sip of his Sprite. "Well, consider me shocked."

"There's something he doesn't want us to see. Something he wants attention drawn away from."

"Like what?"

"I don't know."

Dixon hesitated. "You deal with this type of thing much?"

He shook his head. "No. I think we have what's called a sexual sadist. They're really rare. The rarest type of criminal. They have a mis-wiring in their brains where sex, torture, and death are all the same thing. The mating instinct and the aggression instinct are merged. Even among serial killers, they're rare."

"You can tell that from what we saw?"

"Sexual sadists don't kill. They torture, and the vics just die during the torture. They don't want them dead. The dead don't scream."

Dixon inhaled through his nose and leaned back in the seat, tapping a finger against the table a long time. "I'm not sure this is gonna work."

"What's that, now?" he said, his eyes fixed on Dixon.

"This. Me and you."

The waitress brought over the food. The sandwich looked greasy, sopping with runny mayonnaise.

"You want another partner, just say the word."

Dixon shook his head. "It's not you, necessarily. I think I work better alone."

Baudin shrugged, picking up the fork. "Do whatever you think is right. But I want this case."

"You kiddin' me? A body that's been out there for weeks? There isn't gonna be a collar on this. But you wanna spin your wheels, be my guest. I want cases I can clear off the board."

Baudin stabbed at some lettuce and shoved it into his mouth. He chewed a while and said, "That girl went through more pain than you or I can even imagine."

Dixon watched the man eat before pushing the greasy sandwich away and staring out the window.

9

As he walked back into the precinct, Dixon watched Baudin stop on the steps and answer his cell phone. Dixon had seen enough craziness. He didn't want another partner so soon and regretted not telling Jessop. He'd figured the department wouldn't hire someone so quickly and hadn't thought he had anything to worry about.

When he got to his desk, Jessop shouted out his door, "Kyle, get in here."

As he rose, he wished Jessop would learn to use the damn intercom on their phones. "What is it?" he asked at the door.

"Chief wants to see you. You and Ethan."

" 'Chief' as in our chief?"

"Yes, dipshit, the chief of police. Get over there and see him."

He hesitated. "What's he want?"

"How the hell should I know? But he signs my paychecks, so get your ass over there."

Dixon folded his arms. "I wanted to talk to you about Ethan."

"Later. Go see the chief first."

He nodded. "Right."

As he turned, he saw Baudin hurry over to his desk and go to his computer. He typed something into Google, and Dixon could see the search results. It was a search for crucifixion symbolism in murders.

"This what they do in LA?" Dixon said, sitting down across from him. "Google how to solve killings?"

"Google's the best friend a detective ever had. If I'm right and that girl was posed for us, he's communicating as much as if he'd written a letter. We need to know the language he's speaking."

"See, that's dangerous thinking. Sometimes a cigar is just a cigar, right? You may think we're just simple country folk, but we got a ninety-eight percent clearance rate for homicides. You show me one other precinct in the country that's got ninety-eight percent."

"I'm not talking about walking into a house and seeing a husband covered in blood with his dead wife on the floor. This is something else entirely. Something new. For me, too." He looked at Dixon. "Or maybe it's something old that nobody's recognized before. Maybe he's done it a long time, and no one put them all together."

"You said this was his first."

"His first crucifixion. I doubt it's his first vic."

Dixon swiveled in his chair. He glanced up at the homicide board. Someone had written "Jane Doe: Dixon & Baudin" in red marker. He sighed and stood up. "Chief wants to see us."

"What chief?"

"Chief of police."

Baudin took his eyes off the screen and fixed them on Dixon. "What for?"

"I don't know, but he specifically asked for me and you, so let's go."

The chief, the assistant chief, and most of the administrators were in a different building. The recent structure across the street looked like an office building—brown, two stories with large windows, and brick exterior.

Dixon kept his head low as they crossed the street, looking up only once. Baudin appeared lost in thought, probably wondering what he'd done wrong for the chief to call him in on his second day on the job. Dixon wondered if it had something to do with the policies the department had been instituting since last February. A secretary had sued the department and won on claims of discrimination and sexual harassment, costing the city a cool million. Maybe all new detectives and their partners had to meet with the chief to ensure they understood what the department's policies were.

The building was much more pleasant than the station. It was cool from air conditioning, and the secretary was young, perky, and blond. Dixon smiled at her and said, "Hi."

"Hi, how can I help you?"

"Detectives Dixon and Baudin to see the chief. He called us in."

"Okay, one sec." She picked up the phone and spoke quietly before saying, "You're all set. Go right in."

Dixon went in first. He'd been here only once before, on a tour when it was completed, but the building was empty and undecorated then. It looked a lot different now.

Chief Robert Crest sat behind his desk, staring at his computer screen. He was a pudgy man with a large face and a flat forehead that gave him the appearance of always being angry. Most people found him intimidating, but Dixon saw him as the perfect boss: one who left him alone to do his job. Until now.

"Kyle, good to see you again," he said, rising and shaking hands.

"Thank you, sir."

"And you must be Ethan. Good to meet you, son."

The men sat. The chief finished up something on his computer and then unbuttoned his jacket, resting his interlaced fingers across his protruding belly.

"I've been told about the one you caught this morning, the girl on McCabe's property." A pause followed. Dixon waited until the chief spoke again. As he'd seen before, Baudin seemed off in his own world. "The reason I brought you boys in is because I spoke to the sheriff about this earlier. There's some special circumstances where I thought it might be better if we brought this one in-house. That's why you were there."

"What circumstances, sir?" Dixon said.

He hesitated. "The mayor is up for reelection in four months. To put it bluntly, we can't have people thinking about a killer on the loose while he's out there pressing the flesh. Makes him look weak. Inept. We all know he ain't got shit to do with it, but he's the face of this department."

"Then it could've stayed in Laramie County," Dixon said. "No one would've pointed the finger at him. It would've been the sheriff's deal."

Chief Crest chuckled. "That ain't how people think. They're stupid, son. Like sheep. A brutal killer on the loose will be put on the mayor's neck, guaranteed. It's his city."

Baudin said, "And your neck."

Baudin and Crest glared at each other in silence until Dixon asked, "What is it you need from us, sir?"

"I need this closed quickly. Even if it's a cold case and transferred down to the open-unsolved files in the basement." He looked from one man to the other. "As far as we know, this is a one-time deal. Could be a jilted lover, could be someone she ripped off, could be anything."

"Could be a serial murderer," Baudin said.

"Sir," Dixon quickly interjected, "we don't know what it is. But we keep our mouths shut until we do know."

"That's all I'm asking. Discretion and speed." He smiled, but it looked odd, as though his face wasn't used to it. "I'm glad you both understand. Get to it then, boys. Keep me in the loop on any developments, would you?"

"Sure thing, sir," Dixon said, rising. He held out his hand, and the chief shook it. Baudin didn't offer.

As they were crossing the hallway to the front entrance, Dixon said, "What the hell is your problem?"

"Fuck him. Take it down to the open-unsolved? He wants us to bury this to save their asses in an election."

"So what?"

"So what? You don't care that he brought us in there to intimidate us into closing this case?"

"That's what's gonna happen anyway. You ever seen a homicide solved where there's no suspects and the body's been out in a damn field for a month?"

Baudin stepped in front of him. "She counts, Kyle. She counts." He spun around and left the building.

Dixon stared at the closing door. He put his hands on his hips and glanced back at the receptionist, who was chatting on her cell phone and giggling.

Evening fell quickly as Dixon worked. No matter how many files he closed, there were always more. The bin on the filing cabinet was for cases that were to be transferred to the open-unsolved storage in the basement of the precinct. Transferring a case down there took it off the homicide board, or the active cases calendar if it wasn't a homicide, and off a detective's schedule. Only once before had he felt the urge to put a case in that bin before he felt it was necessary.

A homeless man had been found stabbed to death below a freeway underpass. The man had been positioned flat on his back with his hands on his chest as though he had been preparing to die. No one saw anything. The man had no relatives and likely no possessions to steal. Dixon had caught the case on the heels of several check fraud cases and was enthralled by it. Seemingly no one had any reason to hurt this man.

After six months of investigation, he had turned up no additional evidence—not even a place to start. The turnover at the shelter meant that even two months later, there was no one left who'd known him.

Dixon had filed it in the open-unsolved bin and then had a knot in his stomach the entire day. He stayed awake in bed that night, staring at the ceiling. At two in the morning, he rushed back to the precinct, took the file out of the bin, and returned it to his desk.

Three months after that, he was interviewing another homeless man on a drug charge. The man had been found with cocaine. On a whim, Dixon told him he would cut him a deal if he had any information on the murder case he was working. The man had not only known the victim, but he also knew who killed him. Within two weeks, Dixon had a collar. The victim had been killed over a coat that the killer had wanted.

Dixon wished he could remember the name of that victim now. He felt that he owed him that. But no matter how much he thought about it, the name wouldn't come to him. He'd never put a file in the open-unsolved bin again.

It was past seven, and Dixon stretched and got to his feet. Baudin was still at the computer, sipping an energy drink and poring through websites and internet archives, studying cases of murder by crucifixion.

"Heading out," Dixon said.

"Have a good night," Baudin said without looking up.

Dixon nodded. "Yeah… so you really think that's what we got? A sexual sadist?"

"I don't know, but I think so, yeah. To do something like that to another human being… it's not something just anybody could do."

"So this person, this sexual sadist, if his urges are as strong as you say they are—"

"He'll kill again. If he hasn't already."

Jessop stepped out of his office and said, "I'm taking off. You still need to talk?"

Dixon hesitated, watching Baudin on the computer, his eyes glistening as though he weren't blinking enough. "No," he said. "It's nothin', Cap. I'll see ya tomorrow."

10

The image of the girl wouldn't leave him as Dixon drove home. The interstate wasn't packed, but because it was dusk, all he could see was an ocean of red brake lights. He glanced toward the city center on his left. The tallest building in Cheyenne was only twelve floors, but from the interstate, the city looked larger than it was. Dixon thought of a story he'd read in high school English about some Russian monarch who built a city of cardboard to drive dignitaries through. That was what the city felt like sometimes: cardboard buildings with cardboard people. It was an unnerving image he always had to push out of his mind as quickly as possible.

He took a different exit from the one he needed to get home and looped around a curving ramp. At the stoplight at the bottom, he pulled up next to a car full of teenage girls. They glanced over and then spoke to each other for a second. One of them lifted up her shirt and pressed her breasts against the window, to the uproarious laughter of the others in the car. When the light changed, they sped away.

Dixon pulled in at Lion's Park and stopped in a parking space near a gazebo. The large pond was empty, with the exception of a couple in a paddleboat. He sat on a bench and watched them. Hillary and he had been that young once, but it seemed like a lifetime ago now. They'd met at the University of Wyoming when he was working as campus police and she was working on her art degree. A showing of hers had drawn him in. Her show, *Homeless of Wyoming,* was all black-and-white close-up photos of the men, women, and children who lived on Wyoming's streets. In a move that was quite unlike him, he strode right up to her and asked her out on a date there and then, to which she agreed.

Five years later they were married, and two years after that Randy was born.

Dixon had never pictured his life turning out that way. A wife, kid, mortgage, steady paycheck… it was more than his father, an alcoholic construction worker, ever had. His mother ran out on his father and him when Dixon was three years old. After that, his father just had a series of flings that never amounted to much.

Dixon wondered if his parents had ever ridden in a paddleboat like the couple on the water—if they'd ever truly been in love.

He tried to get the image of the girl on the cross out of his mind. He knew it wasn't good police work to push the victim away—that wasn't detective's work—but he couldn't help it. Thinking about it gave him that familiar knot in his stomach.

Most detectives might complain about their workload, about their cases not making a difference, about all sorts of things, but Dixon didn't have many complaints. He liked his graffiti cases and check frauds. Seeing what he'd seen that day reminded him that there were cases he didn't like.

When it was dark, he rose and drove home.

Every time he pulled into his driveway, he was amazed by the kind of house he could afford. Anywhere else in the country, he might be living in the poor area of town, but in Cheyenne he could afford three thousand square feet and a big backyard. He got out of the car and was heading inside when someone said his name. He turned to see a man walking toward him from across the street.

"Kyle? It's Chris, man. Chris Stuttle."

"Oh, yeah, Chris. Hey, how are ya? What're you doin' out here?"

Chris gave him a big smile. "Just moved in across the street there at the duplex."

"Really?"

"Yeah, Hillary told me about it like a month ago, and I looked into it, and it fit the bill."

"Well, that's great. I had no idea you were even interested in moving out here."

Chris looked back at the duplex. "Yeah, I was sick of where I was. The apartment was too loud, surrounded by people half my age, you know."

"Yeah. I will say this about my father's generation: they knew how to shut the hell up at night."

Chris nodded. "Yeah. Well, hey, I just wanted to say hi. Maybe we can grab a beer sometime."

"Yeah, I'm actually having the WC game on Saturday. Few people over. You should come."

"I'd love to."

"Great. Two o'clock. See ya then."

"See ya then."

Dixon strolled into his house with a grin. He'd always been fond of Chris and was glad this gave him someone in the neighborhood he could relate to. Most of his neighbors were older, and Dixon found their constant complaining irritating.

"Hey," he said, walking into the kitchen. He kissed Hillary on the cheek as she stirred some meat in a pan, then he took off his shoes, putting them on a shoe rack by the sliding glass doors.

"How was work, babe?"

"Ah, you know. Nothing to write home about. Guess who moved in across the street?" Hillary didn't answer a moment. "Hillary, guess who moved in across the street?"

"Huh? Sorry, paying attention to the food. Who?"

"Chris Stuttle. From church."

"Oh, really? That's interesting."

Dixon got a juice out of the fridge, popped the top, and took a drink. "Yeah, he said you told him about the duplex. I don't know how much of a favor you did for him. That place needs a lot of work."

"Dinner'll be ready soon."

He took another drink, kissed her again on the neck, and went to see his son.

His boy was asleep. He'd sleep for about four hours and often wake up in the middle of the night. Dixon always volunteered to feed him. The boy was curled up, sucking on a pacifier. The moonlight streamed through the window and shone across his face. Dixon adjusted the blinds to block the light on him and hit the wall.

He came out as Hillary was setting the table. He kissed her again, and she kept working as though he weren't even there. With the boy asleep, he was hoping to fool around a little before dinner.

Dixon came up behind her and wrapped his arms around her waist, running kisses along her neck. She pulled away.

"I'm not in the mood right now, babe. I've had stomach cramps all day."

"Uh-oh. Stomach bug?"

"No, I don't think so. Just kind of a dull pain. I think I ate something weird."

Dixon sat down as she served the food. She sat down across from him and began eating. Dixon wanted to say grace but felt he shouldn't bring it up. She looked passively upset, as though she were trying desperately to hide her anger, but it still shone through.

"Any new cases?" she said.

"Yeah, one. Young girl that was killed."

"Mm," she said with a mouthful of food, "how?"

He hesitated. "She was crucified."

She looked up at him. "Seriously?"

He nodded, staring down at his plate and realizing he wasn't hungry. "Yeah, it's as bad as it sounds."

"Who was she?"

"I don't know. We should have an ID from the dental records tomorrow."

She shook her head, putting her fork down and leaning back. "Poor girl. I hope you find who did it."

"I don't think we will. See, if a homicide isn't solved in the first two days, its chances of being solved don't just drop a little. They drop to, like, almost zero. There's few cases you can solve if there's no witnesses to tell you who did it." He looked down at his plate. "I don't really want to talk about this now, if that's okay."

"Of course. What do you want to talk about?"

"I wanna talk about what's wrong."

"Nothing."

"I can tell when you're lying, Hil. Something's bothering you."

She began eating again. "Nothing at all."

11

Baudin finished work around nine and took a folder with him when he left. His cousin should've been at his house watching Heather, but when he called, there was no answer. He headed out of the precinct and stood on the sidewalk, staring up at the moon and enjoying the warm night air on his skin. Winters were rough here, and he wasn't looking forward to it. But his worst enemy was monotony. The year-round warmth and sunshine of Los Angeles had worn him down until he was begging for a change.

He lit a cigarette and leaned against a streetlight. A few cars drove by, and he watched them. He opened the folder tucked under his arm and glared at the photos he'd printed off: close-ups of their Jane Doe.

When his cigarette was done, he flipped it into the gutter and drove up to the Motel 6 with his windows down. The wind whipped his face and hair. The more it whipped him, the faster he went until he was going almost ninety in a forty. He slowed down and rolled the windows up.

Several women were already on the corners. He came to a stop in front of a group and rolled down his window.

"Ladies," he said.

"Whatchoo need, honey?"

"I'm looking for Candi Carlson. She out here?"

"You a friend of hers?"

"I am," he said, flashing his badge.

"Oh, well, we ain't seen her."

"It's not like that."

"I don't know where she is. We just out here chillin', ain't breakin' no laws, Officer."

Baudin put the car in park. He stepped out and leaned against it, watching the girls as he lit another cigarette. "So I guess if I search you girls I won't find anything. No H or crystal, no weed. 'Cause you're just chilling, right?"

She folded her arms. "What you want with Candi?"

"Just to talk. I swear it."

She nodded. "She up in room 210."

"Thanks."

He got back into his car and drove through the parking lot. Room 210 was right above him, overlooking a small pool. He got out, watching the way the lighted water reflected off the walls, and took the stairs up to the second level. He slipped the folder into the back of his waistband.

The room had the blinds drawn but the lights on. He pressed his ear to the door and could hear a woman's groans. He leaned his back against the wall and smoked, watching the pool below him.

When the groans reached a fever pitch, he heard a male voice, too, swearing. Then the voices calmed, and a minute later a man stepped out. He was wearing tight jeans and a trucker's hat.

"She good to go, brother," he said to Baudin.

Baudin waited until the man was gone and then peeked into the room. Candi was lying on the bed in see-through lingerie, a sheen of sweat covering her face. Her eyes drifted over to him, and she smiled.

"Officer, are you here for a freebie?"

He stepped into the room, the reek of sex hitting his nostrils, and sat down in a recliner.

"Could I have one of those?" she asked. He lit a cigarette and handed it to her. Her fingers caressed his hand a moment before she slid them up and took the cigarette, setting it gently between her lips. "So what exactly can I do for you?" she asked.

Baudin sat back down in the recliner. "How many johns you get in a night?"

"Good night? Twenty. Maybe twenty-five. Bad night, nobody."

"Do you enjoy what you do?"

"I don't think anybody enjoys what they do. That's the curse of modern days, I guess. Nobody's happy... Are you happy?"

He blew out a puff of smoke through his nose. "Do I look happy?"

"No. But you don't look sad, neither. You look... angry. Like the world's done you wrong and you got a score to settle."

He raised an eyebrow, watching the red tip of her cigarette. "You out here without protection?"

"I got protection."

"The woman in the car I saw the other night?"

She nodded, inhaling gently and blowing out in a whisper. "She's got some gorillas on her payroll. Big beefy guys that just got outta the WSP. They look out for me."

"How much do they take?"

"Fifty percent."

"That's a hefty tag for some protection."

She shrugged. "I don't wanna be alone out here. A lotta sick bastards."

"I bet." They smoked in silence for a second before Baudin said, "I need a favor. I'm going to give you some pictures, and I want you to ask around with the girls and see if anybody knows anything."

"What kinda pictures?"

He took the folder out and leaned forward, tossed it on the bed, and watched her face. She picked up the photos, took a drag, and then put them down again. Almost no reaction, except that she swallowed when she looked at the first one.

"What happened to her?"

"She was crucified and disemboweled. Her breasts and genitals were cut off. I need to know if she was a working girl around here or not. And johns talk to their ladies. Maybe someone mentioned something about this."

She smirked. "I'm anything but a lady. You can call me what I am."

"What are you?"

"I'm a whore, Officer. Just a plain old whore tryin' to get by in the world."

He rose. "You are whatever you think you are. Everything is energy, Candi. You want something different, just attune your thoughts to the energy of what you want, and the universe will respond in kind."

She chuckled. "You some sorta priest?"

"I'm not talking about God. I'm talking about energy. Thoughts are energy, matter is energy, even your soul is energy. You just gotta align all three to what you want, and you'll get it."

"If there was truth to that, I don't think your energy would have you in this room with me chasing down perverts."

He took a last puff of the cigarette and put it out in an ashtray on the nightstand. "No, I think this is exactly where my energy would bring me." He took out a fifty and put it on the nightstand under the ashtray. "You have yourself a good night."

As he was going out the door, she said, "Officer?"

"Yeah?"

"What was your name again?"

He watched her. "Ethan Baudin."

She nodded. "I'll remember that next time. I promise."

He grinned, turned, and left.

12

Dixon woke with an erection. It wasn't something that happened often since he'd turned thirty-five, but occasionally he would wake with one and feel like a young kid again. He turned to his wife and wrapped his arm around her. Laying kisses on her neck, he snuggled next to her, pressing his erection against her. She roused and for a moment pushed back into him. And then, as quickly as the moment came, it was gone. She withdrew. Not physically, but he could feel that she wasn't into it anymore as surely as if she had risen and walked away.

"What's wrong?" he said.

"It's just early. I'm not feelin' it."

"You used to feel it."

"I know, but… I don't know. I'm sorry, I'm the worst wife."

He kissed her gently on the lips and then rolled away to sit up in bed. "No, it's fine. I just thought it would give me something to think about during the day."

She rubbed his back. "Well, it's better to have something to look forward to than a memory."

He grinned. "I'll take you up on that, you know."

"Please do."

Dixon rose and strolled into the bathroom. He urinated, stripped down, and then got into the shower. "Oh, how many pizzas are you ordering for the game tomorrow?"

"Is three enough?" she said from the bedroom.

"Better make it four. I invited Jerry from work and Chris from across the street."

"Oh."

He began soaping his chest and arms. "Something wrong with Jerry and Chris?"

"No, that's fine. Just a lot of people. I don't know if we have room."

"We'll make room."

He finished showering and got out, staring at his body in the mirror. He'd been a track star in high school and had always been lean and muscular. But a slight belly protruded, and skin sagged in places it hadn't ten years ago. To him, age seemed to be little more than the cumulative effects of gravity.

"Hey, hon?" he said.

"Yeah?"

"I love you."

There was no answer for a moment. "I love you, too."

When he was done showering and dressing, Dixon went to his son. He picked him up and tickled his belly, which always made him smile. He played with him for twenty minutes until it was breakfast time, and then he brought the boy out and put him in a high chair at the table.

"What do you two have planned for today?" he said, sitting down as she shoveled eggs and bacon onto his plate.

"We're going with Kelsey to the mall and then lunch."

He took a bite of eggs then rose and retrieved the Tabasco from the fridge. "I'll probably be late for dinner. Wanna catch up on some stuff so I don't have to go in tomorrow."

"Okay. I'll keep a plate hot for you."

She brought him orange juice, and he took her hand, staring up at her eyes. Kissing the soft skin of her fingers, he let go, and she slipped away. He didn't know much about women, but something was wrong. For the past few months, Hillary had been making intimations that perhaps it was time for another child, but she'd stopped in recent weeks. Dixon didn't understand it, but women somehow intuitively knew when their biological clocks were ticking down. The window of having more kids, for her, was closing.

His phone buzzed in his pocket. He took it out. "Hello?"

"Hey, it's Ethan. You at the precinct?"

"Not yet."

"We still partners?"

"I'm eating breakfast with my family right now. Can this wait?"

"When you're done, meet me at the coroner's office. He's got the preliminary ready for us."

Dixon hung up and stared at the phone. Then he slipped it back into his pocket. It hadn't been a request. Baudin had just told him where to be as though he were his boss. Maybe he'd be better off alone again after all.

"Who was that?" Hillary asked.

"New partner," he said, rising and kissing his boy on the cheek. "Gotta run." He grabbed a piece of toast out of the toaster, kissed her quickly on the lips, and was out the door.

The coroner's office was next to the county fairgrounds with nothing else but a few government buildings nearby. As Dixon drove, he again got that feeling of being on a different planet. He wondered if somewhere out in the universe, another creature was looking at a deserted stretch of nothing on its own planet with the same feeling.

He pulled up to the government complex and saw Baudin sitting on the trunk of his car, doing something on his cell phone. He wore a red shirt with a black tie today, looking like some sinister preacher. Dixon got out of the car and scanned the area.

"They should develop this land," he said, a cloud of dust swirling over him.

"Why? The world need more strip malls and movie theaters?"

"Be better than dirt."

Baudin hopped off the trunk, and they entered the building. The doors were open, but there was no receptionist at the front counter. Down a long linoleum corridor, the sound of clanging metal echoed, as though someone were moving pots and pans around. They headed in that direction.

In a room off to the side, a man was stocking pans and trays on a shelf. He saw them and his eyes went wide. "Who are you?" he said.

"Detective Kyle Dixon. Gil here?"

"Oh," he said, relieved. "Yeah. Yeah, he's down in his office."

"Thanks."

Baudin followed him. Dixon had been to the office several times. It was, in his estimation, the worst office he'd ever been in. Tucked away in a corner with no windows, Gil was a hoarder. He didn't call it that himself, but that was what it was. No paper with even a hint of importance was ever thrown away. No files were shredded. It meant his office was stacked from floor to ceiling with papers, trinkets, boxes and folders.

"That man's a junkie," Baudin said. "We need to remember that if we ever need something Gil's not giving us."

Dixon looked back at him. "How you know he's a junkie?"

"He had that droopy appearance, like his arms and shoulders were too heavy for him. And he was missing his shoelaces."

"So?"

"So they use those to tie off injection sites."

Dixon shook his head. "No way, man. They test 'em here."

"Yeah? And who does the testing?"

Gil's office was overflowing with junk. Paper binders were now stacked outside of the office in the corridor. Dixon sighed as he stepped over them.

Gil was behind his desk filling out a paper form with a pen. He looked up, and it seemed for a moment he didn't recognize Dixon. Then a smile crept over his face, and he said, "Detective Dixon? So glad you chose to light our dreary day."

"Gil, you gotta clean some of this shit out, man. This isn't healthy."

He shrugged. "Nothing's healthy. You ready to see your gal?"

They followed Gil down another corridor to the elevators. The old, creaking elevators jolted several times as though cables were snapping above them. Baudin didn't seem to notice. He was studying Gil's face.

They stepped off in the basement, where the bodies were kept. Gil opened one of the old-style refrigeration units and pulled out the metal panel the body lay on.

Their Jane Doe looked different from when Dixon had seen her last. She was much whiter. The genitals were where his eyes went first, to the gaping, open wounds that revealed the dried, crimson interior. He had to look away, down to her feet and the mangled toes with the skin falling off the bone. He'd once watched something on the Discovery Channel about a caveman who had been found frozen into the ice. They thawed him out and determined that he'd been murdered. Jane Doe looked like that caveman, with ancient, crusted flesh.

Dixon closed his eyes and said a quick prayer for her.

"She suffocated," Gil said, staring down at her face. "Suffocation's what kills someone when they're crucified. Their lungs can't get enough air, but it's too painful to put pressure on your feet to stand and give your lungs space. So they slowly suffocate. It takes days."

"About three days, wouldn't you say, Doc?" Baudin said.

"Guess so. Though I'd guesstimate she'd been out there at least twenty days. She's got maggots inside her. We can get an ento person out here from UW to take a look and give you a date certain."

Baudin walked around the table to the head and looked at her eyes. "Was there anything in her throat?"

"Like what?"

"Anything that shouldn't be there?"

"I didn't see nothin'."

Baudin leaned over her. "What was she cut with?"

"Something sharp, a knife or razor. Some organs missing."

"Which ones?"

"The pancreas and thymus. Odd ones to take. That heart, though, that ain't hers. That's a deer's heart, best I can figure."

"Deer heart?" Baudin said, looking up at him.

"Yessir, her heart was still in her chest. Couldn't get through the breastplate, though it looks like he tried. See right there? She's got scrape marks on it. He tried to lift it like a lid on Tupperware. But you gotta cut the ribs first to release the breastplate. Don't reckon this fella had any medical knowledge. Shoved the deer heart right where her stomach goes."

Dixon said, "What about the breasts?"

"Those were torn away. Nothing sharp there. Just cut a little bit and then torn right off. Damn brutal."

"Can you tell if she was raped or sodomized?"

"Nothin' there for a SANE kit to analyze. The rectum's so deteriorated I can't tell. Any semen or hair from this fella's long gone. Sorry, boys, but there just ain't enough here for me to tell you anything."

Baudin said, "How long were the nails?"

"Fingernails?"

"No, the nails she was hammered in with."

"Oh, four inches, about. Why?"

"Christ's nails were supposedly between seven and nine inches long. If this was symbolic, he should've used the same-sized nails. Anything else you can tell us?"

"She bled out, so I can't get enough to test for drugs in the system... There just ain't much there."

Baudin nodded. "I appreciate the rush, Doc. Thanks."

"You're welcome."

Baudin stepped away, but Dixon remained, staring at the girl's eyes. "How old you think she was, Gil?"

"Maybe seventeen, eighteen. Probably no older than twenty-one or so."

"You take the dental impressions?"

"Yeah, we had Marvin come out, and we did 'em. And again, not enough."

"What do you mean?" Baudin said, staring at an anatomy poster on the wall.

"Some of her teeth are missing."

"How many?"

"'Bout fifteen."

Baudin stepped closer to the body. "Can you open her mouth?"

Gil grabbed her chin and upper lip without gloves and forced them open, a slight *crack* escaping from the desiccated flesh. Baudin and Dixon both peered inside. Every other tooth was gone. Dixon saw ragged flesh in some of the holes.

"They were pulled," Dixon said. "And not softly."

Baudin shook his head. "They pulled enough so we can't identify her."

Damn, Dixon thought. He didn't have medical knowledge, but he knew that ninety percent of the time bodies were identified through dental records.

"Anything else you can tell us, Gil?"

"Well, fingertips was cut off, too. No prints. And some birds got a hold of her—crows, probably. So not all the wounds you see are from him. I'm sorry. I'll keep lookin', but don't expect much."

Dixon nodded. "I appreciate it just the same. Have yourself a good day."

As the men walked out, they glanced into the room where the young assistant had been. He was gone.

"Fucker pulled the teeth," Baudin said as their footsteps echoed in the corridor.

"Why the organs?" Dixon said. "What the hell does he want with the pancreas and thymus?"

Baudin was quiet a moment. "They're called the sweetbreads in cooking. I think he took them to eat."

13

Dixon wanted to come up with a picture of what Jane Doe had looked like, based on the photos the forensic techs had taken. Then he could get the photo out to the media and hope a parent with a missing child or a roommate would call in.

The computer artist the department had on contract was located in a graphic design studio. The place was the opposite of the coroner's office: full of light and color, walls painted yellow and red. The tables and desks were all glass, and the artist hummed to himself as he worked, Dixon sitting across from him in his office.

Dixon glanced out the office door and saw Baudin at the conference room table, working on his iPad.

"How's this looking for the nose?" the designer said.

Dixon looked at the photo of Jane Doe's body that they'd printed up and then at the computer model. "Close. A little narrower up top, I think."

The artist, whose name Dixon couldn't remember because he'd never used him before, hummed again as he narrowed the nose.

"Now?"

"Better." He leaned to the side. "You wanna take a look?" he yelled.

Baudin set the iPad down and hurried over. He hovered over the artist's shoulder, glaring at the image on the screen. "That's her."

Dixon nodded, and the designer touched up a few things and printed the photo.

"Gimme about twenty copies and email me a digital, would you?" Dixon asked.

"No worries."

When he had the printouts, Dixon couldn't help staring at them. The girl was beautiful, someone who would stand out in any crowd. Baudin wouldn't look at the photo again. Instead, he paced near the entrance to the studio until Dixon was done.

"You got contacts in the news?" Baudin asked.

"Yeah. I'm gonna head over there now."

Baudin's phone rang. He answered it. "Hello?... Yes. Yes, I'm her father... Today? What happened?... I'll be right down."

"Everything okay?"

"My daughter got into some trouble at school. I'm gonna head down there for a minute. Can you give me a lift back to the precinct?"

On the drive over, Dixon glanced at Baudin, who was busy again on his iPad. The man had an intense look of concentration that never broke. Even when he appeared to be relaxing, his face and body posture betrayed the fact that he was thinking furiously about something.

"So that 9-11 bullshit," Dixon said. "You really believe that?"

"I do."

"Well, what else you believe?"

"Whatd'ya mean?"

"I don't think conspiracy theorists are ever happy with one conspiracy. I'm sure you got more."

He grinned and lowered his iPad. "You trying to get to know me, Kyle?"

"I've always been interested in what crazy people believe."

He went back to the iPad. "You ever heard of the Tuskegee experiments?"

"No."

He looked out the window at a woman on the corner. "Government researchers wanted to study the progression of syphilis but didn't want to use whites. So they studied it in the black population in Alabama. They never told the participants they had syphilis. In Guatemala, these same government doctors purposely infected people with syphilis, too. They knew penicillin could cure it, but they never gave it to them or to the blacks in Alabama. They let them die, so they could study them."

"Bullshit," Dixon said.

"Look it up, man. Don't take my word for it. But a government willing to kill its own people just to study syphilis… Imagine what that government would do to its own people if it wanted to go to war and needed an excuse. We been at war for a hundred years with almost no periods of peace, man. Somewhere in the world, American soldiers are fighting, all the time. We're a nation built on war. Our government doesn't know how to function any other way."

Dixon shook his head. "You believe in UFOs, too?"

"I don't know."

"You don't—what? That's just stupid."

"How the hell do I know what's up there? Could be giant spacewomen for all I know."

"Giant spacewomen infecting people with syphilis?"

He shrugged. "Maybe they get around?"

Dixon chuckled as he merged onto the interstate.

Once he'd dropped Baudin off at his car, Dixon headed to KBS 5 News. The studio was in what appeared to be an office building with a private two-year college on the first floor. Dixon parked at a meter and put coins in before heading inside and up to the main floor.

The station had no security, which always surprised him, considering that these people were on television every night and the offices had nameplates on all the doors. Everyone seemed to be preparing for the mid-morning broadcast, and he stood by for a second and watched them on the monitors, practicing and warming up their voices.

He continued to the last office, which had a nameplate on the door: "Carol Billings."

She was typing away on her computer so quickly that it sounded like pounding rain rather than typing. When she didn't notice his presence after he'd stood there for a few seconds, he cleared his throat. She jumped as though he'd just grabbed her purse.

"Oh my gosh," she said.

"Sorry," he said, sitting down across from her. "Didn't think you were so jumpy."

She exhaled as though forcing herself to calm down. "You always sneak up on women?"

"Just the ones I'm gonna rape."

She threw a pencil at him. "Asshole."

"How you been?"

Carol took a sip from a bottle of water and then leaned back in her chair. "Good. Did you see my piece on the water dispute between the mayor and Frank Herbert?"

"I didn't. I don't watch TV, Carol."

"Like, at all?"

"Like, at all. Just takes away my time or upsets me."

"What about the news? You're a detective, you gotta know what's going on in your city."

"I figure it's none of my business. World's always been a mess, I ain't gonna fix it."

"That's one way to look at it, I guess."

Dixon brushed a piece of lint off his pants. "Listen, I don't wanna take up too much of your time, but I got a photo that needs to go out on the five o'clock and the ten o'clock."

"Both? Mm, this must be juicy."

"On the record, it's a body that was found on Brett McCabe's property that needs to be identified. We're still determining cause of death and need help with identification."

"And off the record?" she said, leaning forward like a child listening to a bedtime story.

"You sure love this gory shit, don't you?"

"I live for it. Now, what's really going on?"

"Murder vic. She was crucified, and her breasts and genitals were cut off. The guy pulled half her teeth out and cut off her fingertips, so we couldn't identify her."

"Whoa."

"No shit. So can you run it?"

"Of course. Gimme what you got."

"I'll email you the photo. She was probably eighteen to twenty-one years old, found about two miles in on McCabe's property, on the county border."

"You got anybody you're lookin' at?"

He shook his head. "Not a one, except for McCabe himself. He looked old and feeble to me, though. It's a completely cold case. We'll probably just file it in the open-unsolved, but I wanna run with it a little first."

She nodded, staring at him a moment. "I'll get it on air. In exchange for something, of course."

"Of course."

"I want first release of anything you guys make public. If you catch the prick, I want twenty minutes with him in the holding cell."

"No way."

"You just said you're not gonna catch him, so what does it matter?"

He grinned. "You shoulda been a lawyer. Always an angle, huh? All right, he's yours if we get him."

She smiled and leaned back, taking her water and holding it up as if she were delivering a toast. "Well, here's to catching him, then."

14

Baudin raced down to the middle school, parked out front, and rushed inside. Anger billowed out of him like clouds of frosty mist from dry ice. He didn't know how he would react when he actually saw his daughter, but anger wasn't the emotion he wanted to show.

He stopped halfway down the hall and leaned back against the lockers, staring into a classroom down the hall. Some of the children were paying attention, but most were doodling, daydreaming, or—an option he hadn't had in middle school—playing on their cell phones.

Fury was like a drug and, like a drug, it dissipated over time. The body expelled it forcefully from the systems that saw it as poison. Within a minute, he was calm, and he continued down the hall to the principal's office.

Inside the school's office, past the reception desk, he saw Heather sitting on a bench. He walked over to her and knelt down.

"What happened?" he said.

"It wasn't my fault, Daddy."

"Heather, what happened?"

The principal, a heavyset black man with a sweater vest, rose from the desk and came over. He held out his hand, and Baudin shook it.

"You must be Detective Baudin. I'm Martin. I'm the principal here at Moss."

"I appreciate the call. I just asked Heather what happened."

"Why don't you two step into my office?"

The principal's own office was covered in photos of him with people Baudin didn't recognize, except for one with George W. Bush at some black-tie function. The chairs were uncomfortable, and Baudin was taken back to the hours he'd spent in principals' offices, probably for offenses no different from Heather's.

"Detective, we take drug use very seriously. Normally, we would call the police and deal with it that way. But I knew who you were and thought I would do you the courtesy of giving you a call."

"I appreciate that."

"She was caught behind the school with a few other students, two boys and another girl, sharing a joint. I've spoken with all four, and Heather doesn't seem to be the one who supplied the marijuana."

Baudin looked at her. He remembered her as the little girl who would throw her arms around his neck and kiss his cheeks, who would hug him every morning and say, "I love you, Daddy." The one he would watch while she slept and hope he could spare her all the pain that life was waiting to thrust upon her. It was difficult for him to see she was turning into her own person, with her own value system that was different from his.

"Is that true?" he said.

"It wasn't... Yes," she said quietly.

Baudin looked back at the principal. "I appreciate you contacting me, Martin. I also appreciate your discretion. I promise you that this will be dealt with."

He nodded. "I understand. And I hope you understand that some punishment must be imposed. I'm going to suspend her for two days. Monday and Tuesday. She can come back on Wednesday, and she'll be spending her lunch hour eating in detention for a month."

Heather was about to object before the principal cut her off.

"That," he said, looking directly at her, "is the price instead of calling the police."

"It's fair," Baudin said. "And it won't happen again."

Baudin shook his hand, thanked him again, and left with Heather in tow. They didn't speak until they were outside and heading for his car.

"How could you do that?" he said. "I'm a cop, Heather."

She was quiet until they were in the car and the doors were shut. "I just wanted to try it."

"How many times have you done it?"

"Never."

"Don't lie to me."

She shook her head vigorously—the actions of someone desperate to be believed, Baudin thought.

"I promise. I've never done it. Becky just had some, and we went out to try it. I just wanted to see what it was like."

"Why?"

She shrugged.

He exhaled and looked forward, debating what to do. "In addition to what the principal's doing, I'm taking away your cell phone for a month."

"Daddy! You can't do that. I have assignments due, and I need to talk to my partners. We work in groups. And I have to look stuff up, my notes are on my phone, there's no way I can do my assignments without it."

"Well… a week, then."

"I have a history paper due, and my partner's totally slacking, and we need to—"

"Okay, the weekend. You can survive the weekend without it." He reached into her breast pocket and pulled out her phone. "One weekend."

She folded her arms. "Fine."

Baudin started the car and pulled away, wishing her mother was here. She had always been the one who punished and disciplined. He had no tolerance for it, no knowledge about what was too much and what was too little. When he looked at her, she was just his little girl.

"I'm gonna drop you at Molly's."

"Now? Why?"

"I have to go meet with someone."

"I can come, too."

"No, not with this person."

15

Baudin was already back at the precinct when Dixon came in after lunch. He walked up to their desks and sat down. Baudin had several windows open on his computer, and he began going through them, closing the unnecessary ones.

"Your kid okay?" Dixon said.

"She's fine."

He nodded. "Fight or something?"

"Or something."

Dixon leaned back in his seat and put his feet up on the desk. "Jane Doe's going on the news. I know the chief said to keep it quiet, but I ain't revealing any details. Hopefully he don't chew our asses for it."

Baudin looked at him. "I have a feeling it's not going to matter what we do. I don't think he'll be happy with any outcome."

"What makes you say that?"

"Just a hunch."

"Well, what'd your hunches say about Brett McCabe?"

"I was gonna head up there now, actually. He declined to come down here yesterday."

"He seems really frail to me."

Baudin stretched his back from side to side. "Frail or no, he didn't look too pleased we were up there."

"Well, you drive."

Dixon pulled his feet from the desk and headed out, Baudin following. The air outside smelled like factory exhaust. Not entirely unpleasant, but that could've been because Dixon was used to it now. He wondered if Baudin found it repellent.

Once they had pulled out of the parking lot, Dixon rolled down the window and rested his elbow on the edge of the door. He'd spent most of his life in Cheyenne and wondered if that was why most people stayed. He couldn't think of many people he knew growing up who had left. Almost his entire high school graduating class was right here, as was everyone he'd gone to church with as a child. His daddy used to say Cheyenne was the crib and grave of people born there.

"Who's your contact with the news?" Baudin asked.

"Girl I used to date. We're on good terms. She wants first release of anything going public, and if we get a collar she wants an interview in the holding cells with him."

"Did you agree to that?"

"I would've agreed to a whole helluva lot more. Where else am I gonna go to get her face out?"

"Did you post on any websites or blogs?"

"Wouldn't help. This isn't LA, not yet. People out here still get their news from the TV. Few folks got Netflix or DVRs. They just watch whatever's on." He looked at Baudin. "How you likin' it out here?"

"It's… different. Slower. But people are the same everywhere. That doesn't change."

Dixon hesitated. "I'm havin' some folks over for the game tomorrow. Two o'clock. You should come. My wife needs to meet you anyway."

"Your wife?"

"Just… something she does. She needs to meet you."

"I'm not really good with the social stuff."

"Don't matter. You gotta be there and be met. Otherwise I'll catch an earful every day until you do. Bring your daughter, too."

"If you insist, I guess I can't be rude."

They rode in silence until they were back out on the border of Laramie County and surrounded by desert and brush. The air was dryer out here and had a different smell. Dixon slipped on his sunglasses.

"You don't have any?" Dixon said.

"Sunglasses? No, man. I like to see things as they really are, not filtered with that shit."

"Don't hurt your eyes? All the sun?"

He shook his head. "Sun's natural. Sunglasses are not natural. You tell me which one poses the risk to my eyes."

The winding road up to McCabe's property was empty, and they got there without seeing another soul. Baudin parked and got out. He went over to the intercom, glancing around the whole time, and pushed the call button.

"Yes?" a voice came through from the other end.

"Detective Ethan Baudin. I need access to your property again, Mr. McCabe."

A string of profanities came through the intercom before he said, "Can't it wait?"

"Afraid not, sir."

A few more F-bombs and then the gate clicked open.

When they were riding up the dirt path, Dixon watched the way the trees moved with the wind. He'd never seen a painting really capture the bending and twisting to avoid being broken. He'd always thought it was like a beautiful dance. Hillary had wanted to move to bigger cities several times in their marriage, but he couldn't imagine a day going by where he didn't get to look at trees.

"How you think it is people can live in the big cities?" he asked. "Didn't you miss bein' outside in LA?"

"I got outside. There were palm trees and the ocean. Don't really miss nature."

"You grew up there?"

He nodded. "Born and raised. You?"

"Cheyenne. My mom took off when I was young, and my dad worked at a factory making engine parts. Made twenty-five thousand a year, and we had a home, a car, and went on good vacations every year. Not to mention a full-time nanny. Can't do shit on twenty-five grand now."

"People always degrade the present and elevate the past, man. It's bullshit. World's always been the same as it always is."

Dixon saw the home up ahead, and McCabe was standing there with his dog and a cane. The grimace on his face was that of a person about to do something extremely unpleasant but with no choice.

They parked near him on the horseshoe driveway in front of the house, and McCabe had to limp over.

"Thought you was goin' to where that girl was killed," he said, standing a good ten feet back as the two detectives got out.

"We will," Baudin said. "Just needed to speak with you first."

"'Bout what?"

"Got someplace we can sit?"

He pointed with his chin to a stone slab surrounded by several chairs. Dixon sat first and leaned back, watching Baudin. There was something different in the detective's eyes. He had a challenge in front of him, Dixon guessed. Baudin was a man who thrived on challenge. He wondered what Baudin was like when there was no challenge.

Baudin stood but leaned against the stone table. "This is a lot of property, Mr. McCabe. How many acres you got?"

"Fifteen hundred all told. Used to be closer to three thousand, but I gave some of it away to save on the damn taxes."

"I bet." He looked down at his shoes before pushing away from the table and strolling around as though studying the house. "You walk the property much?"

"Yeah, with my dog."

"How often?"

"Every day."

"You ever see that girl up there?"

"No, of course not. I would've called the police."

Baudin stepped to within a couple of feet of the man. "You telling me you walk this property all the time, and a dead girl was hanging on a cross not a mile from here and you never saw her? Not in the entire month she'd been up there?"

"Just what the hell are you saying?" he spit, his face flushing red.

Baudin shook his head, turning back to the house. "Nothing. Just talking. What did you do for a living, Mr. McCabe?"

"Real estate. I was a developer. I built Cheyenne from a desert into a city. Me and my father and his father before him, when there was nothin' out here but dirt."

Dixon asked, "Anybody else live on the property? Squatters, maybe?"

"No, no one else here. I see to that."

Baudin said, "You have any idea who could've done something like that?"

"No, Detective, I don't make a habit of spending time with psychopaths. I have no idea who did that to the girl."

"Did you know her?"

"No," he said loudly. "I told you I would've called the police."

Dixon said, "What about the hiker? The guy who called it in? He come down here and see you?"

"No. I didn't know anything about this until that first cop from the sheriff's office showed up and made me let him in."

Baudin turned suddenly, so fast that Dixon was afraid he'd drawn his weapon. But instead he marched up to McCabe and stared into his eyes. "I don't believe you."

McCabe was flustered, his mouth agape with no words coming out. "I don't give a shit what you believe," he finally snapped. "And I'd like you to leave my property now."

"I'll be back with a warrant to search your house. And I won't take it easy, either. Or you can let me search it now, and I promise I won't disturb anything."

McCabe stepped close to him, so close their noses almost touched. "Get the hell off my property."

Baudin grinned and turned away. Dixon rose, nodded to McCabe, and followed Baudin back to the car.

"Well, he was pissed," Dixon said.

"Don't think it was him. He can barely walk. Did you see his feet?"

"No."

"He was wearing sandals. Both his feet were nearly black and swollen. He couldn't put much pressure on them, much less haul a body onto a cross and then pull it up."

"Unless he had help."

"True. But he'd have to be a fool to put the body up on his own property, even if there's nobody else out here. He didn't strike me as a fool. I still would like to search his house, though. You know any judges that would give us a warrant?"

"McCabe's well known in this town. You're gonna need somethin' good for a judge to let you look through his home."

He grinned. "I think I got just the thing."

Baudin waited until evening, filling out paperwork on another case. The chief had given his word that they weren't supposed to be given anything else, but Jessop didn't care. He knew they wouldn't go complaining to the chief about it, and he sure as hell wasn't going out himself to investigate a convenience store robbery or credit card theft.

Baudin looked up and saw Dixon concentrating on his screen. He leaned forward casually and pretended to need something at the far end of his desk, but he actually glanced at Dixon's screen. It was the Wikipedia page on the Tuskegee experiments. Baudin grinned and leaned back in his chair, pushing the credit card theft case file away from himself.

"What ya reading?" Baudin asked.

"Nothin'. Just bullshit to pass the time."

He nodded, not taking his eyes off him. "You staying late?"

"Nah, I'm gonna head home and have a beer, relax on the couch and just forget about chicks with their vages missing."

"You haven't seen many vics, have you?"

"Homicides? I've had some. Maybe ten. Nothin' like this, but still homicides. Most murders in this town are drunken brawls that ended bad. I had one that might've been somethin' like this, but I don't know."

Baudin put his hands behind his neck, revealing the sweat stains under his arms. "What was it?"

"Girl from the strip club, the Eastern Exposure. Don't exist no more. The owner went under 'cause of back taxes, but it was big business years ago."

"What happened?"

"We found one of the girls—I can't remember her name, but her stage name was Diamond, I remember that—we found Diamond in the backseat of her car in the lot, dead. Just starin' up like a fish that'd just been caught and thrown in a cooler to suffocate. Just starin' up. We found some track marks, and her system was filled with so much smack it woulda killed a horse. It was ruled overdose, but... I don't know."

"Just didn't sit right in your gut, huh?"

"No. Never. Not even now. Somethin' about the way she was looking. They found semen and evidence of rape, vaginal tearing, but her previous boyfriend said she liked it rough."

"You look into him?"

"For three months. I followed him around so much he filed a complaint against me. I was ordered to back away. Before I could do anything, he took off. Left the state. I let sleeping dogs lie after that." Dixon stared off into the distance for a moment, and Baudin could tell he was gone, in some distant place considering distant possibilities that no longer mattered. "What about you?" he said after a time.

"I've had similar, but nothing this brutal. Sometimes in the canyons you'd find bodies. We found a young mother once who was pregnant. He'd torn out her throat like an animal. Left teeth marks in the flesh. Real vicious. I started scanning the open-unsolved files, mostly because I had nothing. Nobody saw anything, nobody reported her missing, no relatives. So I'm scanning the files and I come across a woman from 1975 who was killed in an identical way. Throat ripped out, teeth marks, but the vic had been sodomized and mine hadn't. That was the only difference."

"You ever find him?"

Baudin nodded as he took a sip of coffee out of a Styrofoam cup. "Some uniforms went into a house because the neighbors reported a bad smell. They found the owner, Randall Dupas. He died of congenital heart failure. When the uniforms were going through his stuff, waiting for the paramedics to call it and get the ME out there, they found photo albums. Like, five of 'em. They were filled with women, pictures he'd taken of 'em... after he'd bitten out their throats. About twenty women over a forty-year period. But he was a long-haul trucker, so I bet that figure's closer to one or two hundred. He didn't sodomize my vic because he was too old at that point to get it up."

Dixon didn't say anything. Baudin was now the one staring off into space. He blinked several times as though wiping memories away and said, "Better to leave ghosts alone." He rose, finishing his coffee and tossing the cup in the trash. "Need me to bring anything tomorrow?"

Dixon shook his head. "No. There'll be plenty of everything."

Baudin turned and walked away. As he neared the glass doors heading out of the detective's floor, he could see Dixon's reflection in it. He was staring at him, all the way until the moment Baudin had opened the door and gone through.

Baudin ate a slow meal at a Mexican restaurant. He sat in the corner by himself and called Molly. She didn't answer but called him back after a few minutes.

"How is she?" he asked.

"Sulking. Listening to some awful music in my bedroom."

"Can you make sure she eats something? If you don't push it, she won't eat."

She chuckled. "I raised five of my own, you know."

"I know. And I can't tell you how appreciative I am, Cousin."

"Well, bring me a burger and fries, then. From Shakey's. None of that cheap fast-food garbage."

"You got it."

He hung up and put the phone down next to his plate. He'd only taken a few bites of the meal but couldn't eat. Food was hard for him to get down, and it seemed to be getting harder, as though his body were rejecting it the older he got. An image of himself withering away would sometimes come to him. His ribs stuck out, his face gaunt and blackened with malnutrition. When he didn't feel like eating, he would picture that and then take another bite.

"Excuse me," he said to the waitress. "Could I get a beer, please? Corona with lime."

The beer was warm, but he didn't mind. He sipped it slowly and kept his eyes on the people around him. Personal intelligence, the ability to read and understand people, was, in his view, the most important type of intelligence. But they didn't teach it in college, and they didn't measure it in IQ tests. That was why people like the man who crucified Jane Doe could get away with things like that for so long: no one suspected them, because they were geniuses of personal intelligence. They could fit in and seem no different from the people they were around, just part of their world.

When darkness came, he left cash on the table and went out to his car. He leaned his head back and closed his eyes, leaving the keys on his lap. Rest wasn't something that came easily or often, but sometimes it would come in fleeting moments that would make everything else melt away.

Baudin wasn't sure how long he'd sat there, but when he opened his eyes he knew he'd been asleep. He started the car, and pulled away.

In Los Angeles, sometimes he would just go for long drives. Take the Santa Monica Freeway and drive until he was someplace new, someplace he'd never seen. He'd roam the neighborhoods with a small colored spotlight and shine it on houses in the dark, lighting them up a soft blue. He could spend hours driving around the city and still feel like he hadn't seen anything.

Cheyenne wasn't like that. The city wasn't sprawling with hidden nooks to explore. The streets were laid out plainly, and the people were even plainer. Everything had the appearance of being straightforward here, although he knew what lurked beneath that veneer. He'd seen it really close, felt it, tasted it on his tongue… and every city had it.

The Motel 6 parking lot was so packed that there were no spaces available. He had to park across the street in the lot of a payday lender. He stepped out into the warm night air and lit a cigarette, taking a puff before he began the trek across the intersection.

The girls were already out, more of them than before. The new ones were more beautiful and didn't have the worn appearance of junkies and alcoholics. Housewife hookers… women who came out part time to sell themselves, usually behind their husbands' backs. In his time in the vice squad, Baudin had even busted a medical doctor who would sell herself through Backpage when she grew bored. Baudin didn't fully understand it but believed it came from some need to degrade themselves. He tried talking to them about it, but their insights into themselves were clouded with layers of rationalizations and denial. Most of them hadn't the slightest idea what they were doing out on the streets.

He passed groups of women who smiled and asked him innocuous questions, awkwardly gauging his interest. Keeping his head low, he sucked at his cigarette, amazed at his sudden realization that there was no litter on the sidewalks.

One of the women he recognized from the other night. He stopped and offered her a twenty-dollar bill. She took it without asking what it was for and shoved it into her bra.

"Where's Candi?"

"You ain't heard?"

"Heard what?"

"She outta the game for a while. Got beat up by some john and spent the night in the hospital. Gave her thirty stitches in the face. Ain't no one gonna hire a whore lookin' like Frankenstein."

Baudin tossed the cigarette. "Where is she?"

"Home."

"I need to know where that is."

She folded her arms in a gesture of defiance. He took out another twenty and handed it to her.

"She's at the motel. One of the rooms on the first level. I don't remember which one."

He hurried back, pushing his way through two girls who stood in front of him, asking him something about a party. A man with glasses was eating Chinese food out of a carton in the motel office. Baudin stepped to the counter, but the man didn't look up from his food.

"Excuse me," Baudin said, showing him the tin. "Candi Carlson, please."

"What you want with her?"

"None of your damn business."

"Well, then, maybe her room ain't none of your damn business."

Baudin chuckled. The fact that this man was fighting him on this at this time was unbelievable. Life, he had always been convinced, had a sense of humor.

"Your tongue has a green tint."

"Yeah, so?"

"So there's nothing green in that fried rice you're eating. Weird thing for a tongue to be green. Only thing I ever seen do that is someone smoking a joint. Burns the tongue a light green in some people for a good half hour afterward. How much weed am I gonna find I start going through this desk of yours?"

The man swallowed and set the carton down. "She's in 112."

"Thank you for your help."

Baudin left the office, pushing the door so hard it hit the wall and bounced back. He strode to room 112 and put his ear to the door, hearing a television—canned laughter from a sitcom coming through at regular beats. He knocked with the back of his fist, but no one answered.

"Candi, it's Ethan Baudin. Answer the door."

For a good thirty seconds, nothing happened. Then he heard the chain slide off the door and the lock click open. The door opened a crack, revealing a bruised and battered face.

She had a large black eye, the bruising reaching halfway down her nose. Her lips were swollen and cut, and down the side of her cheek was a pattern of stitches like two pieces of cloth sewn together badly.

"What happened?" he said.

She swallowed, unable to look him in the eyes. "Just the cost of doing business, I guess," she said gently.

"That's bullshit. Who did this?"

"I don't want no trouble with him. He's a big man around here. He owns a lotta businesses, knows the mayor personally… I don't want trouble with him. It's done and over with, anyway. Arrestin' him ain't gonna do nothin'."

He exhaled, watching the way the light reflected off the eye surrounded by bruising. "You need money?"

"I got a little saved up. Hopefully won't be too much of a scar that I can't cover with base."

Baudin nodded, looking over as someone left their room and hurried to their car. "Who's the bigwig? I promise I won't arrest him. Just wanna know who he is so he's on my radar."

"Ted Holdman. He owns a buncha gas stations. That's how he made his money."

He reached up slowly, gently laying his fingers on her cheek. She kept her eyes low.

"Will you... I mean, do you want to come in?"

"No, I got work to do. I came by to see if you got a chance to show those pictures around."

"Oh, yeah, I was gonna call you before... well, before everything. One of the girls said she saw something."

"What?"

"I don't know. I think she said she saw a picture in some john's car. Picture of that girl."

A quick shot of adrenaline raced through him as if he'd injected it. "What girl?"

"Dazzle. She should be on the corner now. She's black, straight hair, real pretty."

"Dazzle?"

"Uh-huh."

Baudin took out his wallet, but she put her hand on it. "No," she said. "You don't need to pay me. I just… well, you're nice to me." She smiled shyly. "I think you're the first person in my life that's been genuinely nice to me."

Baudin held her gaze, absorbing the sadness and tragedy of her words. He leaned in close, kissed her on the cheek, and rushed back to the street.

Several girls stood near the motel. He wasn't in the mood for niceties and conversation. He grabbed the first one, spun her around to the shock of the other two, and slapped cuffs on her. One of the women pulled out her phone, and he held up his badge.

"One of two things is gonna happen," he said. "I'm taking all three of you in, or you're gonna point out Dazzle to me."

The two girls left standing glanced to each other. One of them said, "She ain't here now. She gone all night. But she be here tomorrow."

Baudin hesitated and then took the cuffs off before letting the girl go. "If you're lying to me, I'll make sure you're locked up as long as I can get. No money comin' in. Get me?"

"Yeah, we got you."

Baudin went back to his car, watching the gray-black clouds slowly drift past the crescent moon.

17

The precinct on a Friday evening was about as empty as it ever got. Dixon signed some files before he put them in a bin where the secretary would forward them to the screening team at the District Attorney's Office.

The front desk had someone at it twenty-four hours a day. Tonight it was Martha, an older woman with her hair up in a poof. She wore a plastic sheath over it when it rained. He went over after checking the coffee and finding it cold. He tossed the cup in her trash.

"We got anything?" he asked.

"A lotta interesting people calling about your Jane Doe."

"Interesting how?"

"Well, they said they saw it on the news, and they know her."

"How many?"

"'Bout fifteen of 'em."

He nodded. "Email me the info, and I'll follow up."

Dixon was heading out of the doors when she added, "One of them said her son did it."

He stopped. "She said what?"

"She said her son killed her."

He returned to the desk and set his hands against it. "Give me that one now, please." After Martha printed out the woman's name and address, Dixon headed out of the precinct, took out his phone, and dialed Baudin.

"Yeah," Baudin said.

"Had someone respond to the broadcast sayin' her son killed our Jane Doe. I'm gonna head over there now."

"Gimme the address."

Dixon was the first to pull up to the trailer. It looked like any other double-wide in the trailer park. Dixon had been to this park several times before as a beat cop. Domestic violence was common, as were drunk and disorderly and methamphetamine charges. Many junkies found it a safe haven, since the cops didn't patrol around the park and only came when someone called them. Usually the uniforms didn't put much effort into the investigation. The abuser in a domestic violence situation there would be the victim next week and then the abuser again the week after that. After a year or so on the beat, cops got jaded and got out of this place as fast as they could.

Baudin pulled up behind him and stepped out. Dixon grabbed his suit coat from the passenger seat.

"Who is she?" Baudin asked.

"Ran her name through Spillman. Nothin'. No history whatsoever. Ran the son's name, too. Same thing. No history."

"Well, that doesn't mean anything. Sometimes these guys can go for years without doing anything. That gives them a lotta time to fantasize and plan. They're good at what they do."

"You sound like you admire them."

"I just think it's interesting, that's all. That moment when someone decides the universe is chaos and they're gonna be part of that chaos."

"Shit. They're nothin' but horny fuckers with mommy issues."

Baudin grinned. "We're all horny fuckers with mommy issues. That don't make us killers. This it?"

"That's it."

They walked along the road winding through the trailer park. The double-wide of Vickie Connors was tucked away in a corner. Even in the dark, Dixon could see the equipment in the small playground next to it was coated with rust.

The stairs leading up to the door could only fit one person at a time, and Dixon took them and knocked.

Vickie Connors wore glasses so thick that Dixon was amazed they didn't fall right off her thin face. Her hair was a black-gray from a bad dye job, and she had yellowed teeth.

"What?"

"I'm Detective Kyle Dixon with the Cheyenne PD. We got a call from this address regarding a photo that was run on the news tonight."

"Yeah. Come in, I guess."

The interior was cluttered to the point that Dixon didn't know if he could find a place to sit. Old wrappers and paper cartons covered the couch. The single table in the trailer could barely be seen through the pile of dishes and cups sitting on it, all of them coated with rotted food and dust. The place smelled putrid, like the city dump on a hot day.

"Ma'am, is your son here?"

"Bobby? Oh, no. He's over in WSP."

Dixon glanced back at Baudin, who was scanning a small bookshelf against the wall. "He's in prison?" Dixon said.

"Yeah. I keep going to that parole board and telling them my Bobby's a good boy. That's what I say. And I got a letter from our pastor about what a good boy Bobby was growin' up and how it's just plain unfair they keepin' him in there."

Dixon pulled out his phone and its note-taking app. "How long he been inside?"

"Oh, let's see now… Two years and three months. That's right."

"I didn't find a history for him."

"Oh, he got lotsa names. Lotsa names. His real name is Richard Bellows, after his daddy. Then he had an adopted daddy, my second husband, and then my maiden name, Connors, and his adopted daddy liked calling him by his middle name, Bobby."

Dixon slipped his phone back in his pocket. "Well, we'll follow up with him." He put his hands on his hips, glancing around the trailer. "Why do you think your Bobby killed that girl?"

"I didn't say he killed her. I said he knew her. I seen her a few times. Nice girl."

Dixon's stomach dropped, and that familiar thrill of the chase sent shivers up his spine. He had to remind himself that this was probably nothing. This woman was likely delusional, and anything she told them was immediately suspect. Still, delusional didn't mean lying.

"How did he know her?" Baudin asked.

"They were an item. Cute couple. They'd do everything together. But he went away, and she moved on. Used to call and check up on me, sweet thing."

"Do you remember her name?"

"Alli was her first name. I don't know her last."

Dixon glanced at Baudin, who was scanning the interior of the trailer. "You sure about that?" Baudin said.

"Positive. Alli. She would call and check up on me."

"Do you remember where she lives or have her phone number?" Dixon said.

"No, no… I don't have none of that no more. My Bobby might remember."

Underneath the table, Dixon noticed an amber bottle of prescription pills. He bent down. The bottle was empty and expired almost a year ago. The label said it was Saphris.

"It's an anti-psychotic," Baudin said, seemingly reading his mind. He looked at her. "Are you out of medication, ma'am?"

"Oh, no, no… I don't want no pills. Not no more. Don't need 'em."

Baudin nodded, taking a final look around the trailer. "Thank you for your help."

He stepped out of the trailer, and Dixon followed, asking, "You wanna head up to WSP on Monday?"

"I think we should go now."

He exhaled. "Lemme call my wife and tell her I'm gonna be late."

18

The Wyoming State Penitentiary sat on sixty worthless acres. The compound was a two-hour drive into the wasteland, away from places people might congregate. Dixon remembered that when it had first been built, no one thought it would stick around for long. It was too out of the way. The buses shuttling prisoners to and from court would eat up too much gas, or the guards wouldn't want to drive that far, or a whole boatload of other reasons people thought it wasn't going to work.

Not only had it worked, it'd become a model of how states should run prisons: clean and efficient, with no amenities. The warden wanted to make sure not a single prisoner ever wanted to come back. He wasn't cruel, at least not that Dixon had heard; he just denied everyone the simple pleasures. Like television, working out, writing, or drawing.

Baudin drove and was waved through the gate after the guards inspected their ID badges and called somewhere to confirm them. The guest parking lot was nearly empty. Dixon stepped out of the car, and immediately the warm rush of desert air hit him. Later on, the warm air would turn so cold that the guards on patrol on the perimeter would have to wear coats. He had never understood how the desert could be hot during the day and ice-cold at night.

A path led to the front entrance, and the doors buzzed and opened for them. At the solid-concrete façade of a counter to the right, a guard pushed a clipboard in front of them. Both of them signed it.

"Who you need?" the guard said.

The glass edges of the metal doors leading into the prison allowed Dixon to see through. "Bobby Connors, or maybe Bellows."

The guard scrolled through his computer. "Richard Robert Bellows, twenty-six years old. That him?"

"That's him."

"I'll buzz ya in."

They waited as the doors slid open and disappeared into the walls. Inside, a guard nodded at them as they went past. Down the corridor was another door with metal detectors and two guards, leading to the general-population cells. To the left was protective custody, where they kept informants and sex offenders—people likely to be harmed by those in the gen pop. And to the right, where Dixon led Baudin, were the visiting rooms.

Though the general public had to meet with prisoners through bulletproof glass and spoke into a phone, detectives could have contact visits, meaning they were seated in the same room. The two of them entered visiting room two and sat at a conference table.

"This is nicer than the prisons I've been to," Baudin said.

"Guess it depends on what you mean by *nice*."

Baudin looked at the conference table. "If this is him, we'll know it right away."

"Just by lookin' at him?"

Baudin shook his head, his eyes never leaving the table. "No. He'll be superficially charming. One of the most charming people you'll ever meet. So charming that an alarm will go off in your head that something's off about this guy. He's too nice, too good looking, says all the right things. You'll feel that it's him."

"That ever happen to you?"

"Once. Dupas, that man I told you about. I'd interviewed him as part of the investigation and cleared him. But something didn't sit right with me. He had an alibi and seemed like a kindly old man, but bells were going off in my head when he was talking, like blood was seeping out of his eyes as he spoke, and no one could see it but me. I didn't follow my gut, though. We had other people good for it. I won't let that happen again."

The door opened on the other side of the room, and a prisoner in a white jumpsuit, shackled at the wrists and ankles, was led in by a guard. He sat at the table across from the two detectives.

"We got him," Dixon said to the guard.

The guard stepped out of the room and shut the door. Dixon watched the prisoner for a second before Baudin rose and began pacing the room.

"Bobby, how are ya?" Dixon said with a wide smile. "My name is Kyle, and this is Ethan. We're with the Cheyenne PD. Just had some questions for you. Hope we ain't pullin' you away from anything."

Bobby looked back at the door where the guard had left. "You guys got any rings?"

"Rings?"

"Yeah. You wanna talk, you gotta gimme a ring. Or a cigarette."

"What do you want a ring for?"

Baudin said, "They make tips for shanks. Metal you can sharpen's hard to find in here, ain't it, Bobby?"

"Ring or cigarette if you wanna talk."

Baudin slipped out the package of cigarettes in his pocket. He put one in his mouth and lit it with a match. Then he put one in Bobby's mouth and lit that with another match before placing the package in the single breast pocket of the prison jumpsuit.

"We cool?" Baudin said.

"We cool," he said, inhaling and blowing it out to the side. "What you guys need?"

Dixon pulled up the photo of Jane Doe on his phone, the doctored photo of what she would have looked like alive. He handed Bobby the phone.

"You know her?" Baudin said.

"Yeah, man. What she do now?"

"Who is she?"

"Alli, man."

"What's her last name?"

"Um… Tavor or Tevor. Somethin' fuckin' European."

Baudin tapped his ash onto the table. "How you know her?"

"We spent time together, fooled around some months."

"Then what?" Dixon said.

"Then she took off, man. She wasn't no good. I woulda married her if she'd've had me, but she ain't like that. So what she do now? Rob some bitches? Sell coke? She loved the nose candy, man."

Baudin glanced to Dixon. "She's dead, Bobby."

He was silent a second, glancing between them. "Dead? What you mean dead?"

"As in a doornail. She in the bone yard, brother."

"Shit... How she die?"

Dixon said, "She was murdered." Bobby's eyes grew wide. "Don't worry, she's been dead about a month, and you've been in here two years, right? We'll clear you pretty quick."

"Yeah, man. Almost two and a half. Got me another three left and I'm gone."

Baudin sat and leaned back in the chair. "Tell me about her."

"Whatchoo wanna know?"

"About her. What was she like, where'd she come from, what kinda people she run with..."

He shrugged, holding the cigarette between his fingers, the shackles rattling as he raised his hands to his mouth. "She was wild, man. Partier. Sometimes too hard for me. She was always goin' to them parties at the colleges, biker parties, shit, I think she was at a party every night. I didn't mind it for a while, but sometimes you just wanna chill and watch TV, you know? She never could do that shit. Always had to be doin' somethin'."

"Do you know any of her friends we can speak with that may have seen her more recently than you?"

"She only got one friend back then. Um... Dora, that was her name. Like that cartoon. Dora. I don't know her last name. But she worked over there at Macy's in the, like, makeup."

"She got parents or siblings here?"

"Yeah, man. She got a mama that live in Belmore. Tammy."

Dixon said, "What was her drug of choice?"

"She would do X and loved coke… She'd do whatever was around, I guess. She loved yayo. The rush. She never touched weed, though, 'cause she said it slowed her down, and she didn't like that."

Baudin was quiet a moment. "She was tortured to death, Bobby. Real brutal. About as bad as you can imagine it, that's how bad." He leaned closer to the man, putting his elbows on the table. "You know anyone in her life that could do that?"

"Nah, man," he said somberly. "Nah. People loved her. She was funny, man. And always had the hookup. Willin' to share if you didn't have nothin'."

Baudin nodded and rose, setting his palm on Bobby's shoulder. "We'll stop by if we think of anything else."

Dixon rose and followed him out. When the guard retrieved Bobby, they saw him staring down at the floor, his eyes reflecting the pain of what they'd just told him.

"How far is Belmore from here?"

"Two towns over. About thirty miles back toward Cheyenne."

"Good, maybe we can catch her before she goes to bed."

Dixon stopped. "Now?"

"Yeah."

"I'm goin' home, man. My wife's waiting for me."

"You kiddin' me? We just found out who she is. Don't you wanna talk to the mom?"

"Of course, but I ain't stayin' out till midnight to do it. She'll be there Monday. And don't you have a daughter to get to?"

Baudin bit his lip. "I'll go. I'll give you a call after." He hurried back to the car. "Come on, I wanna get there quick."

19

After Baudin dropped his partner off, he hit a drive-through and ordered a large Coke. He put Belmore into his GPS and took the interstate out of Cheyenne. Soft New Age music played through his speakers, something with piano and bass. It didn't matter; he wasn't listening anyway.

His eyes drifted to the white lines on the road, zipping past him so quickly they blended into one solid line. Beyond was desert and the rocky, jagged mountains. Even with the moon hanging over them, spilling light over the peaks, they looked black, as though they had no form or function. Just a blackness carved out of the sky.

He pictured ancient Indian civilizations living here, living off the land, worshipping gods in the trees and rivers. Even with the cities and cars, the airplanes overhead and the campers at the base of the mountains, the wilderness was still the wilderness and still had a pull for him—for every human, he figured—that he couldn't explain. Wonder, fear, and awe all at once.

The exit for Belmore was a small road leading to a cluster of lights that looked less like a city and more like an encampment of Boy Scouts with lanterns. The road narrowed farther into the desert, and he entered the town without any indication he had done so. No welcome signs, no street names or Wal-Marts. The only business he saw was a gas station that doubled as a butcher shop.

He had dispatch run Tammy Tavor through Spillman and got an address. The GPS led him through town, down a long road with nothing but rundown barns and shacks that no one used anymore. The grass was overgrown and shaggy, slowly swallowing any manmade construction.

The house was on its last legs, dull white with red shutters that were falling off the hinges. A chain link fence surrounded it, but the fence was even more dilapidated than the house. He parked in a driveway with garbage strewn across it and climbed out of the car. Taking a moment to absorb the scene, he was instantly transported back to his childhood and the foster homes he would bounce around. One of the couples had a house not unlike this. In back was a set of stairs leading below to a dark cellar. He would lie awake at night imagining what was in that cellar, what the darkness held for him. In the year he stayed there, before the father was arrested for meth distribution and the mother took off with another man, Baudin never once went down into the cellar. He still wondered if what he'd imagined down there was worse than it really was, or better.

The front porch had a mat that said "Leave your worries at the door" and a rug caked in dog fur. Baudin knocked and then took a step back. No lights were on in the house, and he couldn't hear anything coming from inside. Not until he rang the doorbell, and a light switched on upstairs.

A few minutes later, an older woman in a nightgown came to the door. A gray mole thrust out from her chin, taking up more space than it seemed it should. Her eyes fixed on him, but she didn't say anything.

"I need to talk to you about your daughter, Ms. Tavor."

Her eyes suddenly widened and grew moist. Wordlessly, she opened the door and let him through. She waddled over to the dining table and sat down. Baudin followed and sat next to her, close enough to touch her arm in comfort if he got the chance. He knew touch was powerful, more powerful than any words he could possibly say.

"When was the last time you saw her?"

"You police?" Her voice was gruff, a lifelong smoker's voice that was near giving out.

"I am."

"What type of police?"

He hesitated but somehow knew she could tell if he was lying. "Murder police."

She nodded, looking down at the floor. "She dead then?"

"I'm sorry." He reached out and gently rested his hand on her forearm. It felt too forced, and he withdrew it. Instead he reached for his cigarettes, and when he touched an empty pocket, he remembered he'd given them to Bobby.

"When was the last time?" Baudin said.

"You want a drink?"

He watched her and could almost see the loneliness in her. The type that hope and optimism couldn't touch. The type that had given up a long time ago and didn't even remember what it was like not to be alone. "A beer if you got it."

She waddled to the kitchen and came back out with two cans of beer. She popped them both and handed one to him. He took a long drink, letting the fluid coat his mouth and throat. Half the can was empty before he set it on the table.

"I seen her 'bout five months ago. She came here checkin' up on me. Sometimes she did that. Would clean up the house and such. She cleaned the house, spent the night in her room, and then left."

"She say where she was going?"

"No. I didn't ask. We ain't have that type of relationship."

"What type did you have?"

The woman grew visibly uncomfortable and the moisture in her eyes grew more pronounced. "She blames me... she blames me for what her father done to her. Sayin' I didn't protect her. That I knew about it and didn't protect her none when she was young."

Baudin didn't have to ask what she needed protection from.

"Her father live here, too?" he asked.

"He died some five years ago. Liver failure from all that drinkin'. Hard drinkin', since he was eight years old."

Baudin finished the beer. He belched quietly and let alcohol-soaked air out of his nose. "So she didn't tell you who she was spending time with or where she was living? Anything like that?"

"No, nothin' like that. We'd talk about gossip in the town, what her cousins were doin', stuff like that. We wasn't like a mother and daughter. We was like neighbors, if that. But she was sweet. She'd come clean my house ever' month."

He gave a melancholy grin. "That does sound sweet."

She nodded and quietly mumbled, "Uh-huh."

"Any idea who would want to hurt her? Maybe an ex-boyfriend she was worried about or something?"

"No, I don't know any of that. I just know she'd show up at my house once a month, clean, sleep here, and kiss me goodbye in the mornin'. Don't know nothin' else that could help." She sipped her beer and played with the can. "She go quick? I wouldn't want her to suffer none."

He pushed the can of beer away, not looking her in the eyes. "Yeah, real quick. She didn't feel anything."

"That's good at least."

"Do you have a recent picture of her I could have?"

"No. I got some baby ones but nothing recent. Her high school might, though."

Baudin felt an icy chill up his back. "How old was she, Ms. Tavor?"

"Sixteen."

20

Baudin left the Tavors' home in a stupor.

A child.

Alli had appeared so much older on the cross and at the morgue. The behavior that Bobby described was of a wild twenty-something sowing her oats. Not a kid barely older than Heather. The thought that Alli was only a handful of years older than his own daughter filled him with an unidentifiable dread that churned in his stomach as if he'd eaten something bad.

On the drive back, he didn't speed. Molly's house wasn't far from his own, but it was close to ten by the time he pulled up there. Only when he arrived did he realize he'd forgotten to get her food.

He went in without knocking and found Molly asleep on the couch, some sitcom turned low on the television. He quietly made his way down the hall to the empty guest room and opened the door to see if Heather was sleeping, too.

As his hand touched the doorknob, he heard giggling, and then two voices. One was his daughter's. The other was a male voice.

Baudin opened the door and saw something he knew he'd never forget: a boy pulling his daughter's skirt down to her knees, exposing her panties.

"Dad!"

Baudin felt nothing at that moment. No fury, no sadness, no regret… it was as if everything went dull, as if the volume of the world went down a notch. But what had to happen next was something he knew couldn't be avoided.

Baudin rushed forward as the boy jumped to his feet. He was older than Heather by at least four years. Baudin swung as the boy tried to say something, connecting with the boy's jaw. The blow sent him spinning onto the bed, unconscious.

Heather screamed, and Molly ran into the room as Baudin picked the boy up by his hair and cocked back his fist for another vicious blow. Molly grabbed his arm, holding him back, pleading with him to stop.

Heather sprinted out of the room, hysterically crying.

Baudin calmed down and pushed Molly off. "What the hell, Molly?"

"I'm sorry. I fell asleep. She must've snuck him in through the window."

Baudin stormed out, looking for Heather, but he didn't see her. He ran outside. "Heather!" He scanned from one end of the neighborhood to the other. He ran out into the street, his hands on his head as though in surrender. Panic gripped him now. When he looked back at the house, Molly was helping the boy out the front door. Baudin ran back.

"Where is she?" he asked, grabbing the boy by the collar.

"Ethan, let him go."

"I said where is she!"

"How in heaven's name is he supposed to know? You knocked him unconscious, remember?"

The boy wobbled and said, "I think I'm gonna be sick."

He vomited over the lawn. Molly held him up as well as she could, but he toppled over. "We better call an ambulance," she said.

21

Dixon lay on his couch, staring blankly at the television. Dinner had been odd. When he got home, it was sitting in the microwave. Hillary was taking a shower and had been in there a long time before she came out and announced that she would be reading in bed.

"What's wrong?" he'd asked.

"Just not feeling well."

When she didn't feel well, he was the one she came to for comfort. Something else was going on, something she didn't want to discuss with him.

He rose from the couch and moved to the door of the bedroom. Hillary was asleep on her side, the book lying flat next to her on the sheets. He watched her breathe for a while, watching the way her chest rose and fell, admiring the smoothness of her legs and the two or three wrinkles that were beginning to appear on her face. She was self-conscious about them, but he didn't care. He wanted a woman who was real, not plastic, but it seemed she would never accept that.

Feeling ashamed, he still went into the kitchen and found Hillary's cell phone. He turned it on and flipped through the recent call log, then the text messages, then her emails. Nothing out of the ordinary. He suddenly felt foolish for doubting her. The poor woman was sick, and here he was going through her cell phone as if she were a criminal.

As he went to the fridge to get a beer, his cell phone vibrated. It was a junior detective from the precinct, Cory Hatch on the night shift.

"This is Kyle," he said.

"Kyle, hey, man, it's Cory."

"What's up, man? You bored whacking off over there?"

"Yeah, I'm bored, and your dull ass is the first person I thought of calling."

"Hell, I wouldn't call your wife first either."

"Me neither, actually."

Dixon grinned as he got his beer and popped the top, holding the phone between his cheek and shoulder. "So what can I do you for?"

"Um… well, we got your partner here. Thought you might want to deal with this personally."

"Ethan?"

"Yup."

"What about him?"

"He broke some kid's jaw. Seventeen years old, man. Guess he caught the kid in bed with his thirteen-year-old."

"Shit. You holdin' him?"

"I don't know. The kid's father is talking lawsuit and newspapers… I just thought I should call you."

"I'll handle it. Be down in ten."

Dixon put the beer back in the fridge and rushed to his bedroom. He was getting dressed when he heard Hillary stir. She rolled over in bed and watched him.

"Where you going?"

"Looks like my dumbass partner broke some kid's jaw. I'll be back in, like, an hour."

"What happened?"

"Caught him and his daughter in bed. Don't blame the guy for somethin' like that, but I gotta get down there and deal with it."

He kissed her on the forehead before grabbing his gun and badge and rushing out the door.

When Dixon arrived at the station, he realized he'd sped down there and wasn't sure why. Everyone would've waited for him.

The precinct was calm and quiet. No phones ringing, no faxes coming through, no detectives laughing and telling stories. He found Hatch getting some coffee.

"Hey, where are they?"

"Ethan's at his desk. The kid's in interrogation three. His dad's pacing the halls, waiting to hear back from his lawyer."

Dixon looked toward the interrogation rooms. "What happened?"

"The boy was on top of his kid when he came into the room. Knocked him cold with a single punch."

"You called IAD yet?"

"Fuck them."

Dixon nodded. "Thanks, Cory."

"No worries."

Interrogation 3 was at the end of a long hallway, tucked back from the main floor. Dixon peered in through the one-way glass. The boy looked even younger than he was, and the left side of his jaw was swollen and red. He was running his finger along the top of the table, resting his chin on his other arm. Dixon walked in.

"Hey," Dixon said, sitting down across from him.

"Can I go home now?"

"What's your name, son?"

"Billy."

"Billy, I don't think you're goin' home just yet. We need to talk first. You want a soda or anything?"

"No thanks. My fucking jaw hurts. And the ambulance guys didn't do shit."

He nodded, keeping his eyes locked on the kid's. "We'll get you to a hospital in a minute. Detective Baudin's daughter—I'd like to talk about her, Billy. Will you talk about her with me?"

"I didn't do anything. We were just fooling around, and that guy nearly killed me."

"You bang her?"

"What?"

He leaned forward. "Did… you… bang… her? Did your fingers go inside her pussy?"

"No, nothing happened."

"That's not what Detective Baudin is saying. He said you were fucking her when he walked in."

"What? No, I wasn't! I was bangin' her a little, but she wanted it. That's it. I fucking swear it."

Dixon grinned and pointed to the camera in the corner. "See, what you just did, son, was confess to sexual abuse of a child. She's thirteen. Which means under the law, there's no difference between her and a six-year-old." He leaned back in his seat. "Did you know minors in this state over fourteen who're convicted of sex crimes involving children have to register as sex offenders for the rest of their lives? That's if the DA doesn't charge them as adults and send 'em to prison first. *Prison*, Billy. Where the big dogs are. Pretty young kid like you, they are gonna have some fun, I'll tell ya."

"I was beat up. Why are you messing with me, man?"

"I'm not messing with you. Detective Baudin will be punished. He'll probably be suspended for a while and get a black mark in his folder for brutality. That's nowhere near what's gonna happen to you, son. Do you understand what I'm sayin'? Your daddy's out there tryin' to talk to his lawyer right now and sue Detective Baudin." Dixon stood up and went over to the camera. He unhooked the wire, which turned off the red blinking light on top. "I promise you, Billy—if anything happens to Detective Baudin, I promise you that you will be charged as an adult for this, and you will go to prison. I'll call in some favors to make it happen."

Billy swallowed. "What do you want me to do?"

"Say you made it up and nothing happened. It was a friendly misunderstanding."

Billy nodded, his mouth open as if he'd seen a ghost. "Friendly misunderstanding."

"That's a nasty bump, though. How'd you fall?"

"I... I fell and hit my cheek on the bed. It was really stupid."

Dixon bent down, staring into the boy's eyes from only a few inches away. "That's right. It was."

Dixon left the room, leaving the boy with a blank stare on his face. He went to his desk and saw Baudin on the computer. He sat down across from him and didn't say anything.

"You okay?" Dixon asked.

"Just peachy."

"It's taken care of."

"Thanks."

Dixon swallowed, inhaling deeply through his nose and scanning the precinct. Hatch was speaking to the man he guessed was the boy's father. "I'm sorry," Dixon said. "Sorry you had to see that."

Baudin stopped what he was doing on the computer and leaned back in his seat. "She's thirteen, man... thirteen. She should be playing with toys and running around parks."

"It's a different world from when we were kids. Magazines and TV force them to learn about sex too early. Whatever you're exposed to early in your life, that's what you'll have a problem with later. For me, it was violence. My daddy was an alcoholic and came home some nights and whooped my ass for no reason. He wore this ring on his pinkie finger, some fuckin' high school football ring. I remember one night lookin' in the mirror and seein' the imprint on my cheek."

Baudin was silent for a moment. "Made you stronger, though. Sex doesn't make anybody stronger. It just destroys." He exhaled, leaning his head back on the chair. "What the hell am I gonna do, man?"

Dixon hesitated. "Why'd you really leave LA?"

"This. I saw what was happening to her. The people she was spending time with, the boys that were attracted to her. I thought I could get away from it by moving someplace like this, but there's no running from it. The black cloud follows you around."

Dixon checked the clock on his phone. "You feel like a beer?"

22

The bar was a place Dixon knew from back when he was a teenager. It used to be a place for college kids to hang out, but now it was rundown. The only people that went there wanted to hook up with the other people soaking their souls with booze. When he was younger, they hadn't checked IDs and hadn't cared who was drinking; black, white, biker, gangster, or gay. It was a different world back then.

They sat at the bar, and Dixon ordered two beers. Baudin stepped away for a minute to the cigarette machine and bought a pack of Luckies. He then searched his pockets for change and put a dime in the jukebox, a price that hadn't changed in twenty years.

The Who's "Rain on Me" started playing. Baudin leaned against the jukebox and lit a cigarette, taking a few drags before closing his eyes, blowing the smoke out through his nose. He strolled back to the bar and sat down.

"I'm glad I had a boy," Dixon said, sipping the icy beer. "I wouldn't want to raise a daughter in this shitty time."

"World's no worse than it's always been, man. That's just our species. I see fathers in Babylon knee-deep in this shit, too."

"I don't believe that. My father never had to deal with what you're dealing with. I had two sisters, and he never had to deal with something like this. The boys knew that was grounds for being shot. Something's changed in people. Sex is all over the TV, kids is wearin' clothes that hookers back in my father's day wouldn't wear, every punk wannabe in every ghetto in this country's got a gun... something's changed."

"Promises."

Dixon took another drink. "Whattaya mean?"

"I think it has to do with promises. Couple generations ago, a man's word was his bond. He didn't break it for anybody, at least not publicly. Now, nobody believes in promises anymore. Everyone's expected to break them. When you lose that trust in people, everything else crumbles, including morality. Morality is just promises."

"You talk about morality a lot for someone who thinks our own president killed thousands of Americans."

"You believe the Vietnam War was justified?"

"Stopping communism seems okay."

"Did we stop it? Did we even come close?"

Dixon shook his head. "Guess not, but that wasn't somethin' we could've predicted."

"Bullshit. They knew. And they sent those boys to die. Presidents kill people all the time. This time was just in a more dramatic way."

Dixon put his elbows on the bar, leaning forward. "Lemme ask you somethin'. You believe in God?"

"Personal God? No, man."

"Well, I guess there ain't no evidence of it for a man like you."

"If there were, what would be the point of faith? That's the problem with creation science, man. If they ever actually do get some good evidence of God's existence, they'll destroy their religion. Faith won't be required anymore."

"What about you, though? You got faith?"

"I got faith that people will screw you in the end if they get the chance. That's what I got faith in."

"Well, that's fucking awful, Ethan."

He shrugged, puffing at his cigarette. "Why'd you become a cop?"

"I don't know. Good insurance, didn't need a college degree, pay was fine for out here. Seemed like a good choice."

"You regret it?"

Dixon pointed to his empty beer, and the bartender got another bottle. "No, mostly 'cause I don't know what else I would do. Why'd you become a cop?"

He blew smoke out. "You wouldn't believe me if I told you."

"Now I gotta hear it."

"I joined up as, like, recon. I was part of an organization that advocated for transparency of the police department. We needed to know what went on inside the LAPD. This was, like, ten years after the riots, though, man. Everyone still thought the cops were as big an enemy as any of the gangs."

Dixon was silent a second. "You're shittin' me? You were a terrorist?"

"I wasn't a terrorist."

"You were part of a criminal organization that wanted to take down the police. What would you call it?"

"We didn't want to take them down, we just wanted transparency. Like I said. I'd wear, like, recorders and shit. Stupid nonsense. Just kids playing patriots."

The beer was as cold as the first, but Dixon found it didn't taste as good. The second one never did. "Why'd it stick?"

Baudin stared down at the tip of his cigarette and swallowed. "We raided this gangbanger's house. It was, like, my fourth day. Still a noob. The warrant said we were looking for pot, big bricks of pot that the CI said would be there. We were securing the house, and I went back to this, like, closet. Not really a closet, more like a really small room. The door wouldn't open, and I busted it down. This guy was taking off his shirt, and this young girl, maybe like eleven, was on, like, a twin size bed. She was staring out of this little window they let her have, just blank eyes. These eyes that, like... I've never seen them before. Some of the esés had kidnapped her right from her walk to school in the morning. They'd been shooting her up with H and raping her for days. The whole gang.

"I popped the guy with the back of my weapon. It busted his nose, blood just everywhere. I picked her up and carried her out of the house. At the hospital, she wouldn't talk to no one, so I went down to see her. I sat next to her and just talked about stuff. She started crying and buried her head in my shoulder. I must've let her cry for hours before she stopped."

Baudin blinked several times, as though he had been somewhere else and was just coming back to his surroundings. "Anyway, next day I turned the recordings off. I was a cop."

Dixon didn't know what to say. He drank his beer while Baudin smoked, and the two of them whittled away some time.

At around one in the morning, when at least six empty bottles crowded the bar in front of Dixon, he turned to Baudin, who'd been talking about his time as a beach bum, and said, "You think we're actually gonna find this guy, don't you?"

"I don't know. He might just be some trucker that came through town and is gone. These guys aren't stable. I can't predict what he'll do."

Dixon finished the last of his beer and stood up. "Well, that's it for me, man. I'm goin' home."

Baudin stood up and left some cash on the bar. "Thanks," he said.

"For what?"

"For taking care of that kid for me."

Dixon watched him as he put on his jacket. "Well, don't let it go to your head. According to you, I'm gonna fuck you over in the end."

23

Kaitlin Harris had been going to clubs ever since she turned seventeen. The fake ID, her older sister's, was enough to get her into any bar in the city. None of the bouncers cared. Everyone in Cheyenne drank from the time they could drive—all except the Mormons, but she didn't have anything to do with them.

The music was loud and the space black with flashing colored lights. Young men and women were grinding against each other, the men hoping to take it further, and the women hoping the men would go away. The dealers in the corners mostly sold X, but some had meth and coke, too. X was her favorite thing to do. It made the world the place it should've been rather than the place it was.

Her friends were at the bar doing shots while she sat at a table and smoked. The ritual had grown boring. Drink at home, drink here, end up at some guy's house and drink there. Booze and sex. The X would break up the monotony, but she couldn't afford it that often. Only one dealer here sold the pure stuff, and he sometimes charged $50 for two pressed pills, which was way more than she could spend every week. Sometimes he'd take blow jobs instead, but he was disgusting and she had never been able to bring herself to do it.

She glanced at the bar and caught the eyes of a man. He was handsome, though a little older than most. His blond hair was cut short, and he wore a black turtleneck and blue jeans. He smiled, and she turned away. She didn't feel like playing the nice girl right now.

Before she knew it, the man was at her table, sitting down across from her.

"Buy you a drink?" he said, his face revealing a dimple when he smiled.

"Long Island."

"Quickest way to get drunk. You looking to get drunk?"

"Aren't you?"

He kept her gaze, the smile never leaving his face. "Be right back."

The man went to the bar, ordered the drink, brought it back to the table, and sat down again. Kaitlin drank down a good third of it before putting her cigarette out and leaning back in the chair, the alcohol warming her stomach.

"You seem kinda older to be in here," she said. "No offense."

"None taken. I'm forty-three. How old are you?"

"Twenty-two," she lied.

He smiled again. "How old are you really?"

"You saying I'm lying?"

He held up his hands. "No, no. I would never do that to a beautiful woman looking to get drunk. Especially one with the nails you got."

She grinned. "I like 'em long."

"What else do you like long?"

She giggled in spite of herself. "What's your name?"

"Casey."

"I'm Kaitlin."

"Kaitlin, I couldn't help but notice your friends over there. You don't seem to be hanging out with them much."

"Nah, they don't want to get drunk. They wanna find boys to go home with."

"Hm. Both worthy goals, I guess."

She took a long drink. "What about you? What are you lookin' to do?"

"I am looking to take you back to my house and eat Oreos and watch a movie with you."

She laughed out loud and covered her mouth with her hand. "Bullshit."

"Scout's honor. I think it'd be fun, and honestly we're both too drunk for much else."

She nodded. "I think you just got yourself a date."

Kaitlin had ridden down to the club with her friends, so she just told them she wouldn't be needing a ride home. None of them protested.

Casey drove a nice Lexus. When Kaitlin got into the passenger seat, the warm smell of new leather hit her nose, and she closed her eyes.

"I love that smell," she said.

Casey opened the center console and took out a vial filled with a white powder. He put some on his hand and offered it to her with a rolled-up dollar bill. She snorted and felt the numbing burn of coke and then, only a moment later, the rush that sent her heart into a frenzy.

He peeled out of the parking lot, the tires squealing as the moon roof opened and Kaitlin howled. She felt good, better than she had in a long time. The streets were empty at this time of morning, and she stuck her head out of the moon roof and wailed like an animal.

Casey was smiling at her when she sat back down.

"You're beautiful when you scream like that."

She leaned over and kissed him, thrusting her tongue in his mouth. He let go of the steering wheel, focusing on the kissing, and the car veered to the right. He grabbed the wheel, and she laughed.

When the car finally stopped, they were in front of a house. This wasn't a neighborhood she knew or had even been to before, and she thought she'd been to them all. The house was up on a hill overlooking the rest of the neighborhood.

"Nice house," she said.

"Thanks."

They went inside. She noticed there was no alarm, which seemed odd for a house this nice, though she wasn't surprised. Not enough happened in Cheyenne for people to be worried about locking doors around the clock.

The furniture was black, the carpets red. The only decoration on the wall was one painting: a crescent, a sideways M and a U that looked as if it were bleeding down. She flopped onto the couch, feeling the effects of the coke slowing down.

"Got any more?" she said.

"Oh, I got something better."

"What?"

Before she could react, Casey was sitting next to her. He pushed a pill into her mouth and gave her some water.

"What is it?"

"Prescription pill. They call it Circle B. Makes you feel like you're floating on clouds. It'll work nicely with the coke to keep you feeling good."

Kaitlin swallowed the pill and leaned her head back on the couch. She slipped off her heels and placed her foot on his stomach, slowly sliding it down to his crotch. "You sure you wanna watch a movie when there's other things we can do?"

He grinned. "What else could we possibly do?"

She giggled. "I can think of a few things."

"You wanna go upstairs?"

She nodded. He took her foot in his hand roughly, squeezing it until it turned white, then he let go and stuck her toes in his mouth. He sucked on them a moment and then stood up, taking her hand.

The stairs were wide and carpeted the same color as the front room below. There were no decorations on that floor either. A bathroom faced them at the top of the stairs, but there was no shower curtain, no towels or soap.

"You just move in or something?" she said.

"Or something."

The bedroom was large, at least as large as the front room, but it was difficult to tell because the walls were all mirrors, as was the ceiling. A bed with red velvet sheets sat in the middle of the room. She ran and jumped onto it. The velvet was soft against her skin as she got up to her hands and knees. Running her tongue across her lips, she beckoned him over with one finger.

The smile was gone from his face now. He flipped off the light and then flipped another switch. The room was lit again, but a blacklight this time.

"This is wild," she said.

He joined her, lifting up her chin in his fingers. "You have no idea," he said softly.

Behind him, Kaitlin thought she saw movement, but it was hard to tell in this light. To the left, she saw the same thing. To the side, she heard something: the sound of breathing. Movement and breathing surrounded her.

It took a moment before the full horror of it dawned on her: they weren't alone in this room.

"What's going on?" she said.

"You should start feeling dizzy, but don't worry, you'll be awake. I told you, you are beautiful when you scream."

In a flash of movement and pain, hands grabbed her. Fingers clawed her body as they ripped off her clothes. She screamed and heard piercing laughter in response. Casey was laughing as he stripped off his clothes and approached the bed, while the hands held her down from behind.

24

When Baudin woke up in the morning, his daughter was gone. Panic seeped in, and he searched the house. He was on the phone with Molly when he suddenly remembered that she had soccer practice, and it was his neighbor Rachel's turn to drive the girls out.

His head pounded as he took a shower. Afterward, he took a thousand milligrams of ibuprofen and had some coffee, the only thing he ever had for breakfast. Two cups later, he felt awake, and he read a few articles on the Philosopher's Mail website and then headed out.

He picked up more coffee and some bagels and cream cheese at a bagel shop before driving to the Motel 6. The parking lot in daylight was nearly empty. He parked, got out, and headed to Candi's room. She answered before he'd even knocked.

"You brought me breakfast?" she said.

"Just coffee and bagels." He eased past her into the motel room. Setting the coffee and bagels down on the only table in the room, he noticed a copy of a check, signed by a name that wasn't Candi's.

"Check fraud," he said. "I didn't see a working girl like you as white collar."

"It's my uncle's."

He didn't speak or move, just held her gaze.

"Fine, it's mine. I got bills to pay, and how the hell am I supposed to work all cut up like this?"

Baudin sat down at the table. He'd brought two coffees, and he took his and sipped at it. "I wasn't judging."

"So you ain't gonna bust me for it?"

"I'm not the check squad." He slipped out his pack of Luckies, lit one, and told himself he had to remember to pick up some more matches. "I tried to speak to Dazzle last night, but they said she wasn't out there."

"She was. They're scared of her. She can get really mean. The younger girls are all scared shitless."

"Are you?"

"Nah," she said, grabbing a bagel and flopping onto the edge of the bed. "She leaves me alone. She knows I been in the game a long time."

"*The game*. Funny you would call it that. Does it feel like a game?"

"I don't need a lecture 'bout what I do."

The coffee was already cold, and he flipped the lid upside down on the table to use as an ashtray. "No lecture. I'm just curious what it feels like."

"Why do you care?" she said, with her mouth full of bagel.

"My mother was a prostitute. At least, I think. She left me on the doorstep of a police station when I was six months or so. Just always been curious about what it's like to be out there on the streets."

She chewed a bit and then said, "It's hell. But that's life, ain't it?"

He shrugged, dropping ash into the lid. "Fuck if I know."

She looked him up and down. "So you gonna catch this guy, or what?"

"I don't know. Depends how much Dazzle can help me."

"Well, she'll be out on the corners whenever it gets dark. She's got a couple of girls who work for her, and she takes the higher-end tricks. The ones who drive up in BMWs and Infinities."

He put his cigarette out and rose. "Just wanted to check in on you."

"Ain't you sweet."

"Sweet as molasses." He laid his card on the table. "That has my cell. If you see Dazzle here, you call me."

As he was leaving, she came to the door and said, "Ethan?"

"Yeah?"

"Ain't no one ever been nice to me. Especially no cop."

He turned and walked away without replying.

The Spillman database, exclusively accessible by law enforcement, had just about everything the police could want to find out about a person. Baudin hadn't yet been assigned a new login with the Cheyenne PD, but he still had his old one from the LAPD. He accessed it from the app on his phone and typed in the name "Ted Holdman." Several addresses came back, all of Holdman's businesses and his home address on Blueberry Hill.

Baudin put the home address into the GPS and drove up to Blueberry Hill, which must've been the upper-income neighborhood: no graffiti on the walls, convenience stores without bars on their doors and windows. Maybe all of Cheyenne was like that; he didn't know. He hadn't seen enough of it yet. But this area at least was the opposite of South Central Los Angeles, where he'd worked as a beat cop.

The Holdman residence had a horseshoe driveway, and he drove right up to the door and parked. The trees and bushes were trimmed well, the grass freshly cut. He could hear a sprinkler on in the back.

He climbed the steps to the front door and pounded on it with his fist. A moment later, an older man with a beard answered. Baudin recognized him as Ted Holdman from the photos on Spillman.

Before Holdman opened his mouth, Baudin popped him: one solid left in the nose that sent the man's head snapping back. Baudin slammed his fist into the man's kidneys before spinning him around and into his wall, his head causing a dent in the plaster before he flew onto his back.

A woman screamed—he guessed Holdman's wife. Baudin climbed on top of him and slammed his fist into the man's face again.

"You like cutting girls? Huh? You like cutting fucking girls?"

He punched him again, so hard he heard his nose crack. Grabbing Holdman by the collar, he pulled him near. "You ever go near those girls again, I'll put a bullet in your fucking skull."

Baudin rose and caught the eyes of the wife. She was holding her robe closed, her toenails freshly painted. The ring on her finger was the size of a decent strawberry.

"Excuse me, ma'am."

He headed home to pick up Heather and go to Dixon's house.

25

The car was silent as Baudin drove. Heather sat in the passenger seat with earbuds in, listening to music that Baudin couldn't hear. Which wasn't good; it meant she didn't want him to hear.

"What're you listening to?" he asked. She ignored him, and he pulled the earbuds out. "What're you listening to?"

"Just some band."

"Some band?"

"Yeah. You wouldn't know them."

A minute of silence followed. *But at least she didn't put her earbuds back in.* "I ever tell you I was in a band?"

"No," she said, staring out the window.

He glanced at her. "Are you not interested at all in what instrument I played or what kind of music it was?"

"Sure, Dad, I would love to know what type of music your shitty band played."

"Hey, what the hell is the matter with you? Ever since we came out here you've had a damn attitude like I'm just some jerkoff for you to talk down to."

"Whatever."

"No, not 'whatever.' I catch you having sex in my cousin's house—*my cousin's house*, Heather—and now you won't even talk to me. I should ground you for the rest of your damn life for that. You know what getting pregnant or getting AIDS would do? Do you even care?"

"We weren't gonna have sex, we were just gonna do other stuff."

He looked out the windshield. "You make me sick."

Instantly, he regretted saying it. And he could tell it cut. He'd found that no matter how tough a daughter acted, no matter the armor covering her, a dad could always cut her.

"I'm sorry, I didn't mean that. I'm just worried. We used to talk about everything, you know? Anytime you wanted to talk you never went to your friends, you always came to me. Now I can't get two words out of you."

"I wanna go home."

"Sweetie, I told you, we'll just stay half an hour and say hello before—"

"No, I wanna go *home*," she said, looking up at him.

"Home as in California?"

"I miss my friends. I miss Aunt Sarah."

Baudin didn't have the heart to tell her Aunt Sarah didn't give a shit. She was his wife's sister, and after his wife was gone it was as if he and Heather never existed. One day, out of the blue, he'd gotten a call from Sarah asking that he not bring Heather around anymore. It was too painful, she said. Too painful… Baudin'd had some choice words for her, and they hadn't spoken since.

"This is our home now, Heather. I promise that if you give it a chance, it will grow on you. I promise it will."

Dixon's home seemed nice, far nicer than he would've guessed for a cop's salary. He waited for Heather outside the car as she texted someone on her phone and then stepped out. Baudin knocked, and a beautiful brunette answered with a pearly smile.

"Hi, you must be Ethan. I'm Hillary, Kyle's wife."

"Nice to finally meet you. This is my daughter, Heather."

"Heather, it is so nice to meet you."

"Thanks," Heather said, not looking up from her shoes.

She opened the door wider. "Well, come in, everyone's here."

In the front room, a crowd of men were gathered around a television.

"Hey," Dixon shouted, "this is my partner, Ethan Baudin."

A few people said hello, and he nodded back. He recognized some of them from the precinct, but most he didn't. They were wearing baseball caps and T-shirts with the same team's logo. Baudin had once read a book on primate behavior that said they acted in groups because they were insecure as individuals. He tried to push that type of thought from his mind but couldn't. The thoughts were always there, and he would make connections, much of the time without wanting to.

"Heather," Hillary said, "this is my niece, Anna."

A young girl of twelve or thirteen was standing against the wall. "Hey," she said.

"Hey," Heather replied.

And just like that, they began talking—mostly about the schools they went to and if they knew any of the same people. Baudin stood by until Anna said, "Let's go out back."

152

The girls made their way through the house. That ability to instantly make friends was something he had never had in his life. As a child, he had been painfully shy, and bouncing from foster home to foster home left him unwilling to ever get too close. Whoever he happened to care about, who were few anyway, would eventually leave.

"Pull up a seat," Dixon said.

Baudin sat down in a folding chair. Within a few seconds, everyone exploded when something happened on the television. The noise was so sudden it startled him and filled him with anxiety. Rather than showing it, he rose and walked into the kitchen with his hands in his pockets as though just looking around.

Hillary was preparing snacks. She smiled at him as she went from the oven to the toaster and back.

"She's cute," she said.

Baudin saw where she was looking. Just outside, past a line of trees, Heather and Anna were on swings, another young girl, younger than them, leaning against the swing set and staring at the other two.

"She's my heart."

"Will her mother be coming?"

Baudin hesitated. "Her mother passed."

She stopped what she was doing and looked at him. "I'm sorry. I hadn't heard."

"What about your little one?"

She turned back around. "He's at his grandma's. He's really sensitive to noise, so I thought it better for him to be there during all this." She glanced at him and then back at the food. "You're not into sports, are you? I can tell."

"How do you know I'm not just new and don't have skin in the game yet?"

"No, I can tell. You don't care."

He turned to the sliding glass doors, watching the girls. "It seems like what men are supposed to do."

"Some men. But not you."

He grinned. "No, not me… Do you have a bathroom I could use?"

"Sure. Just down the hall, right there."

Baudin strolled down the hall, taking his time, studying all the photos. Dixon was a hunter, and there were at least thirty photos of him out in the woods or with a kill or smiling while wearing green and brown camouflage. In one photo, he held the head of a massive buck and was smiling widely at the camera. Baudin could see the ragged edges of flesh on the head. The deer hadn't been killed efficiently; something had torn the head off the body. Probably a cougar, and Dixon had found it later.

The bathroom was small and white, with a blue rug and blue toilet seat cover. Baudin shut the door behind him and stared at himself in the mirror. He turned the faucet on and splashed cold water on his face before exhaling loudly, his elbows resting on the sink. He used the new towel on the rack to dab at his face, taking his time drying it. When he was through, he stepped into the hallway.

There was an office across the hall. Baudin went in and sat at the desk. He leaned back, staring at a poster of Dirty Harry on the wall. The poster made him grin, mostly because it was Dixon's. He wondered if the movie was responsible for his becoming a cop, as it had been for an entire generation of young men.

He turned on the desktop computer, opened the browser, and looked in the history. The most recent things searched had been several conspiracy theory sites. Baudin typed in an address for his favorite blog: a government worker who allegedly worked for the CIA but wrote a blog about all the deviant acts of the government. His superiors, according to him, had spent $58 million the previous year trying to track him down and weren't able to do it. Baudin bookmarked the site, leaving it open when he rose.

The bookshelf in the corner drew his attention next. He didn't think there was any better way to know what a person was thinking than to look at their bookshelf. Dixon's was filled with biographies of athletes and presidents, a handful of civil war histories, and a multi-volume work translating the Bible into modern vernacular.

He stepped back out into the hall and heard voices.

Without making a sound, he crept closer to the kitchen. Hillary was arguing with one of the men Baudin had seen when coming in. He couldn't hear what they were arguing about—it was one of those conversations that was shouted in angry whispers—but he made out the words, "He's mine, too."

The two of them stopped the moment they saw someone else was in the room. Baudin looked into the man's eyes. Not a quick glance—a real, long look, seeing what was there.

"Chris, I don't think you've met Ethan. This is my husband's partner."

"Pleasure," he said.

"Likewise."

"Chris is our neighbor."

The two were so awkward, so absolutely uncomfortable, that Baudin knew instantly what the problem was.

"Well, better get back," Baudin said. "Nice meeting you."

He waited a few minutes in the front room while everyone was dipping dried meats and chips in the cheese and guacamole dip. Baudin watched Dixon, the way he would interact with others and get them to laugh, and always be willing to render support when they felt others were teasing them. Everyone seemed to like him. Baudin, despite himself, liked him, too.

Baudin went back to the kitchen. Hillary was busy with the food again and something she had simmering on the stove.

"How long has it been going on?" he asked.

"Excuse me?"

He held her gaze. "You're a cop's wife. You can't hide things like that forever. He'll find out."

"You don't know anything about me," she said, anger in her voice.

"No, I don't."

She put her hand over her eyes, rubbing her temples. "I think I'd like you to leave my home."

He nodded. "Of course." He went to the sliding glass doors and opened it. "Heather, let's go, baby."

Baudin thought she would put up a fight, but she said bye to her new friend and hurried over. She followed him to the front room, where he said, "Got an appointment to keep. Better bounce."

"Now?" Dixon said. "It's the first quarter."

"I'm sure the recap will be on ESPN. I'll see ya."

He left without any fanfare and no other goodbyes. When they were walking to the car, Heather said, "I miss my friends in LA."

"I know, baby," he said, getting into the driver's seat. "I do, too."

26

Baudin sat on the couch, Sartre's *Being and Nothingness* open on his lap but facedown. He'd been staring at the clock for the past hour. It was dark now, and Dazzle would be out. All he could think about was running down there to talk to her.

Most people thought prostitutes were local to whatever area they were working, which couldn't be further from the truth. The majority of prostitutes roved from city to city, usually led by pimps who didn't want to stay in any one place for too long. Dazzle could vanish tomorrow, and he would never get to see her again.

He dialed Dixon.

"Yeah?" Dixon said.

"Hey, sorry, I know it's getting kinda late."

"No problem, I'm just in bed watching TV. What's up?"

"There's a lead I've been running with. A prostitute thinks she saw Alli Tavor before she was killed. She's out on the street right now."

"You wanna go talk to a hooker now?"

"My daughter… I've asked a lot of my cousin already and can't ask her to sit."

"You want me to babysit her?"

"No, man. I thought if Hillary and the baby could come over here, we could go do it. It won't take more than an hour."

A long silence on the phone. "Ethan, there is no way in hell my wife would ever do that in the middle of the night. The hooker'll be there on Monday. You gotta relax. All this work, you take it this seriously, you're gonna burn yourself out. Caring about people this way has a price. It ain't free."

"I know. It was a stupid idea. I just thought... I don't know what I thought."

"Get some sleep. After church tomorrow, if you still want to, I'll come with you. You can drop Heather off here. Hillary's niece is staying with us a few days, and Hillary said they hit it off."

"Yeah, I think they did."

Another silence, though shorter this time. "Why'd you really leave so early?"

"Just wasn't my scene. I'm not a sports guy."

"Hillary said you weren't feeling well."

"Yeah, man. That too."

"Well, I'll give you a call tomorrow."

"Yeah, tomorrow."

Baudin hung up. He pulled another beer off what was left of the six-pack at his feet, cracked it open, and chugged half of it. He was drunk. He could always tell because the room would start spinning. He didn't hold his liquor well, and four beers was enough.

He rose and, as carefully as possible, tiptoed to Heather's bedroom. He stood in the door and watched her. When she'd been a child, he found himself doing the same thing, sometimes. The way she breathed comforted him. The rest of the world didn't matter as long as that little person was drawing breath.

The feeling was still there, only now it didn't comfort him. When she'd been a kid, a toy or an ice cream solved all problems. Now, he didn't know what she needed, and that terrified him.

He shut the door and went back to his beer. Within a few minutes of sitting down, a soft knocking came from the front door. He sat quietly a second, unsure if he'd really heard it, and then it happened again. He slid the beer behind the couch and answered the door. Hillary Dixon stood there in a coat, though it wasn't cold.

"Can I come in?"

"What are you doing here, Hillary?"

"I just… can I please come in?"

He held the door open for her. She brushed past him, the scent of body wash on her skin. He shut the door and sat down in the recliner as she took the couch.

"I like the house," she said. "You're an austere."

"What do you want?"

"I just wanted to talk about what you think you heard."

"If it wasn't what I thought, you wouldn't be here right now." A moment passed between them where they held each other's gaze, and nothing else needed to be said. They understood each other perfectly. "I won't tell him. That's not my place."

"I just… when it started I was all alone."

"I don't need to hear this, Hillary. You don't owe me anything."

"No, it would help if I could just tell somebody. You don't know what it's like carrying around a secret like this. It feels like I'm always being crushed. Like I can't breathe." Tears formed in her eyes, and her voice cracked. "I sometimes just think everyone would be better off if I just died."

"You can't die. You have a child now. One of the advantages the childless have over us, I guess. That child has no one else to take care of him. He'd be raised in daycare until Kyle could remarry. And stepmothers aren't exactly known for their kindness to children from previous marriages."

She wiped the tears away, drawing in a deep breath. "You must think I'm such a horrible person."

"No, I don't. I think we're all learning as we go."

"Yes," she mumbled, "we certainly are." She sniffed and glanced around the room. "There's no pictures of your wife."

"No."

"How'd she pass?"

Baudin swallowed. "She killed herself."

Hillary was silent as she watched him. "I'm sorry."

He nodded. "Like I said, we're learning as we go."

"How old was Heather?"

"She was eleven. After that, things started to unravel. Her grades dropped, her friends changed... I lost control of her. That's why we moved out here. I thought if I could give her someplace that didn't remind her constantly of her mother, maybe things would be different." He grabbed a package of cigarettes and lit one. "But there's no running from it. You're stuck in life where you are, no matter where you run to."

She folded her arms, staring at the floor. "Are you going to tell him?"

"I already told you I wouldn't."

"I know I have to tell him someday. He deserves to know, but he's so good with Randy. I just..."

"Randy's not his?"

She shook her head. "I don't think so. He looks like Chris. I haven't done a paternity test or anything, but it's obvious—obvious to everyone but Kyle."

"The world's just a construct in our minds. We see in it what we want to see in it. Maybe somewhere inside him, he knows and can't bring himself to think it."

She nodded, though he could tell she hadn't heard what he'd just said. "I better go. He'll wonder where I am. I told him I was just going for a walk."

Hillary stood and hurried to the door, but then she turned around and watched him for a moment. "It was good just to tell someone. It feels like it doesn't hurt as much."

"Glad I could help."

She shut the door and was gone. Baudin slid the beer out from behind the couch and took another drink.

When Baudin awoke the next day, he found that he'd slept on the recliner in the front room. Heather woke him after she showered.

"Sorry," he said. "Musta passed out from exhaustion."

"Exhaustion or beer?"

"Both." He sat up, the room still spinning. "Get ready, would you? I'm dropping you off with Anna at Kyle's house."

"Why?"

"Just got some things I gotta catch up on."

"Well, I was gonna hang out with Gina and them at the mall."

He shook his head, afraid that if he stood he might fall over. He tried it anyway and got to his feet without wobbling. The effects of the alcohol must've long since faded, and he wondered what was causing his vertigo. "I don't know who Gina is."

"She's fine, Daddy. Just let me go to the mall, and I'll call you after. Gina's mom is gonna drive us. What could happen with her there?"

He watched his daughter, the way she looked up at him with her doe eyes… the eyes that were exactly like her mother's and reminded him every day of what had happened. "Okay, sweetie. I'm trusting you, though."

"Thanks, Daddy," she said, leaning in and kissing him on the cheek.

Baudin went out and met Gina's mom when she came to pick up Heather. She was about the same age as he was, and attractive. She smiled widely and flicked her hair at one point. Her clothing was something a twenty-year-old would wear, and she was certainly attempting to appear as young as her daughter.

"I'll bring them back safe, I promise," she said.

"Thanks."

Baudin watched them drive off, then got into his car and called Kyle.

They agreed to meet by the Motel 6. Baudin got there first and waited by the sign, smoking and watching the cars pass. Even this early in the morning, a few girls were out on the corners. One got into a Cadillac, and they drove away only to return ten minutes later and dump the girl out on the corner again.

Dixon parked near the entrance and walked over. He was wearing jeans and a T-shirt but had his badge clipped to his belt.

"Lose the badge," Baudin said. "It makes them nervous."

He slid it into his back pocket. "So who we meeting?"

Baudin motioned with his head. Dixon followed him over to Candi's room, and he knocked. Candi answered wearing a robe that was open in front, revealing her breasts. Baudin reached in and closed the robe.

Her eyes were bloodshot, and her face drooped as though she couldn't flex the muscles in it.

Baudin slipped in, Dixon behind him. They stood in the center of the room and Baudin scanned the place. He saw what he was looking for on the nightstand: a spoon and hypodermic needle.

"I need to know where Dazzle lives," Baudin said.

"She ain't here," Candi mumbled. She collapsed onto the bed, her eyes rolling back before she snapped her head back then forward. "She gone."

"Gone?" Baudin said, approaching her. "What do you mean, 'gone'?"

"She heard some cop was askin' for her and she gone. She don't want… she don't want no trouble."

Baudin bent down so he was at eye level with her. "Candi, I need you to listen carefully. I need to speak with Dazzle. You need to get her on the phone and get her back here."

"She at the airport. She ain't comin' back."

"Where's she going?"

"California. She got family there."

Baudin rose, his hands on his hips as he watched the young woman. Drugs were glamorized in celebrity culture, but as he watched her turn into little more than a heap of conscious meat, with no direction, emotion, or reason, he wondered why anybody would want to turn into that.

No, he didn't wonder. Not really, he thought. He knew why: escape so deep that it ripped them away from their current lives.

"Who the hell is Dazzle?" Dixon asked.

"We need to get to the airport," Baudin said as he headed out the door.

27

Cheyenne Regional Airport was in the middle of the city. Baudin drove over ninety the entire way, expecting to have to explain himself to some highway patrolman who pulled them over, but none ever did.

He parked just outside the sole terminal and ran in, Dixon not far behind him. Baudin stood in the center of the terminal, staring past the metal detectors. A line was forming for a flight that was about to leave, and a few people were scattered in seats across from the gate waiting for their plane to come in.

Baudin rushed past the metal detectors, showing his badge, but the TSA stopped him and forced him to go through.

"You gotta be shitting me," he said.

"Sir, please just comply or we won't let you through at all."

He did as he was asked and then checked the information on the gates. The flight leaving right then was heading to Denver, the other one to LAX. Seated in one of the blue plastic seats was a young lady matching the description Candi had given him: straight hair, dark skin, purple eyeliner. He walked over casually and sat down.

At first, he didn't say anything. He wanted to watch her, the way she moved and interacted with her surroundings. She moved with confidence and defiance. If she didn't feel like it, she wouldn't be giving them anything.

"I thought you'd be gone by now, Dazzle."

She looked at him, an even expression on her face. Dixon was a few seats away, watching her face.

"Don't run," Baudin said. "I just want to ask you about ten questions, and then we're outta here. Is that cool?"

She looked at Dixon and then Baudin before nodding her head.

Baudin pulled out his phone and the photo of Alli. He showed it to her and let it sit for a while before saying, "You recognize her?"

"Nope."

"I'm not here to get you involved in anything you don't want to be involved in. We think a john murdered this girl. I know you're hard, you have to be, but you gotta care about these girls. They went through the same shit you've gone through. I know you don't want to see them hurt." He looked at the photo on his phone. "She was only sixteen."

Dazzle sighed and looked away. "Yeah, I recognize her."

"From where?"

"She and this other dude rode up on me about seven or eight weeks ago."

"You remember her face from that long ago?"

"They was real strange, that's how come I remember. The dude had this big smile and a Lexus. She was just sittin' there, like, staring into space. They wanted a three-way. I was gonna do it, too."

"Why didn't you?"

"I got this, like, feelin' from it, you know? Just a feelin'. I didn't trust that dude. Sometimes in this game you got nothin' but your gut to go on, and my gut said that muthafucker was trouble."

Baudin slipped his phone back into his pocket. "Did they say where they wanted the threesome?"

"No. Didn't say nothin' about it other than they wanted one."

"Did you catch his name or any part of his license plate?"

She shook her head. "Wasn't lookin' for that."

Dixon said, "Did you see anything that might help us identify this guy?"

"He had, like, symbols hanging down from his rearview. Like a sideways M and a U with a line at the bottom, like you drew the first line too long on a regular U. I remember that 'cause I axed him what it was. He said just letters."

Baudin thought a moment and then took out his phone again. He Googled the ancient Greek alphabet and showed her sigma.

"This the sideways M?"

"Yeah."

He pulled up another letter. "This the U?"

"Yeah, that's it. It was them two."

Dixon said, "You remember what color the car was? The model of it, maybe?"

"Nah, nothin' like that. I think it was either blue or black, though."

"If we put you with a sketch artist, you think you could help him draw this man you saw?"

"I don't know, I guess. But I can't. I'm headed home, fellas."

"We could arrest you for solicitation," Baudin said. "Keep you here."

"What? I ain't done no soliciting."

"Sure you did. You asked to give me a blow job for twenty bucks. Isn't that right, Kyle? Isn't that what you heard?"

"Clear as day."

She sighed. "Crooked-ass cops."

Baudin moved seats and sat closer to her, close enough that he could smell her breath. "You would not believe how far I'm willing to go to catch him," he whispered.

"Well this is some bullshit."

"It is, but one way or another, you're gonna help me."

The sketch artist said he was unavailable for Sunday work, and Baudin and Dixon each pitched in twenty bucks to get him out to the precinct. The only things he said when he arrived were "Where's my money?" and "Where is she?"

The sketch artist sat in a conference room with Dazzle for over an hour.

Baudin researched fraternities. Sigma Mu was a local frat at the University of Wyoming. It was on a block next to the university called "frat row," which he told Dixon they'd have to visit. "Those symbols... I'll bet you he's an alum or a current student and was in that frat."

"I worked there as a uniform when I first got POST-certified. You don't just run up on the frats. They'll lawyer-up right away. You gotta set an appointment."

"Shit, they aren't gonna talk to us. I want to talk to the *sororities*."

"For what?"

"They go to all the parties. They'll know if someone plays a little rough."

The door to the conference room opened, and the sketch artist came out. He slapped a drawing on Baudin's desk and left without a word. Dazzle came out and said, "'M I free to go?"

"Have fun in LA."

She shook her head as she walked out, slamming through the double doors hard enough to get one of them to bounce off the doorstop on the wall.

Dixon rose. "Well, I'm headin' home."

"Now?"

"Yes, now. And you should, too. This is one case. Don't get a hard-on over it. That shit never ends well."

Baudin was left sitting by himself. The only other detectives had been the two on call, and they'd been summoned to the scene of a home invasion. Baudin sighed and rose to go home.

28

Dixon waved to someone on the street who waved to him as he drove past. He wasn't sure who the man was, but he didn't want to be rude. He thought for a moment that the guy might be crazy, but it didn't matter. He missed the days when everyone said hello to strangers on the street.

He parked at the grocery mart near his home and went in. It wasn't one of the large grocery chains, but it had enough. Dixon grabbed some beer as he knew he was out and some flowers on the way to the register.

When he was back in his car, he laid the flowers on the passenger seat and wondered whether Hillary would really like them or if she would just pretend to like them. She had a tendency to spare his feelings in all things, and he knew there were gifts he'd given her that she hated but never said anything about.

He drove home with the windows down and parked in the driveway. As he was getting out, Chris was coming from across the street, a smile on his face. In his hand was a leash, and on the end of that leash was one of the ugliest dogs Dixon had ever seen.

"Holy shit," Dixon said.

"I think it's a dog," Chris said playfully. "Picked it up from the pound yesterday. Just needed a little company."

Dixon bent down and rubbed the dog's head. "Well, I'm sure he's got a sweet spirit."

Chris shrugged. "Someone else to talk to."

"If you're lookin' to hook up, Hillary has this friend who just went through a divorce. Blonde, skinny, an accountant… If I weren't married—"

"You sold me at blonde."

Dixon grinned. "You'll like her."

"Mind if we make it a double date? I'm a little awkward on first dates."

"Don't see why not." Dixon reached into his backseat and pulled out some files before getting the flowers.

"Those cases you working?"

"Yup."

"I always wanted to be a cop," Chris said. "Just never had the stomach for it. Too scared of getting shot or something."

"Yeah, there's that. But you put it outta your mind most of the time. Sometimes you can't help it, but officer deaths are rare. Especially here." He paused, thinking of his last partner, and then reached for his suit coat.

"I bet. That's one of the reasons I chose to live here—how safe it is." He hesitated. "Hillary like it here?"

"Yeah, I think she does. She's more big-city-folk than me, but I think she generally likes it."

"Huh. Her family here?"

"No, they live in Kansas City. Like I said, big city folk. She came out here for college and just never went back. Probably 'cause we got married."

Chris smiled. "Well, I'm sure it was worth it."

Something in the way he said it made Dixon think that he didn't think it was worth it. Almost as though he were mocking him somehow, though Dixon couldn't see how that was an insult.

"Yeah," Dixon said. "I better head in. You have yourself a good one."

"Will do."

The house was cool as Dixon entered. He hated wasting money on air conditioning, so he turned it off and opened a few windows, tossing the files on the couch. He left the flowers on the coffee table where he knew she would see them.

"Hil?" he shouted.

"In the backyard."

He headed that way and saw her lounging in a deck chair in her bathing suit. The baby was in a covered bassinet next to her. Dixon leaned against the wall and watched her. Her skin wasn't as tight as it had been when she was younger, but it was still toned and turning a caramel color from constant tanning. She had little body fat, and her abdominal muscles showed. A vein running down her shoulder was visible because of how lean she was, and—Dixon's favorite—another ran down her stomach and disappeared below her bathing suit.

He walked over and kissed her and attempted to put his tongue in her mouth. She giggled and pushed him away.

"Let's do it out here," he said.

"The neighbors will see."

"Let 'em watch. Old Mrs. Dodd needs to see some sexing."

She giggled as he bit her neck and ran kisses down to her shoulder. "Stop, stop. I'm embarrassed. But maybe tonight you'll get a treat. If you're a good boy."

Dixon pulled away, an erection pressing against his pants. "Well, a cold shower for me, then."

Inside, Dixon went to his son's bedroom and leaned over the empty crib. Even without him in the room, it still held his scent. This room—having a child's bedroom, even having a son—was something he never thought he would have. In high school they'd called him Dirty Dixon because of how many girls he'd bedded. It took a woman like Hillary to change him. Before her, he'd pictured himself a lifelong bachelor.

Dixon took another cold shower. He didn't believe hot water killed germs any more effectively than cold, but it did cost money to heat.

When he was through, he came out wearing sweats and toweling off his head. He began going through a stack of bills on the kitchen counter.

"Hey, hon?"

"Yeah."

"What's the name of your friend who just went through the divorce?"

"Tiffany."

"We need to set up a double date with her."

"For Ethan?"

Dixon grimaced. The thought of setting Baudin up with one of her friends was repellant for some reason, as if Dixon would be revealing some secret to a stranger. Though maybe meeting a good woman was exactly what Baudin needed to quit being so damn weird. "No, not for Ethan. For Chris across the street. He bought the nastiest-looking dog I've ever seen 'cause he's lonely."

An envelope addressed to him had no return address. He opened it and found an advertisement for a new car.

"You hear me, hon?"

"I did. I don't think they'd get along."

"He's not bad looking."

"She likes manly men. He's kind of feminine."

"Well, you're right there, but I already told him we'd do it. Set it up for Friday, would you?"

"I really don't think it's a good idea."

Dixon threw the last of the envelopes back on the counter and regretted going through them. Reading bills was the quickest way to put him in a sour mood. He trudged over to the couch and collapsed onto it, staring at the ceiling fan. "Why you fightin' me so hard on this?"

"I just don't think they'd be a good fit. And she's a friend—I don't want to set her up on a bad date."

"So we'll go have dinner, and if she hates his guts, we'll call it a night. No biggie."

"If you say so."

As Dixon closed his eyes and began drifting off to sleep, he thought about Hillary's friend and Chris. Hillary was right; he was feminine. And Tiffany's last husband had been an avid hunter and ex-rugby player. Chris had once told him that his favorite sport was volleyball.

Still, Dixon felt sorry for the guy. He was alone and didn't have a woman like Hillary to come home to every day. If he could, he would find someone for Chris.

29

Ethan Baudin was nearly out the door to find Heather when she called and asked if she could stay and have dinner at Gina's house. They were having spaghetti, and her mom, whose name was Keri, he learned, had specifically asked for him to join them.

"Maybe later," he said. "I have something to do tonight."

"Dad, don't be a douchebag. She invited you."

He sighed. "All right. Dinner, and then I gotta go."

Baudin went to a back closet. Inside was a large trunk. He took out his keys and unlocked it. It took some rummaging, but he found what he was looking for: a black nylon mask, a canvas bag, and a 9mm Smith & Wesson without a serial number, along with latex gloves.

He changed into black pants and a black T-shirt before putting the mask, gun, and gloves in the canvas bag and heading out.

Gina's house was in a more upscale neighborhood, and a BMW— not the car she'd been driving earlier—was parked in the driveway. Baudin parked at the curb and got out. Poor neighborhoods were all unique in their own ways, but rich ones were all the same. The quiet was what he always noticed; a deep quiet that never existed in a poor neighborhood. He smoked a cigarette by his car, enjoying the silence before going inside.

Keri had showered and changed, putting on fresh makeup and tight jeans with boots that came up to mid-calf. Gina, Heather, and another girl their age were seated at the table.

"I'm glad you could make it," Keri said.

He sat at the head of the table. All the family photos on the walls and on top of the shelves had one thing in common: no man.

"You didn't have trouble finding the place, did you?"

"No, I just did a GPS search."

The girls dug in and began eating. Keri slapped Gina's hand and said, "We say grace in this house."

Everyone bowed their heads, so Baudin did the same as a courtesy, though he didn't close his eyes. Keri said a quick prayer thanking the Lord for the food and asking that he bless it so it would nourish and strengthen their bodies. When the prayer was done, the girls dug in again and began laughing and joking among themselves.

"So Heather told me you guys moved out here just a few weeks ago," Keri said, spooning out spaghetti sauce from a white dish. She poured it over a plate of spaghetti and passed it to him.

"Yeah, we moved from Los Angeles. Change of scenery, I guess."

"Well, this must be quite a change of scenery. Most people I think move to northern California when they want something different from LA."

"I don't know. I wanted somewhere quiet. San Francisco's just as loud. What about you?"

"We're from Seattle originally. We moved out here for my ex-husband's work. And of course that didn't turn out so well."

"What happened?"

"We were always kinda drifting apart. I think we both knew the inevitable was coming. So he decided to get started early and began sleeping with a girl who worked at a tanning salon in town. I found out when I ran into them at lunch and saw them holding hands."

"Men's appetites control them, not the other way around."

She snorted. "Don't tell me you're making excuses for him, too. Gina does that all day, Daddy this and Daddy that."

"I'm not making excuses. We all have a choice in what we do. But I think maybe women don't understand how powerful the sex drive is in a man. We're designed to breed with as many women as possible at all times. Then comes civilization, and societal norms don't allow that. We have to repress our most basic urges. That's why there's so much violence in society. We're all sexually frustrated adolescents that gotta get it out somehow."

A long silence followed, and Baudin knew he'd offended her somehow. Social situations weren't his finest moments.

"What about you?" she finally said.

"Me included. Although sex has never had the appeal for me that it does for most men."

"Why's that?"

He tasted the spaghetti. It was good. The noodles were perfectly *al dente*, and the sauce had a spicy sausage flavor. "I don't know. Maybe I just always thought it saps you of your strength. Some research suggests that excessive sex actually lowers IQ, in males."

"Hm. I could see it." She twirled some spaghetti on her fork and took a bite before delicately wiping her mouth with a napkin.

Baudin desperately wanted to change the subject and knew he'd talked too much about it, but he couldn't think of what else to say.

"It must be hard raising a daughter as a single mom."

"I guess I could say the same thing for a single dad."

"Sometimes I don't know the difference between a girl and a woman. I don't know how to guide her in that transition."

She reached out and gently set her hand on his. "Well, if you ever need advice, I'm here."

They ate for a solid hour and talked. Despite his initial reluctance, Baudin actually had a good time. Speaking with someone who wasn't his daughter and wasn't a cop or a CI was rare for him. It was refreshing to talk about the mundane and meaningless.

He left later in the evening after Heather convinced him that she should be allowed to sleep over. Keri told him he could come over any time he had questions or wanted a home-cooked meal. He said he would, and got into his car.

Laramie was only about forty-five minutes from Cheyenne. When Baudin arrived at the University of Wyoming campus, he was taken back to his own college days. He had been studying history and was on track to enter graduate school when he tried his experiment with the police department. Policeman would have been last on his list of possible careers, and yet here he was, working a case in the middle of the night.

"Frat row" was on an incline, near the top of the hill. He found Sigma Mu and drove past. He found a parking lot up the block and left his car in a stall in a dark corner. He got out and brought along his canvas bag. He had fully planned on breaking into the car of the man Dazzle had seen, if he could find it. But now he didn't have the urge. He would find the car and, if possible, see if the man he was looking for was a current member of the frat. Still, he brought along his bag just in case.

Across from the Sigma Mu house, a thicket of trees stood like giants looking down over the house. Baudin simply stopped between them and sat down, making it nearly impossible for someone on the street to see him unless they were specifically looking for him.

There was a lot of activity in the house: people playing pool, some drinking in the front room, others upstairs in the bedrooms or watching television. He had stared long enough at the composite drawing the sketch artist had made that he could recognize anyone even resembling the man in the drawing. But no one he could see through the windows resembled the drawing. He wished there was a way for him to actually get inside the frat.

As he watched a couple of the boys playing pool and several more standing around and watching, he caught a look at a wall in the kitchen. The wall was painted red and appeared to be covered with photos.

Baudin debated what to do. He could go in with his badge, but he had no doubt a call to both campus police and the dean would be placed. Not long after that, a lawyer would be asking him if he had a warrant. After that, if the man he was looking for really was in there, his guard would be up. He'd be more careful, more selective.

Baudin opened the canvas sack and took out the gloves and the mask. He slipped them on and slung the bag's strap around his head and one shoulder. Looking down both sides of the street, he dashed across and to the back of the Sigma Mu house.

The backyard was enormous, with unlit tiki torches spaced every five feet or so. The fence gate was open, and he just slipped inside. Ducking low, he made his way cautiously to the back door. The canvas bag had a lockpick kit in one of the pockets, but he hoped the door would just be open. He tried the knob, but it was locked.

The lockpick kit was something he'd confiscated from a man who'd described himself as a professional burglar. More advanced than anything someone could buy on the market, the man had designed and created it himself. He'd told Baudin that a person could open over 99% of the world's locks with it.

Baudin inserted a long thin piece, almost like an Allen key, into the lock, and then slid what appeared to be a pin on top of it. With a few turns and tugs, the lock was open. He slipped inside the frat house.

The smell was something he remembered well: young men. Whenever young men lived together, the house always had a certain smell. Musky, almost as if the place had been coated with sweat and allowed to dry.

The kitchen was empty. Baudin, crouching in a duck walk, headed straight to the wall of photos. Most were of drunken parties, girls that had come through the frat, and photos of the members at sporting events or concerts. Up in the corner were at least twenty photos of each year's members in front of the house, almost like a school picture. Baudin counted them as he took them all down and shoved them in his sack.

"Hey! What the fuck?"

He looked back to see a young man standing at the kitchen entrance with a beer in his hand. Without a word, Baudin dashed out the back door.

"Hey!"

Sprinting out the fence gate, he heard the stomp of shoes as the men poured out of the house. They were coming out of the front door by the time he got to the sidewalk, and one of them got in front of him. Baudin ducked low, drawing the man's attention there, and came up with a hook that slammed into the man's jaw, sending him reeling back.

He ran the opposite direction of his car. Men shouted behind him, and car engines were turning. At the bottom of the hill he sprinted through the tennis courts and out the other side into a small park with playground equipment. As fast as he could, his heart pounding in his ears, he jumped inside a large cement tube that was coated with rubber on the bottom: something for children to crawl through.

He lay still, the pack still clamoring for him. He debated getting out the gun but knew even threatening these young men with it was too much. They'd done nothing to deserve that. He would wait in here and hope they passed.

Footfalls grew louder and then quieter as the men ran past the playground. He waited a long time, so long that his heart had calmed. Poking his head out of the tube, he saw no one. Another street near the playground seemed to head up, right past frat row but a block over. He ran for the street, and as he crossed an intersection he saw red-and-blues turning up frat row.

The upscale neighborhood right next to the frat houses was all large homes and well maintained. The easiest way to tell if a neighborhood was affluent was the amount of debris. The rich tended not to have debris in their neighborhoods.

The streets were clean and the lawns manicured. It was quiet, and he stopped for a second and just watched the homes. Through a window he saw a family gathered in the front room. Two children, a mother, and a father. Baudin watched them a long time, feeling as though he'd swallowed lead in his gut, and then hurried up to his car. There was no one in the parking lot, and he stripped off the mask and gloves and threw them in a trashcan at the front of the lot. He started the car and pulled away.

He turned up the hill rather than going back past frat row and soon had looped around and found the interstate again. He reached his hand into the sack and felt the photos. Somewhere in one of them was the man he was looking for, the man who had tortured Alli Tavor to death, and probably several others.

———

184

He grinned and pressed the accelerator down.

30

Dixon was woken by his cell phone, and he silenced it without seeing who it was. Hillary lay nude next to him, only the corner of their sheets lying across her breasts. He watched her a long time, the curves in her soft flesh, the way her chest moved with each inhalation of breath, the perfect lips with the strands of hair that came down over her face… She was even more attractive than when he'd first seen her.

He turned finally to his phone and saw that Baudin had called. Dixon texted him.

What?

You need to come to my house

Why?

You'll see. Just come down

He exhaled loudly and rose from bed, rubbing the back of his head before hitting the shower.

The baby had slept all night, giving Dixon that weird euphoria that the sleep-deprived got when they suddenly were allowed to sleep. The shower went quickly, and he dressed and was eating breakfast before Hillary was even up.

"Morning," she said, heading for the coffee.

"Morning. Little guy slept the whole night."

"I know. Let's hope he makes a habit of it."

She retrieved her coffee and sat next to him. He reached out and set his hand over hers before leaning in and kissing her. "I love you," he said.

She looked down at the table. "I love you, too."

He squeezed her hand, rose, and kissed her again before leaving.

The sky was a light blue, a little hazy but without too many clouds. A breeze blew, and he sat in his car a moment and listened to it rustle the leaves on the trees surrounding his home.

Once he was on the road, he turned on a country station, and Lynyrd Skynyrd was playing. He turned it up, tapping his hand on the door as he took the interstate.

At the baseball field near Baudin's home, a man was walking around flattening the dirt with a machine that looked like a riding lawnmower. Dixon waved to him as he got out of the car, but the man's head was down, and he didn't see it.

He knocked, and Baudin answered a second later. He wasn't dressed, and his eyes were rimmed with red.

"You look like shit," Dixon said.

"Good morning to you, too," Baudin said, leaving the door open.

Dixon shut the door behind him and followed Baudin into the kitchen as he prepared some tea.

"You want some?" Baudin asked.

"No, thanks."

"Tea's good for you. Lots of antioxidants to get all that shit out that the corporations pump into our food."

Dixon sat on a stool. "I thought we'd go interview that friend who works at Macy's today. See if she knew who Alli was hangin' out with."

Baudin nodded while taking a sip of his tea. "I got something to show you first."

Dixon hopped down and followed him to the stairs leading to the dark basement. Baudin flipped on a light, one bare light bulb for the entire basement. Several photographs were pinned above a desk pushed up against the wall. A copy of the composite sketch they'd gotten hung next to the photographs.

"What's this?"

"He's there," Baudin said, his eyes on the photos. "He's in one of these photos."

"How do you know?"

"He's an alum, or he's in the frat now. I know it. No one else would have a Sigma Mu up on their rearview. He's a brother."

Dixon put his hands on his hips, surveying the photos. "How'd you even get these?"

"They got the years written on 'em, but the hard part's going to be the names. There's no names on any of these photos." He thrust his middle finger at a boy with a circle in marker around his face in one of the photos. "It's either him," Baudin said, then pointed at another boy's circled face, "or him."

Dixon leaned in close. The composite sketch was rough, little more than a general outline, as though the artist just didn't have the time, or didn't *want* to take the time, to fill in the details. "Could be, I guess. Could be a buncha other people, too."

Baudin shook his head, taking a sip of his tea. "It's one of them."

"Well, I guess we can take the photos to Dora and see if she recognizes one of them."

Baudin put his tea down. "Lemme get dressed."

Macy's wasn't terribly busy as Dixon and Baudin strode in. Dixon had never liked the store. Maybe something about the lighting or the customer service… something didn't sit right with him. As soon as he walked in, that uncomfortable feeling hit his gut.

Baudin went up to an older woman behind a counter near the clothing and said, "Excuse me. We're looking for Dora."

"She's in the fragrance department."

The fragrance department was completely empty except for a young girl with straight black hair who was busy stocking a shelf. Dixon approached her. She looked fragile, and he was worried that Baudin's direct style might intimidate her.

"Are you Dora?" Dixon asked.

She looked up with soft blue eyes, and Dixon could tell her first response was fear. "Yes?"

"I'm Detective Kyle Dixon with the CPD. Um, did you know Alli Tavor, Dora?"

She closed the shelf she was working on, pulling a transparent plastic sheath over it. "I heard what happened. Her mom called me and told me she was dead. I'm sorry, I told one other person, and now everybody at school heard. They announced it on the PA and had a moment of silence." She looked away. "I had to leave school. I couldn't stop cryin'."

"I'm sorry about your friend," Dixon said.

She nodded. "She was always partying, always hanging out with college guys and going to clubs. She ran away once and moved in with this thirty-year-old guy who was divorced. Her mom got her back, but it didn't do nothin'. I always thought... I mean, I didn't think *this*... but I always thought somethin' bad was gonna happen."

Dixon nodded. He glanced down and saw that the girl was wearing an engagement ring. "Can we talk somewhere private?"

"Sure. Lemme get someone to cover."

Dora left, and after a few moments, another girl had taken her place. They walked outside, and Dora took out a package of cigarettes. Belatedly realizing she was with two cops, she put the cigarettes away again.

Baudin took out his pack and lit two. He handed one to her and smoked the other one.

"Thanks," she said bashfully.

"These guys she was hanging out with," Dixon said. "You ever meet 'em?"

"Sure I met 'em. I met that thirty-year-old guy, too. He always creeped me out."

Baudin said, "You catch his name?"

"Tom. I don't know his last name. He lived in them apartments up on Orem Street. Philip somethin'."

"Philip Arms," Dixon said. "I know the place. Did Alli ever tell you Tom was mean to her or acting strange? Was she afraid of him?"

"No, I don't think so," she said, blowing out a puff of smoke. "He was creepy, though. Made us watch pornos when we was at his apartment. I think he was hopin' to fuck both of us."

Dixon nodded. "What about the college guys?"

"Just college guys. A lot of 'em. She'd go party up at their frat."

Baudin pulled out the photo from a manila envelope he had tucked in his waistband. "You recognize any of these guys as people she hung out with?"

Baudin had erased the circles around their faces. He slowly flipped through the photos as Dixon hung back and watched the girl's reaction. Baudin flipped back ten years, and she didn't say anything.

"Nothin'?" Dixon said.

"I mean, some of 'em look familiar, but it's kinda hard to see. Them pictures is blurry."

Baudin said, "Do you have any photos on your phone of any of the guys?"

She shook her head, holding the cigarette low between two fingers. "No, I don't think so."

"Was she dating any one frat guy in particular?"

"Um… I don't think so."

Dixon said, "Did you go up there with her?"

The girl looked away. "No. Because of them parties."

"What parties are those?" Dixon asked.

"They call 'em slut parties, but only the guys in the frat call 'em that." She took a pull of smoke. "They're really rape parties."

"Rape parties?" Baudin asked.

"Yeah. They, like, throw a party and invite a bunch of girls. Then they kinda, I guess, vote on which one they're gonna do. Then they get her drunk or put, like, roofies or GHB in her drinks. When her friends aren't paying attention, the guys take her upstairs."

191

Dixon couldn't speak for a second and just stared at the girl. "Are you telling me they organize and rape girls at these parties?"

"Yeah, they throw 'em, like, for special occasions, I guess. New people comin' into the frat or somethin'."

"Have you seen one?"

She nodded. "I wasn't picked, but a girl I knew was."

"I'll need her name."

"Ruth Chase. She's a grade behind me. Or was. I dropped out."

Baudin took down the name in his phone. "We're looking for one person in particular, Dora. A man who knew her, spent time with her, and then wasn't that broken up about her disappearing. Can you think of any man like that?"

She shook her head. "No, I didn't go to those parties after what happened to Ruth."

Dixon stood grinding his teeth. Baudin must've noticed because he said, "Thanks for your help. We'll give you a call if we need anything else."

As they were walking back to the car, Dixon couldn't speak. The anger inside of him was too much.

"I worked campus police there, man," Dixon said. "There was nothin' like that back then. What the hell is wrong with the world?"

"You're just seeing more of it. Or you didn't see enough of it back then."

"Bullshit. There weren't no rape parties twenty years ago."

"Maybe not here. I worked some. It's a type of binding oath they have. Everyone in the frat has to rape her, that way none of them can go to the cops because they were part of it, too. Keeps their silence. It started in the Ivy League. The rich kids would invite the poor ones from other schools and rape one. Degradation, man. It's what it's always been about."

Baudin opened the door to the car but stood there a second. "I think we should visit the friend at school before the porno guy. She'll know more about what the frat guys are like than anyone."

31

Hillary Dixon finished her workout and cooled off by walking on the treadmill. The sweat had poured out of her in a way she wasn't used to, and she checked her distance: she'd run ten miles, four miles more than her usual.

The gym was always busy with the stay-at-home mothers who kept their bodies in perfect shape. She saw the way they looked at her as though she were poison but then would all smile and pretend they were her friend when she spoke to them. She didn't understand their jealousy. Hillary had always been beautiful and never gave a second thought to it. Intelligence was more important to her, but she didn't hate those more intelligent than herself. She admired them and tried to learn from them. Pettiness wasn't an emotion she could relate to.

The daycare worker was a skinny woman with a tattoo on her neck, and she was playing with Randy, making him coo and smile. From a few steps back, Hillary stared at her son. The older he got, the cuter he got. But he also resembled his father more and more.

She'd told herself to get a paternity test dozens of times. Once she'd gotten as far as walking into the clinic before turning around. A glimmer of hope still existed that Randy was her husband's child, that she wasn't the worst wife she'd ever known—something she felt constantly—and that life could go back to some sort of normal, without the endless bouts of crying and dread that would eat up her days.

A day would come when Kyle would look at his son and realize he looked nothing like him, and she didn't know what she was going to do on that day.

"Hey," she said, "you miss me?"

Randy cooed as the daycare worker laughed. Hillary picked him up in her arms and kissed his cheeks. Regardless of what she had done, of what she and Chris had done, the child was innocent. He was pure and good... and her son. Even if he wasn't Kyle's.

She walked out of the gym and to her car. As she approached, she saw a man leaning against the driver's side door. Chris stood there with a grin on his face. His arms were folded, and his eyes never left the baby.

"Are you following me?" she said.

"We used to meet in places like this," he said, looking out over the traffic in the street. "Anywhere we thought Kyle wouldn't be. Little nooks of the city I didn't even know existed."

She pushed him away and opened the backdoor. Buckling Randy into his car seat, she saw Chris get into the passenger side.

"Get out."

"I need a ride."

"I said get out."

"I'm serious. Just a ride. I took the bus down here."

She sighed. Once the baby was buckled in, she sat in the driver's seat and closed her eyes for a moment. His scent still gave her shivers down her spine. Every man had a unique scent and, though she had known many lovers in her life, she had only known the scent of two men.

"Please, Chris, if you ever cared for me at all, please leave us alone."

"How can you ask me to do that? We have a child together. Doesn't that mean anything to you? Are you really so cold that you would raise this boy without telling him who his real father is? Do you think he would love you for that?"

Tears were streaming down her face. "Please, I don't know what I'm going to do. Just please leave us alone. Please."

He was quiet a moment. "I'm sorry, I can't do that." He took some papers out of a satchel and laid them on the dash. "That's a petition to force a paternity test. If he's mine, I'm going to sue for custody. Just weekends. Even every other weekend. Just so he doesn't grow up thinking his father's completely abandoned him."

Reason had gone out the window, and Hillary felt nothing but a deep ache that started in her gut and ran up to her head. It dulled everything and filled her with a terror that made her tremble. "Please... please... why are you doing this?"

He gently took her hand. "Because I love him... and you."

"No, no... no."

He kissed her, and she let him. His lips were soft, far softer than Kyle's, and the pit of her stomach quivered at his kiss.

"I'm married," she whispered, pulling away. He brought her head onto his shoulder. "I'm married."

"I know. But you don't have to be. We don't have to be apart, Hillary. Do you still love him?"

"Yes."

"But you love me, too. I know it. I can see it when you look at me."

He held her, his arms wrapped around her as she wept. A single image kept coming to her: Kyle. Her husband. The one who she swore she would always be loyal to. The one who had always been loyal to her. The one who she had betrayed in the deepest way possible. Somewhere inside her, she knew there was a price that would have to be paid. Betrayal this intimate had to be avenged.

She pulled away from Chris, stared into his eyes, and then pressed her lips to his.

32

"Shit, I loved high school," Dixon said as they parked in guest parking.

Baudin scanned the school and then looked at his partner. "I figured you'd be the type."

"And what type is that?"

"Someone who would think this meat grinder was enjoyable." He stepped out of the car and watched as Dixon popped some gum and followed him. A paved sidewalk led up to the front doors and was surrounded by grass and trees.

"I take it Ethan Baudin didn't have a good time in high school. What, did you get picked on by the jocks?"

"How do you know I wasn't a jock?"

"No, you got nerd written all over you."

Ethan began to pull out his cigarettes then thought better of it. "I was an outcast. For gym class I'd sit on the sidelines and read Shakespeare. That didn't win me many friends. Kids, though, adolescents, see, their brains aren't formed like ours. They can't repress what's inside them as well. They're cruel in a way adults would be arrested for. Monsters."

"I wasn't a monster."

Baudin looked at him as he held the door open. "Ask the people you stepped on, and let's see if they say the same thing."

The school seemed small. Baudin remembered high school appearing larger than life, and he didn't know whether it was the school or if he had been shorter. Maybe the perspective of middle age looking back on youth just aggrandized everything.

The administration offices were to the left, and Baudin went inside. Dixon sat down in one of the chairs as if he were waiting for the principal.

Baudin asked the receptionist to speak to the vice principal. He knew the vice principal was the one who did most of the work and would know the students intimately.

A skinny man with hair that was slicked back to cover a bald spot stepped out of an office a moment later. He shook hands with Baudin.

"Roger Daft."

"Detective Ethan Baudin."

"Pleased to meet you. My brother's a highway patrolman, actually."

Baudin ignored his attempt at familiarity and said, "We need to speak to one of your students, Ruth Chase. And then maybe a few more after that."

"I assume this is about Alli."

"It is."

He nodded, solemnly looking down at the floor. "I was wondering when you'd come out. I don't announce things like that without the parent's consent. The mother consented, I want you to know that."

Baudin shrugged, though it was odd that her mother had called Dora and told her that quickly. He wondered why she would want everyone else to know her daughter died. "I don't care. I want to know about her."

"I knew you would. I met with her a lot because of her behavioral problems." He cleared his throat. "She accused me of sexual harassment once. You should probably know that. It was a complete fabrication, of course. But that was the way she was. She was promiscuous at an early age and used her sexuality to get what she wanted. Very underhanded that way."

Baudin stepped close to the man, not breaking eye contact with him. "She was a kid."

"I know," he stammered, "I know. I'm just saying she had certain proclivities... that's all. I'll have someone pull Ruth out of class for you."

Dixon was smiling when Baudin turned around.

"What?" Baudin asked.

"Just interesting the stuff that gets you riled up, that's all."

"Why would Alli's mom call Dora and tell her she's dead?"

Dixon shrugged. "Who the hell knows? Maybe she wants to play the grieving victim and can only do that if everyone knows our Jane Doe is her little girl. Don't matter, I stopped asking questions like that a long time ago."

Baudin paced the offices until one of the staff brought in a girl with glasses and worn jeans.

"May we use this office?" Baudin asked.

"Sure," the receptionist said without looking up.

The office was decorated with motivational posters. Baudin sat on the couch so as not to give the appearance of authority. She sat across from him in a recliner, wringing her hands.

"You're not in trouble, Ruth," Baudin said. "I'm Detective Baudin, and this is Detective Dixon. But you can call me Ethan, okay?"

"Okay."

"I guess you heard what happened to Alli Tavor."

She nodded without looking up.

"It's come to our attention that something like what Alli went through may have happened to you."

She shook her head. "No."

Baudin stared at her a while in silence. He rose and sat next to her, lowering his voice to almost a whisper, his lips close to her ear. "I know you're scared of them, Ruth. But I promise you, you don't have to be. Not anymore. I will protect you. I'm stronger than they are. I have more power than they do. I won't ever let them hurt you again." He took out his card and scribbled a number on the back. "This is my personal cell phone number. If any of them ever even look at you funny again, I want you to call this number."

She took the card, her eyes never leaving the floor. "I told Mr. Daft about it."

"What did he do?"

"He said he would look into it."

"Did you tell your parents?"

She nodded, tears welling in her eyes. "My dad was leaving to play golf when my mom told him. He said, 'Boys will be boys,' and then he left."

Baudin was silent, stealing a quick glance at Dixon, who was leaning forward, listening to the girl. "Ruth, that will never happen with me. Do you understand? I will protect you better than anyone's ever protected you in your life. I swear it."

Finally, she looked at him. A tear was running down her cheek and Baudin reached up and wiped it away.

"Alli was hanging out with those boys. I tried to tell her what happened to me. But she said she loved one of them. I don't know which one, I never met him. But she said she loved him and that he loved her and wouldn't let anything happen to her."

"Which boys, Ruth?"

"The Sigma Mu guys. She was in love with one of them."

Dixon asked, "Did she ever say his name?"

"Dustin. She said his name was Dustin."

Baudin looked at Dixon, who nodded and immediately rose and left the office as he placed the call. A quick call to the administration office of the University of Wyoming should reveal a student named Dustin in the Sigma Mu fraternity.

Baudin turned to Ruth, who was wiping away tears with her sleeve. He took a box of tissues off the desk and handed them to her.

"What did they do to you, Ruth?"

She swallowed. "We went over there, three of us. We thought we were so cool. Hanging out with college guys. And they started giving us booze. I swear, I only had one drink. Not even that. Less than, like, five sips. But I was so drunk. I was so drunk I couldn't move. And one of the boys grabbed me, and he lifted me up and carried me upstairs, away from where anybody could see me. I went in and there was like, maybe twelve of them or more… I don't know. There were so many…"

He rested his hand on her forearm and just let it sit there. A long silence passed between them before she continued.

"And, like, they laid me down on the bed. And they took turns. All of them."

"You saw their faces?"

She shook her head. "They wore these, like… black hoods. I couldn't see any of their faces except the one who carried me up." She began to sob. "I couldn't move, and I tried to scream and one of them shoved a rag in my mouth. And they held me down, and they took turns and…"

"Shhh," he said, wrapping his arm around her. Initially, she jolted as though startled, but then she eased into his warmth. Baudin closed his eyes, pretending that he was taking her pain into himself, that somehow he was lessening the agony she felt.

Dixon opened the door and nodded.

"I have to go," Baudin said. "I'm going to stop these boys, Ruth. Do you hear me? They will never hurt anyone again. I promise."

She wiped the tears away.

"Can you think of any other friends of Alli's I should speak with?"

"She didn't have any friends. There's a girl named Dora Sullivan, and that's it."

Baudin kissed her on her forehead. "You have strength I can only imagine. Use that, turn to it. Hatred has energy, too, more than most things, but in the end it can eat you up—devour everything in your life. You take revenge somehow, whatever way you can, and then you close it like it never happened."

She nodded as he rose. At the door, he looked back and saw her sobbing again. Baudin shut the door behind him and walked into Daft's office.

"Detective, I assume—"

Baudin grabbed him by his tie and pulled him across the desk, knocking over everything on the desktop. Dixon ran over and tried to pull Baudin away, wrapping his arms around the detective. Daft was choking from the tie. Dixon finally got the two men apart.

"What the fuck!" Daft coughed as Dixon dragged Baudin out.

When they were heading back to the car, Dixon asked, "What is your problem?"

"I don't have a problem."

"You can't treat people that way. This is a small town. You'll get a reputation, and you'll be out on your ass. Not to mention that he will never help us again with anything."

"Fuck him."

Dixon stepped in front of him. "You can get more from people if you're nice. Shit, you don't even have to *be* nice, just fake it. Just for a few minutes. Or is that too hard? Would you feel too inauthentic, or some other bullshit you tell yourself to explain why you're an asshole?"

"He covered it up, man. That girl went to him for help, and he didn't do shit. Probably knows one of the frat boys' daddies."

"So what? It's already done. Strangling him with his tie isn't going to do anything, and now he'll work against us. You gotta think, man. These are small town folks. Simple folks."

"Idiots, you mean."

"Well, everybody's an idiot compared to the great Ethan Baudin, right? The nut job who can't handle a big city career so he tries to move to a small town and is fucking that up, too."

Before another word came out of Dixon's mouth, Baudin hit him. The blow was quick, a rabbit punch, and didn't do much damage. But it was enough.

Dixon rushed him, tackling him at the waist. Both men hit the ground hard, Dixon on top. He struck with his fist, bouncing Baudin's head off the ground. When he tried to punch him again, Baudin stopped his arm at the biceps. He headbutted him, Dixon's head snapping back with the blow to his nose. Baudin rolled him off.

He got on top and was now the one hitting. Dixon wrapped his arms around him like a wrestler and pulled him close so he couldn't strike him. Then he thrust his hips up and rolled on top of Baudin again. Dixon scrambled to his feet, holding his fists in a fighting stance.

"Come on!" Dixon shouted.

Baudin rose. He wiped the blood from his lip and instead moved slowly toward the car. He sat on the hood and lit a cigarette—one of the few that hadn't been crushed during the tumble. Dixon watched him a moment and then went and sat on the hood, too. Neither said anything as Baudin smoked, and a bell rang in the school.

33

The precinct was awash in activity. The noise swamped Dixon as he stepped inside. The act of purposeful motion was calming to him, somehow, as if everything was just rolling on despite all the chaos. Life just moved on.

Baudin came in after him. His lip was swollen, and he had a red cheek, but other than that he looked fine. Dixon hadn't looked at himself and didn't know what he was showing.

They sat across from each other without a word and went to work on their computers. Dixon wanted a break from Alli Tavor. He hadn't wanted to know about rape parties or any of it. His mind needed a reprieve.

"Kyle," Jessop yelled from his office, "get your ass in here. You too, tough guy."

They glanced at each other before Dixon rose and Baudin followed him. Inside Jessop's office, Chief Crest sat on the couch, leaning to the side with his elbow on the armrest. A lit cigar held in between his fingers. He looked like a reclining king uninterested in his own kingdom.

"Shut the door," Jessop said.

Dixon shut it.

"Sir," Dixon said, "about the vice principal. It was a—"

"I don't give a shit," he said, his hands on his hips as he paced behind his desk. "The Sigma Mus had their house broken into last night."

"Yeah, so?"

"The only thing taken was a bunch of photographs. A guy dressed in black snuck in through the back door. You two know anything about that?"

Dixon looked at Baudin, who was staring down at Jessop's desk without moving.

Dixon realized he'd been silent too long. He had to say something. "Why would we want to break into a frat house?"

"You tell me."

Dixon shrugged and shook his head. "We ain't got no reason for that. And we're cops. We ain't stupid."

Jessop turned to Baudin. "What about you, hotshot? You know anything about this?"

"No, sir. Probably another frat."

He nodded. "Uh huh." He looked from one to the other. "I find out either of you had anything to do with this… I don't need to finish that sentence, do I?"

"No, sir," Dixon said.

"Get out."

Dixon was the first to leave, glancing back at the chief, who hadn't moved anything but his eyeballs. His gaze was set on Baudin.

Once back at their desks, Dixon didn't say anything. He typed a probable cause statement on a burglary case, finished the entire thing, and emailed it to the office assistant to print and email to the court for a warrant. He rose and headed out of the precinct to grab something to eat.

Once outside, he was walking to his car when he heard Baudin behind him.

"Wait."

Dixon didn't acknowledge him. He kept walking, never looking back.

"Would you wait a second?" Baudin grabbed his arm.

Dixon pulled away violently. "I can't believe you did this," he said through clenched teeth. "Getting *your* ass in a sling is one thing, but I want to keep my job."

"I'm not saying anything about that."

He snorted. "So if I'm ever forced to testify against you, I can say I have no knowledge about the break-in. Nice. What the hell is the matter with you? We're cops, Ethan. We're fucking cops."

Baudin's eyes changed. A gloominess came over him, and he took a step back and put his hands on his hips. A car drove by, and Baudin didn't acknowledge it. "The darkness that's eating this world doesn't care, man. It doesn't have ethics. It doesn't have rules. And without that, it has a natural advantage. If we're gonna level the playing field, we can't think like you think."

"You mean actually following the law? Yeah, I think cops should follow the fucking law, Ethan," he nearly shouted.

"There is no law, man," he said calmly. "There never was. It's an illusion. The people in power exploit the people who have no power. We can stand between them. We can fight for people who have no power. And by the way, before you get too high on your holier-than-thou soapbox, everyone is capable of that darkness. Even you, man. Everyone. So don't judge me for what I did. All my actions are for a greater good."

"Bullshit. All your actions are for Ethan Baudin and to hell with everyone else around him."

Dixon stormed off and jumped into his car. He peeled out with Baudin still standing there watching him. Dixon wasn't sure which one of them he was more upset with: Baudin for lying to him and breaking into that house without telling him or himself for being envious that Baudin could do things like that.

34

Baudin stood in the parking lot, watching his partner drive away. He was a good man, Baudin decided, but damned naïve. Baudin went inside and got his jacket before heading to his car. Chief Crest was just coming out of the building at the same time.

"I hope you had nothing to do with that, son," the chief said. "That fraternity has some members that are... important people. They would be downright furious if they knew the police illegally entered the house and stole property that they weren't entitled to."

Baudin nodded but said nothing. He turned away from the chief and got into his car, watching as the chief spoke into his cell and got into his Mercedes.

Baudin Googled "Philip Arms" and saw that it was only twenty minutes from the precinct. He pulled out of the lot and drove to the interstate. The window was down, and the hot air blew over him. The smell was different here. The city didn't have enough humanity to make it stink yet. It still had the scent of brush and desert, of rains that would pound the dirt and churn dust storms; a wild place in the process of being tamed, of becoming normal. That was most days. And every once in a while, the smell of whatever the factories were spewing out would fill the air, making the city stink like any other.

He stopped at a shack selling burritos. He ordered beans with salsa—he was a vegan—and ate at a bench, wiping his hands with thick napkins. They weren't the cheap stuff he'd expect from a place that should've been cutting costs.

When the burrito was finished, he threw his paper plate and napkins into the trash. A couple of girls seated at a bench smiled at him. He smiled back and headed to his car.

Philip Arms consisted of six apartment buildings surrounded by a knee-high white fence. Everything about the place said ostentation and impracticality. Baudin counted no fewer than five BMWs as he parked and got out.

He walked to the first building, easily stepping over the fence and wondering why they had it in the first place, and scanned a cubby with mailboxes. They had first initials and last names, nothing starting with a T.

The second and third buildings were the same. In the fourth was a mailbox for T. Aaron. Apartment 406.

Baudin found 406 on the first floor, the back apartment in the corner. He didn't check if anyone was home initially. Instead he went around the side of the building and looked in through the sliding glass doors. The curtains were open, and he could see the sliding door was unlocked. He glanced around and went in.

Baudin shut the door quietly behind him and listened. There was a fan on in an adjacent room, and a shower was running. He cautiously stepped through the front room and peeked around the corner. Down a hallway, a door was open: the bathroom. He glided past silently and went to the bedroom.

He searched the drawers, the closet, and underneath the bed. Nothing. The dresser was filled with nothing but socks and underwear. A shoebox in the closet held old family photos. As Baudin was about to give up and leave, he saw something in the corner of the closet: a black box. He bent down and lifted the lid.

Inside were several pipes and a small baggie of marijuana. He smiled to himself, closed the lid, and left the apartment.

Outside, he smoked a cigarette and paced in front of the building. The day was hot and made his neck sticky and uncomfortable. He checked the clock on his phone and saw that Heather would be coming home from school in an hour. Though not something she cared about or even noticed, he liked to be home when she got there.

Baudin remembered his own childhood and the terror of coming home. One foster parent in particular, an old man named Gary, would have five or six foster children at all times, mostly boys, whom he treated relatively well—only delivering the occasional beating for disobedience or if he was drunk. But he always had one or two young girls, too.

The girls were used to make pornography that Gary sent around the world. Gary didn't make a dime off the porn. It was a phenomenon Baudin had never quite understood, even after his degrees in history and behavioral science and ten years as a detective: the need pedophiles had to share with other pedophiles what they had done. Maybe the fact that others out there shared their darkness made them feel better about it, almost human. But what Baudin saw Gary do to those two girls was certainly not human.

One day, Baudin was taken from Gary's home. It seemed Gary couldn't take what he had done and shot himself. But that wasn't what Baudin had seen. He remembered the episode as if it'd just happened. He came home from school and saw Gary slumped over a desk, a little girl of no more than ten standing behind him, and a pistol, the one Gary liked to use to shoot cans behind the house, lying on the floor.

Baudin helped her clean up, and they promised no one would ever know what actually happened to Gary. And they thought no one ever did. But once Baudin became a detective himself, he found that the detectives investigating the case knew almost immediately what had happened and why they chose to ignore it. The death was ruled a suicide.

Baudin tossed the cigarette onto the sidewalk and ground it out before going back inside the building and pounded on the door of 406. A wet-haired man in jeans and a T-shirt answered.

"Yeah?"

"You Thomas Aaron?"

"Yes."

He flashed the badge. "I'm Detective Ethan Baudin with the Cheyenne PD. We got a call of marijuana smoke wafting from your apartment."

"What? That's crazy. I don't have any marijuana."

"Then you won't mind if I have a look around, will you, sir?"

The man thought a moment. "No. No, that's fine."

Baudin entered the apartment. He strode to the center of the room and stood still. "I smell pot here."

"There's no pot. I never touch the stuff."

"Not fresh pot, but pot. Like you've smoked it in the past few days. Carpet absorbs the scent. You get used to it, but for someone coming in, it's clear as day."

The man swallowed. "I don't…"

Baudin turned and strode down the hall. He looked in the bathroom and in a hall closet before going into the bedroom and standing in the doorway. Thomas stood in the living room, his face pale and his eyes wide. Baudin went to step inside.

"Please," he said. "Please."

"Please what, Mr. Aaron?"

"I'm a CPA. I can't have a criminal conviction on my record. Please, I'll do anything."

Baudin crossed the hallway and stood in front of him. "How much pot am I gonna find in that bedroom?"

He shook his head. "I don't know."

"More than five ounces?"

"Yeah, I think so."

"I'm guessing you got a firearm in that closet, too, don't you?"

He nodded. "Yeah. But just a pistol I use for home defense."

Baudin made a clicking sound with his cheek. "See, now that's a problem. Whenever a firearm is in proximity to a stash of drugs, that's an automatic felony. We assume the gun is used in furtherance of buying or selling drugs."

"What? No, I never even take it out of the case."

"Well, you'll have to explain that to the prosecutor and the judge."

"No," he said, grabbing Baudin's arm. "Please, I'll do anything."

Baudin glanced down at the hand.

Thomas immediately withdrew it and said, "Sorry."

"You'll do anything if I let this slide, huh? Well, I want some information, then."

"About what?"

"I was investigating a case about a girl you knew. Alli Tavor."

A light turned on in the man's head. Baudin watched his demeanor go from passive fear to anger. "That's why you're here. Nobody called about pot."

"Whether they called or not, that's what I'm finding in that closet. So do you want to have an honest conversation with me, or should I go ahead and call this in?"

Thomas took a step backward, as though frightened. He leaned against the wall, staring at Baudin. "What do you want to know?"

"You were dating Alli Tavor."

"No, I didn't even—"

Baudin reached into his pocket and pulled out his cell phone. The two men stood staring at each other in silence. Finally Thomas said, "Yes."

"Yes what?"

"Yes, I was dating her."

"You know she's dead?"

Thomas nodded. "Yeah," he said softly. "It was on the news."

"How did you come to date a sixteen-year-old?"

"It just… happened. I didn't know she was sixteen when we first met. She acted like she was thirty. I didn't know. And by the time I found out, it didn't really matter. I was too deep into it."

"We found semen inside her," Baudin lied. "Is it going to match your DNA?"

"No, no way. I hadn't slept with her in months. She was dating some new guy and said she didn't want to see me anymore. She... she came over once after that, and that was it."

"She came over, and you guys had sex?"

He nodded. "She said she had blown some random guy in a bathroom and wanted to tell me about it. She went through everything in detail, and then... we did it. She left after that, and I never heard from her again."

"You saw her on the news?"

"I did."

"And you didn't think to call the cops?"

"Are you kiddin' me? She was sixteen. No way I was gonna call."

Baudin closed the distance between them. At no time did he get the impression that this man was a killer. Going with his gut was the most dangerous type of tool but one that worked often enough that he had come to rely on it. He didn't have a lot of choice. His gut told him Thomas Aaron wasn't capable of killing anybody... but that he might know who was capable.

"Who did she dump you for?"

"I don't know. Some frat guy."

Baudin was silent for a second. "What frat guy?"

"I don't know his name. I saw him only once, when he came by with her to pick up some stuff she'd left here. A toothbrush and clothes."

"What'd he drive?"

"Red Volvo. An SUV."

Baudin held the man's gaze before taking a step back. He scanned the room. "If I find out you're lying to me, I'll be back to hit you with that stat rape. Got it?"

"Got it."

Baudin left the apartment. He shut the door behind him and stood there a second, picturing a red Volvo in his mind. When he had been at the frat house the other night, he'd seen one parked in front.

Baudin rushed to his car.

35

Dixon ate lunch by himself at a little dive sandwich place near the precinct. The restaurant, despite several closings the past year for health code violations, was always packed. The food was just too good. He got the Colossus: a cheeseburger packed with French fries, freshly made mac and cheese, and a fried egg. It was so gooey it dripped down his chin and spotted his tie.

"Damn it," he mumbled, dabbing at it with a napkin.

His cell phone rang; it was Baudin.

"What do you want?" Dixon said.

"He's a current member of the frat. Drives a red Volvo. I ran the plates, Dustin Orridge."

Dixon exhaled loudly and pushed the mass of wet meat away from him. "Shit."

"Hate me still?"

"Just not at the frat house, okay? They're already on our ass. Let's wait until he leaves and stop him."

"Done. Where you want to meet?"

By the time Baudin picked him up, Dixon had eaten half the burger and felt ill. He was sucking on a Sprite when he climbed into the car and Baudin sped away.

"Do I even want to know how you found this out?" Dixon asked.

"Just good old detective work. Nothing fancy." He pulled some sheets of paper off the dash and handed them to Dixon. "His rap and a psych profile."

"What'd he have a psych profile done for?"

"Part of sentencing on a conviction for lewdness. He flashed some sixth-graders at a playground. Read the last paragraph."

Dixon read.

It is this therapist's opinion that Mr. Orridge, though early in his criminal career, has not shown any signs of remorse or correction of behavior. In fact, his statements on the entry-of-plea form to this court indicate that he blames the victims, has no sense of repercussions, and feels that women and young girls somehow "owe" him their sexual favors. I do not believe, based on my seventeen years' experience as a child psychologist, that Mr. Orridge is a good candidate for probation. It would be our recommendation that some form of incarceration be imposed, with immediate and long-lasting treatment.

"Wow," Dixon said.

"Orridge was fifteen when that was written. The therapist says earlier in that report that he comes from a wealthy family, and there're allegations that he raped one of their maids and may have molested a sister, both things the family buried to save themselves embarrassment. This kid's a predator, man."

"One thing, you let me handle him. You don't talk. You come with me, show your muscles and your tattoos, but no talking."

"Sure, whatever you say, man."

Baudin parked the car down the street from the Sigma Mu house, close enough that they could see everyone coming and going but not so close that anyone in the frat would notice two men in a car. The Volvo was parked right in front.

"Why didn't you tell me?" Dixon asked.

"Tell you what?"

"That you were gonna break into the frat?"

Baudin rubbed his lower lip with his index finger as he watched the house. "I thought you'd say no."

"I would've said no, but you still tell your partner. This shit we got goin' isn't gonna work. It's either all trust or no trust. No gray."

Baudin looked at him. "All right, brother. From now on, no secrets. I run everything by you."

Dixon nodded, unsure if he really believed him. But he had to give him the benefit of the doubt.

Baudin's cell phone rang.

"Hello? … Baby? What's wrong? No… it's okay… okay… no, but I promise… I'll be home soon… Heather, we already talked about this, several times… I know… I know… I'll see you soon."

Dixon didn't say anything as he hung up the phone. But he'd heard the girl crying on the other end.

Baudin took a deep breath. "She wants to move back to LA. Says she doesn't fit in here and misses her friends. Somebody was mean to her at school."

"That age, friends are all you got. You can't relate to your parents. Shit, you know that."

"No, I never had parents. Foster parents, at least in the area *I* was in, weren't no parents. They saw me as a paycheck. There was one family who took me in. They really loved me, I think. Talked about adopting me."

"Why didn't they?"

"Didn't give 'em a chance. I ran off."

Dixon shifted in his seat to have a better look at him. "Why would you do that?"

"I don't know. I got close and... I don't know. Maybe I thought it was only a matter of time before these good people turned to bad people. I needed to believe there were good people in the world and didn't want them to ruin that."

Dixon was silent a moment. "Ethan, you are by far the most fucked-up person I have ever known."

He chuckled. "Shit, man. You're not a paradigm of normality yourself."

Before Dixon could respond, someone popped out of the frat.

"That's him," Baudin said.

Coming down the steps with a backpack slung over his arm was Orridge, and two other boys. They spoke at the base of the steps a long while before they split up, and Orridge went to his own car. He threw the backpack into the passenger seat and started the engine. Baudin did the same and waited until the red Volvo pulled away before he merged into traffic and then flipped a U-turn.

The Volvo turned left and headed deeper into the campus.

"What time is it?" Baudin said, not moving his eyes from the car.

"Four. They got classes that start in half an hour up here, the evening ones. Mostly social science, so he's headed to the north side of campus."

Baudin hung back. He let several cars cut in between him and Orridge. The Volvo followed all the traffic laws perfectly.

"This guy's not breaking any traffic rules," Baudin said.

"So?"

"So how many people you know can do that? He's studied up. Even changing lanes, he knows you have to signal three seconds ahead of time."

"That don't mean he kills girls, man."

"Doesn't help his case."

Dixon glanced at him. "Just remember that I'm doin' all the talkin'. I'm serious about that."

"My lips are sealed."

The Volvo made a turn up ahead, and Baudin followed. It went down a long street and then turned again, this time south.

"Shit," Baudin said.

"What?"

"I think he's made us."

"There's no way he—"

The Volvo gunned it up a street, and its tires screeched as it took a turn too fast. Baudin hit the gas, and the car lurched forward. He didn't stop at a red light, and the car was almost clipped by an F-150 truck. Dixon swore at the top of his lungs as Baudin took the same turn Orridge had but at twice the speed.

"Slow down!"

"He's not getting away."

The Volvo was on a narrow road in a residential area. It was passing cars, swerving into oncoming traffic, and then swerving back. Baudin did the same. Horns blared and car tires squealed as people scrambled to get out of the way.

Instead of fighting it, which he knew he wasn't going to win anyway, Dixon strapped on his seat belt and held on to the grip above the door.

The Volvo slammed on its brakes and flipped a U-turn so fast it looked as though it might tip over. Baudin did the same but pulled the emergency brake, flipping the car around at a speed that pushed Dixon into the door. Smoke billowed out from the tires. Baudin hit the gas and peeled out on the pavement.

"Slow down, man."

"We'll never get this chance again."

Dixon took out his phone.

"No," Baudin said. "Don't call it in."

"You shittin' me? We can cut him off with patrols in a New York minute."

Baudin shook his head. "He's ours, Kyle. This is between us and him. No one else."

Dixon lowered the phone and then put it back in his pocket.

36

Hillary Dixon lay in bed and wept softly. The tears flowed down her cheeks and left spots on her pillow. She was nude except for the sheet that covered her lower body. Chris lay next to her, asleep. His arm was thrown over her, and the touch of it was at the same time pleasurable and revolting. She lusted after him. She had no doubt of that. He had thrown her on the bed—her marital bed—ripped off his pants, and forcefully shoved himself into her mouth, nearly gagging her. He then pulled out and thrust inside her so powerfully she screamed.

When they were done, she went to the bathroom and vomited.

On the nightstand was a photo of Kyle. She reached over and turned it face down. She remembered that photo. They'd been hiking at Dinosaur National Monument in Colorado. Her husband had a juvenile fascination with dinosaurs, and whenever they went on vacation anywhere he insisted they see all the dinosaur sites they could.

The trip had lasted four days, and it had gone by so fast she could scarcely believe it. It was four days of pure fun and laughter. She couldn't remember a time when she had been so happy in her life.

And now she lay in their bed with another man on Kyle's side of the bed, the man's child in the other room, being raised as Kyle's own. She rose again and ran to the bathroom. Bending down over the toilet, she retched, but nothing came. Everything in her stomach had already been expelled.

She sat on the bathroom floor and quietly cried. This was too big. A secret this big felt like a noose around her neck, and every time Chris touched her that noose grew tighter. It would suffocate her soon, and nothing would be left.

No matter the consequences, she would have to tell him. She had to.

"Hey, Hillary? You okay in there?"

"Fine," she said, flushing the toilet. She stood up and stared at herself in the mirror.

Her body was perfect, honed with hours of yoga, biking, running, and weight-lifting every day. But her mind, her soul, felt diseased, as if it were poisoning the world around her. She washed her face and hands and took a wet towel and wiped between her legs, breasts, and neck. She threw the towel in the wicker basket they used for their dirty laundry, and she saw one of Kyle's shirts: a blue one with a stain where Randy had spit up on his shoulder. She'd wanted to throw it out, but he said he liked that it was stained, that it provided proof he was a real father and had earned his stripes.

Before she could leave the bathroom, her stomach churned again, and she returned to the toilet.

When she was done, she went to the closet and got dressed. Nothing fancy, jeans and a black shirt with two buttons at the top.

Chris was sitting up in bed smiling, one arm behind his head. "Come back to bed."

"I want to tell him," she said, slipping on her shoes.

"Tell him what?"

"I want to tell him, Chris."

Chris jumped out of bed and approached her. He stood behind her without touching her. "You can't tell him. Not yet. You need to leave him first. Then I'll serve him with the paternity suit."

She shook her head. "I'm not leaving him. He might leave me, but I'm not leaving him."

"You have a child with another man and lied to him about it. He won't stay."

"Maybe not, but I need to give him that chance. I want you to leave."

"Hillary—"

"Leave. Now."

He stood a moment longer, and then anger flashed through him. He swung, and his fist hit the wall behind her. She flinched but didn't move. They stood staring at each other, and then he gathered his clothes and left.

Hillary stood in front of the mirror, trying to look at herself and not being able to lift her eyes to do it.

37

Dixon yelped as the car nearly careened off the road into a building. Baudin yanked the steering wheel into the turn, and the car spun fully around before settling.

The Volvo had made a mistake. It went right when it should have gone left and was now stuck in a cul-de-sac. Baudin spun the car so that it was lengthwise, taking up as much space as possible. He got out and drew his weapon, as did Dixon.

The kid in the driver's seat looked frightened. Not at all the calm psychopath Dixon was expecting. Then again, what was a psychopath if not a good liar? Dixon decided he wouldn't believe anything this boy said or did.

"Turn the car off and come out with your hands up," Baudin shouted.

A long pause followed where the boy simply stared at the two men without moving. Finally, Dixon said, "Kid, I don't want to kill you, but I will if I have to. Get your ass out of that car."

The door opened, and Orridge stepped out. He was short, maybe five six, and had his hands up. Baudin approached him and told him to lie on the ground. He got to his knees, and Baudin shoved him into the pavement and slapped cuffs on him.

He lifted him by his arms and brought him over to their car.

"Yo," Orridge pleaded, "what about my car?"

"Kyle, drive the car and follow us," he said, tossing him the keys that were in Orridge's hand.

A tow would've been proper, but Dixon had driven suspects' cars before when a tow wasn't available. On weekends, Cheyenne had one of the highest per capita DUI arrest rates in the nation, and it only had a handful of tow trucks to service all of them. Once, Dixon had driven back to the precinct a Ferrari that might have been used to transport drugs.

He got into the Volvo and followed Baudin, who'd put the kid in the passenger seat. They left the cul-de-sac, went down University Avenue, and parked in a Walmart parking lot. Dixon wasn't sure what was happening until he saw Baudin turn and begin asking questions right there.

"Shit," Dixon said as he stepped out. He hurried to Baudin's car and got into the back, staring incredulously at Baudin.

"Dustin and I were just talking about a girl we both know. Isn't that right, Dustin?" The boy looked out the window. "See, Dustin is claiming he didn't know this girl, but I think he did."

The boy was fidgeting and biting his lip.

Baudin leaned in close to his ear. "Tell me what I want to know, and I'll let you go. Right now. We'll pretend this never happened. That's why you're not in a station right now, Dustin. I just need the information. I don't need you."

The boy swallowed. "What do you want to know?"

"Tell me about Alli."

"She was cool, I guess."

"She was cool," Baudin said, nodding. "You are a poet."

"What do you want me to say?"

"I want you to tell me about her."

The two of them stared at each other. The boy looked so terrified that Dixon almost felt bad for him.

"I didn't kill her."

"You sure about that?"

The boy turned to face him squarely. "I swear. I didn't know she was dead until someone told me. They saw her mom on the news talkin' about it. I thought she just took off. She was doing that all the time, just leavin' for no reason. I thought that's all it was."

"And when you learned it wasn't, you didn't call the cops, did you?"

He looked back through the window. "I want a lawyer."

"Maybe you don't get a lawyer."

Dixon said, "Ethan, can I talk to you outside?" He opened the door and stepped out of the car. Baudin followed.

"He's asked for a lawyer," Dixon said, once Baudin shut the door. "Anything he says beyond now will be excluded from court."

"No, it won't. We'll just say it's bullshit."

Dixon shook his head. "No, man. I will testify that he asked for a lawyer and you kept interrogating him. I told you to keep your damn mouth shut and let me handle this."

"You'd let this piece of shit walk because he said some magic words? You think that's what this is about?"

"Yes, I do," he said sternly. "I believe in the fucking Constitution, Ethan. Now take him back to the station and get him a lawyer."

Baudin looked at him as if he were insane. He put up his hands as though in surrender and got back into the car. Dixon got into the Volvo, and they drove out of the parking lot.

Once back at the station, the frat was called to tell them Dustin had been arrested. Someone there then called Dustin's father, who sent a lawyer down within an hour. Baudin and Dixon stood in the observation room while the lawyer spoke to his client. Baudin was staring at him through the glass. The room was soundproofed but had a microphone that had been turned off.

"This isn't right," Baudin said. "This kid's gonna walk."

"Maybe."

Baudin began pacing like a caged animal. "All we had to do was work him in that parking lot and promise we'd let him go, man. We would've had him."

"Maybe."

"Maybe? That all you can say to me?"

"What do you want me to say?"

"I want you to say you're fucking sorry for torpedoing this case."

Dixon couldn't help chuckling. He shook his head, watching the way the light played off the linoleum on the floor. "You are unique, Ethan, I'll give you that. That kid may or may not get what's comin' to him, but I can sleep at night with a clear conscience."

"A clear conscience?"

"Yeah, man, a clear conscience. Because I did my job and followed the law."

"There isn't any law, man, I told you."

Dixon stepped away from the wall toward his partner. "That is bullshit. And if you really believe that, you need to find some other work." Dixon left the room and headed for his desk. "Maybe some alien conspiracy theorists are hiring security guards," he said, looking back.

Within twenty minutes, the lawyer was out. He walked straight to the captain's office and spoke to him briefly. Jessop came out and went to Dixon.

"Cut him loose."

"You sure?" Dixon said. "This is the guy."

"Maybe, but you're cutting him loose. All you got is some dipshit who told your partner this guy was dating her. That's nothin'."

"It's enough to make him a person of interest."

Jessop watched him. "Kyle, you don't have anything."

Dixon sighed. "I know."

"Cut him loose," he said, going back to his office.

Dixon rose and walked back to Baudin, who was staring at the kid through the glass. "Let him go."

Baudin looked at him, was about to say something, then changed his mind. He opened the door to the interrogation room and said, "You're free to go."

They both watched as Dustin Orridge smiled and left the precinct.

38

A day later, Dixon was at his desk. As far as he was concerned, Alli Tavor was a cold case. No forensic evidence existed, no witnesses, no real motive, and their only suspect had lawyered up. They could put a twenty-four hour tail on Orridge and see if he screwed up somewhere, but that was fantasy. Dixon had only seen the expense of a tail authorized once when they were following a biker gang selling meth in the high schools. With the lack of evidence in this case, there was no way Jessop would approve a tail.

Baudin was sitting across from him, working on the computer. They hadn't said a word to each other all day other than "Hey."

Dixon finished up a few calls and was about to head to lunch when the doors to the detective squad opened, and Dustin Orridge and his lawyer walked in. The two detectives looked on as the boy, his face down, trudged past everyone and directly into Jessop's office. They shut the door, sat down, and the lawyer began talking.

"What is this?" Dixon asked.

"No idea."

After a few minutes, the door opened, and Jessop stuck his head out. "Detective Dixon, your suspect is ready to confess."

Dixon sat across from Orridge as Baudin stood behind him. The camera was on, and the lawyer was sitting next to Orridge, busy on his phone. Dixon had a yellow legal pad in front of him with a blue pen, and he wrote Dustin's name across the top, more for something to do than for any functional purpose.

"I was told you wanted to speak to us, Dustin."

The boy wouldn't lift his gaze from the floor. His eyes were puffy and red as though he'd been crying.

"I did it."

"Did what?" Dixon asked.

"I killed Alli Tavor," he said, his voice cracking.

Dixon was silent a long time. "How?"

"She said she didn't want to fuck me no more. I got mad. I didn't mean to. It just happened."

Baudin asked, "You just *happened* to crucify her? Like by accident?"

"That was all done later. After. To cover everything up. I choked her until she wasn't moving no more. She died."

"How else did you injure her?" Baudin asked.

"I cut her up with a knife. I don't remember the details of that—it was a blur, all real fast. But I killed her."

"When?"

"Five weeks ago. In a field near where you found her. I told her we were going to have a picnic and hang out with my frat brothers. When we got out there, I started hitting her, and then I choked her."

Dixon didn't know what to say. He looked back at Baudin, who, for the first time since Dixon had met him, didn't know what to say either.

"Um," Dixon said, trying to keep a veneer of cool, "Dustin, I'd like you to write down everything you remember about it on this legal pad, please."

The boy wrote. He wrote for a good fifteen minutes, filling two pages. The entire time, Dixon stared at him and wondered if he really looked like a murderer.

When Orridge was done, he slid the pad back to Dixon, who read it. It said the same things he'd just confessed to orally. Dixon showed it to Baudin.

"I want some time with him," Baudin whispered.

"Why? He confessed. It's done."

"I just want to make sure."

The lawyer finally put his phone away and said, "Gentlemen, this interview is over. Please book my client and let's get on with it."

The two detectives looked at each other. Dixon took out his handcuffs and helped Orridge stand before saying, "You have the right to remain silent..."

When they stepped back into the bullpen and Orridge was escorted down to booking, several of the detectives clapped for Baudin and Dixon. Jessop came out and shook their hands.

"Don't know what you said to that little prick, but it must've scared him. Lawyer said he was confessing against legal advice."

A few detectives slapped their backs and asked them about the case. Someone broke out a bottle of sparkling apple cider he'd had in his desk. Styrofoam cups were passed around. Murders with almost no evidence weren't something that were solved often.

Dixon stood chatting with a few of the officers when he glanced at Baudin. He held up his cup as if in salute, and Baudin nodded.

39

A week went by, and Baudin had thought about little more than the murder of Alli Tavor. He'd never had a suspect come in and confess to unburden the soul. The human soul, in his experience, could take a hell of a lot of burden.

He'd caught other cases since then: a missing person and a convenience-store robbery. He didn't miss the compartmentalization in Los Angeles. The diversity of cases here refreshed him.

But he couldn't get the Tavor case out of his head. It was closed, and he was grateful for that. He'd been the one to tell her mother, and she'd seemed to accept it well, but something didn't sit right. Orridge wasn't the type of person to have a change of heart. Something happened to make him come in and confess.

He was at his desk on a phone call when a woman came in. A detective named Hernandez was walking back to the interrogation rooms with her. The woman was young and attractive but crying profusely. Hernandez had her arm around the woman's shoulders and sat her down before shutting the door.

After fifteen or twenty minutes, Hernandez came out to the squad room.

"Who's that?" Baudin asked.

"Oh, her name's Kaitlin Harris. She says she was raped a couple of weeks ago by some guys at a club."

Baudin didn't have to ask about the time lapse. He knew most victims were reluctant to come forward right away. They felt guilt and shame, as though they were somehow responsible for the assault. It usually took coaxing by family and friends to finally get them through the precinct door.

"More than one?" Baudin asked.

"Yeah, she says one guy took her back to his place, and then a bunch of guys came out and took turns."

Baudin was silent for a moment.

"You okay?" Hernandez said.

"Yeah, sorry, yeah. Just sad is all."

"Yeah, poor girl. Luckily they drugged her, and she only remembers bits and pieces. I was gonna head down and get a crisis counselor."

Baudin nodded and went back to his computer. He waited until Hernandez was out the door before he rose and hurried to the interrogation room where Kaitlin Harris was seated.

She looked frail and weak. As though if he weren't careful with her, she could crumble to dust right in front of him. He sat down across from her, rose and unplugged the camera, and then sat down again.

"I'm sorry," was all Baudin said. "I'm so sorry."

She nodded, twirling the tissue in her fingers. "Are you a detective?"

"Yes."

She sniffled. "I feel so stupid. I just feel like the stupidest person in the world."

He reached his hand across the table, letting it rest near her. "You're not. This was not an act of God, like lightning striking. This was an act of evil perpetrated by men. It had nothing to do with you. It's not your fault."

She seemed to slump in her chair, as though her muscles couldn't hold her up any longer. The long strands of hair came down over her eyes, and she sobbed quietly. He moved his chair next to her, and the action, though he'd been as slow and quiet as possible, startled her.

"Shh," he said.

He didn't touch her until she was ready. And even then, it was only a couple of fingers gently placed on the back of her hand—just enough that she knew someone else was there, someone who cared and empathized.

When she was through sobbing, he said, "I need your help."

"How?"

He pulled out his phone and brought up a photo of the Sigma Mu frat house. "Do you recognize this house?" She shook her head. The symbol over the door was blurry. He flipped to a clear photo of the Sigma Mu symbol. "What about this?"

Her mouth nearly fell open. "I saw that in a painting. When he was taking me upstairs, I saw that painting hanging there."

"Can you tell me anything about the house?"

"It was empty, like no one lived there. There was plastic over the furniture, dust everywhere." She looked up at the ceiling. "I'm so stupid."

"Kaitlin, stay with me… stay with me… what else did you see?"

"Nothing. We went upstairs to the bedroom, and all these guys came out. He'd given me something so I couldn't move. I was just lying there like… I couldn't move. And all these guys came out. And they started… they started."

"Who took you there?"

"Some guy. He said his name was Casey."

"What'd he look like?"

Kaitlin wiped her tears away again, taking a deep breath. "Good-looking. Blond, I guess. He said he was forty-three, but he looked a little older."

"Forty-three?"

"Yeah, but he looked older."

"You sure about that?"

"Positive. I saw him really close. When he was on top of me… when he was…"

She began to sob again, more forcefully this time, as though losing control. Hernandez walked in, the counselor behind her.

"What're you doing?"

"Just making sure she's okay," Baudin said. He rose to leave, but before doing so, he bent down. Close to her ear so only Kaitlin could hear him. "I'm going to find them, Kaitlin. I'm going to find them, and I'm going to kill them."

She looked up. The sobbing ceased. Their eyes held each other a moment, and then he turned and rushed out of the room.

40

When Baudin found Dixon, he was sitting on the hood of his car in the parking lot, eating a bagel and drinking coffee. He sat next to him, and they didn't speak right away. He let Dixon eat for a bit, getting comfortable with his presence before springing it on him.

"I think Dustin Orridge didn't do it. Or at least didn't do it alone."

Dixon chewed and just said, "Why?"

"There's a woman in there right now talking about a sexual assault. She saw the Sigma Mu symbol in the house she was gang raped in. The guy who took her there was in his forties, maybe even older."

"So?"

"So how many fifty-year-olds you see in those Sigma Mu photos? He's alum."

Dixon looked at him. "You think the alum raped her?"

"Why not, man? They get into these rape parties, but they gotta leave the frat sometime. Doesn't mean they can break the habit. They got a taste for it... but you already thought of that."

Dixon took a sip of his coffee. "I did."

"Then why haven't you said anything?"

"Because the case is over. It's closed. And if you think Jessop is ever gonna let us reopen it and start interviewing alums from that frat, you can forget it. The mayor and DA are both alums." He went to take another sip of coffee and stopped. The two of them stared at each other.

"Shit," Dixon said.

Baudin's house was empty as Heather was in school. Dixon entered and followed Baudin down to the basement where the photos of the Sigma Mu brothers were set up. Baudin took down the photos of the past fifteen years, and they had five photos left. They spread them on a table and leaned over them like generals looking at a map.

Baudin got out some reading glasses and went over the faces of each one. In one particular year, 1995, he stopped. In the center of the pack, smiling widely with a bad haircut, was a face he recognized.

"I know that face."

Dixon bent closer. He took the glasses and raised them above the photo, making the face as large as possible. He dropped the glasses and turned away, taking a few steps back, his hands coming up over his head before his fingers interlaced and rested on the back of his neck.

"Fuck," Dixon shouted, grabbing the first thing that came to hand—a plastic bottle from a shelf—and throwing it. The bottle bounced off the wall and hit the floor, rolling to the center of the basement until it lost momentum.

"Who is he?" Baudin asked.

41

Dixon paced the hallway. The secretary was staring at him as though she'd never seen him before. Baudin seemed calm. He was standing against the wall with his eyes closed, as if he were meditating or something. Dixon, on the other hand, felt as though he were about to hurl.

"The chief will see you now, Detective."

"Thanks," Dixon said meekly.

They walked into Chief Robert Crest's office and sat down across from him. The chief was on the phone and held up one finger, indicating he needed a minute. Dixon swallowed and looked around the office.

When the chief was done, he smiled widely, pulled a cigar out of a drawer, and said, "Great job on that crucifixion case, boys. I don't think I've gotten to congratulate you yet. Sorry about that, mayor's got me running ragged on this new drug initiative he's got going." He lit his cigar and took a puff.

"No problem, sir," Dixon said. "We're just happy you could fit us in."

The chief leaned back in his chair, the smile never leaving his face. "So, what can I do for you?"

Baudin said dryly, "You never told us you were a member of Sigma Mu."

The smile instantly disappeared. Dixon's guts tightened. He'd been hoping he could avoid the confrontation and just talk like gentlemen who had found an intellectual curiosity, but Baudin had his own plans.

"What the fuck does that have to do with anything?" Chief Crest said, his face contorting with rage.

"Seems like an interesting little fact you'd want to tell the investigating detectives on a case involving that frat."

"That isn't relevant to anything. I think your partner here worked at U of W. Maybe you should be interviewing him, too."

"If he belonged to a frat that systematically raped women, I would be."

Baudin and the chief stared at each other. The chief's face was flushed red with so much anger that he seemed unable to contain it.

"Get the fuck outta my office now!"

Baudin rose and smirked before leaving. Dixon felt that he should say something—anything—but couldn't think of a single thing. He just nodded apologetically and left the building behind Baudin.

"That's not gonna be good for us," Dixon said.

"I had to feel him out. What did you think? Honestly."

Dixon spit on the ground. "I think if he *didn't* know anything, he'd be more surprised than angry."

Baudin slapped his shoulder and grinned. "See, now you're thinking clearly."

Dixon's phone buzzed, and he looked at it. It was a text from Jessop saying he wanted to see them immediately. "Well, hope you like the taste of shit 'cause we're about to eat a boatful right now."

Dixon gazed out the window. Jessop had screamed so much he'd lost his voice. A vein in his neck looked as if it were about to pop, like a snake writhing up his neck into his head. Dixon tried not to look. He tried to keep his stare out the window, but it was difficult. Jessop was circling the office and, since he'd lost his voice, bent down to whisper hoarsely in his ear when some insult came into his head.

"Sir," Baudin said, "we didn't accuse the chief of anything. We just went in there to talk, and he's the one who flipped out."

Jessop, his voice completely depleted, picked up a pencil and flung it at Baudin's head. The three men then sat there in silence, watching rain beginning to spot the cars outside in the parking lot.

Jessop pointed to his desk. Dixon pulled out his badge and gun. He laid them on the desk. Baudin did the same, and they stared at Jessop before he pointed to the door.

The two of them walked out of the building. They stood in the rain. It wasn't coming down hard, just a sprinkle that would leave droplets on clothing.

"Well, that went well," Dixon said.

Baudin was staring at his phone. "I gotta go."

"Now? Where you gotta go now?"

"Heather's not answering her cell. She should've been at Molly's house."

Dixon sighed. "Well, I may as well come with you since I don't have a job right now."

42

The car rolled to a stop in front of Baudin's home. The truth was, Dixon didn't want to go home. Home meant he'd have to face his wife and tell her he'd been suspended. At least, he thought he'd been suspended. Jessop might very well fire them. Despite not saying much, they had flat-out accused the chief of being involved in the death of a young girl and with the rapes of dozens more.

He followed Baudin up to the doorstep, the rain now pelting him in the face. Baudin unlocked the door and stepped inside. The house was quiet. He checked Heather's room and then went to his bedroom.

"Heather?" he called.

As he was walking by the bathroom, Baudin's eyes went wide. He seemed to have the wind knocked out of him, as though he were collapsing right there in the hallway.

He dashed into the bathroom. Dixon followed.

"No, baby, no, what did you do... What did you do?"

Huddled on the floor, Baudin held his daughter in his arms, both of them now covered in blood. The dark fluid spurted out of cuts in her wrists. The cuts weren't long, but they were deep, and the girl was white. She wasn't conscious.

"What did you do to yourself?" Baudin said, tears on his cheeks. "What did you do? What did you do?"

Dixon called it in and took off his belt and ran over. He wrapped his belt around one of the wrists and tightened it just above the wound. Baudin seemed far away. Dixon grabbed him by the back of the neck, looking into his eyes. "Hey! She needs you right now."

Baudin, seemingly in a daze, slipped off his belt and tightened it around her other arm. Both of them held her, putting pressure on the wounds with towels. The girl responded once—she just said, "Daddy," before losing consciousness again. Baudin wept as he rested his forehead against hers.

The ambulance was there in less than five minutes. Dixon stepped into the hallway with Baudin, both of their clothing looking as if they'd been sprayed with blood from a hose. As the paramedics hauled her out on a stretcher, Baudin cried again. He buried his face in his hands.

Anything Dixon said right now would be cheap. So instead, he put his hand on his partner's shoulder and followed him out as he got into the ambulance.

"I'll follow behind," Dixon said.

Dixon had never liked hospitals. As a kid, his grandmother was a hypochondriac and took him in for the most minor cough or ache because his father didn't care enough to pay attention to illness. He'd come to despise the smell of antiseptic and the stale taste of tongue depressors. Once, a doctor pierced his eardrum to drain an infection. The pain was so intense, so all-consuming, Dixon swore he'd never go to the doctor again. Since then, he'd only been twice.

The waiting area was nice, as far as waiting areas went, decorated with paintings of sunflower fields, plants on the side tables, a rug with intricate designs beneath their feet. Baudin had been rocking gently back and forth for the past hour. His eyes were red-rimmed, and every once in a while tears would stream down his face. Dixon leaned forward on his knees.

"My daddy told me kids are the best and worst thing 'bout life."

Baudin shook his head, his unblinking gaze directed at the floor. "This is my fault, Kyle. She was trying to tell me she's lost, and I didn't hear her. She reached out to me, and I slapped her hand away."

"That's horseshit. We do the best we can with what we have, man. Raisin' a girl on your own without a mother around... I can't even imagine it, man. Hillary knows when Randy is hungry, when he's sleepy, when he has gas, all that just from the way he cries. I don't know nothin'. It's like dealing with an alien."

"I need to take her back. I never should've left California. Her friends were there."

Dixon saw a speck of mud on his shoe. He wanted to kick into the floor to get it off, but the motion seemed inappropriate. "I ain't no psychologist, but my guess is that wouldn't have done nothin'."

"Mr. Baudin?" a woman in a white coat said as she stepped out of the double doors.

"Yes?"

"I'm Dr. Juni, nice to meet you. I've been treating your daughter." She sat next to them. "First, I want you to know she is perfectly okay. She's lost some blood, but other than that she'll be fine. The wrists are actually a difficult place to bleed out from."

Baudin exhaled a puff of breath, but it didn't seem conscious. It was as if a great pain had lifted out of his body and left a quivering sack of meat and blood behind. "Can I see her?"

"She's sleeping now. Why don't you give her an hour or two and then head back there?" The doctor paused. "I've asked that our psychiatrist on call come down and meet with her. I hope that's okay."

"It is."

She nodded. "Teenage suicide is usually a cry for help. She's trying to get your attention. A real attempt is frequently successful. We're not as hard to kill as people think. But I'll let the psychiatrist get into that with you. Her name is Dr. Natalie Leishman, she'll be down soon."

"Thanks."

"You're welcome."

When the doctor had left, Baudin rose from his chair. He stood by the window overlooking the parking lot, staring down at the cars coming and going. "I did this to her."

"You can't think that way, man."

"There's no other way to think."

He turned and strode down the hall.

43

The closest bar to the hospital was a place called the Dirty Raven. Baudin sat at the bar and drank shot after shot, barely tasting them. He wasn't drinking for taste, anyway.

The smoke-filled bar stank so strongly of pot and cigarette smoke that he thought he could feel the stuff permeating his skin, as if he would never get that stink off. And for a moment, panic gripped him and tightened his chest, then it faded away.

Baudin didn't know how many shots he'd had. The bar wasn't the type to cut him off. The bartender, an old man with a balding head, kept pouring the amber drink into the same glass, over and over and over.

A few construction workers sitting next to him were speaking loudly about some NCAA game. Baudin took another shot and dropped the glass on the floor, shattering it.

"Why don't you cocksuckers shut your damn mouths?" he spat.

One of the workers, with a thick bushy beard, turned to him. "What'd you say?"

Baudin lifted the cigarette he'd laid on the ashtray. He took a final puff and then flicked it onto the man's shirt. "I said, why don't you cocksuckers shut your damn mouths?"

The construction worker, without a moment's hesitation, swung.

Baudin ducked and came up with a right into the man's kidneys. Then he swung with a hook and hit the guy hard enough that he stumbled back into his friends. One of them grabbed a bottle and came at Baudin, who jabbed him in the nose, and the bottle went wide. Baudin jabbed him four more times until his nose gushed blood, confusion on the man's face as Baudin's strikes came like snake bites.

Baudin kicked him in the groin just as the bearded one hopped over the bar and came up behind him. Baudin kicked out, connecting to the man's gut, but it wasn't powerful enough to send him sprawling. The bearded one still came at him and got hold of him from behind.

Baudin thrust his head back, smashing into the guy's nose as the third one came up in front. Baudin tried to kick out, but the third one wasn't new to brawls. He brushed aside Baudin's kick and hit him so hard in the face that he thought he might pass out.

The guy kept hitting him, a flurry of punches that Baudin was helpless against. He felt himself going out and made one last attempt to get the bearded one off his back. He ducked low, using all of his bodyweight to fall, and the man's grip loosened. Baudin came up with a left hook that sent the guy in front of him over a table.

The bearded one was swinging wildly, more with rage than anything else. Baudin was bloodied and dizzy, but he dodged as many as he could before grabbing the bearded man with both hands behind the neck. He brought the man down to chest level and came up with several knees into his groin and chest.

But that all ended in one loud crash. A glass bottle broke over Baudin's head. There was no pain, but the noise was deafening. And the last thing he saw was the floor racing toward his face.

Baudin felt coolness against his skin. A breeze. It brought him out of his unconscious slumber and made him aware that he was now in the gutter outside the bar. He felt as though he could sleep right there, even though his back was twisted on the curb in a way that shot pain up and down his leg. But the effort of moving was too great. Instead, he closed his eyes.

"Come on, hon, let's go."

He felt hands on him, soft hands but firm. They helped him to a standing position. As soon as he was on his feet, he bent down at the waist and hurled a putrid mix of alcohol and bar peanuts into the gutter.

When he was through, he wiped his mouth with the back of his arm, and the hands were on him again, helping him up the sidewalk and to a car waiting on the corner.

44

Baudin smelled incense. Before his eyes even opened and he was aware that he was still alive, he smelled incense, and it took him back to college. He'd shacked up with a granola girl who believed in free love as if it were still the 1960s. Baudin would occasionally come home to find another nude man already in his bed. She encouraged him to experience other women, too, but he never could. He liked her. And one day, she was just gone. Her things were packed and the room empty. She dropped out of school and didn't tell any of her friends why.

As he opened his eyes, his first thought was of that girl and where she was now. And then in the periphery of his vision, he saw Candi sitting in a recliner watching television. He inhaled deeply and turned to her, his head pounding as though he were still being punched.

"Where am I?"

"In my room, hon. How ya feelin'?"

Baudin tried to sit up, but the world spun so violently he collapsed back. "What happened?"

"Well, looks like you got into a scrape with a few fellas you couldn't take. You lucky one of my friends was in that place and recognized you."

"I don't need your help."

"Uh-huh. Well, you're free to leave."

Baudin tried to get up again. The pain felt as if his guts had been smashed like a bug on a windshield. He groaned.

"That's what I thought," she said. She lit a cigarette. "What you doin' gettin' in bar fights with three fellas big as bears, anyhow? I thought you was a cop."

"I was. I don't know if I am anymore."

"Oh, one of those."

"Yeah," he said, reaching up and placing his hand on his head. "What's this?"

"A bandage. Your head was bleedin'."

He looked at her. "Why would you help me?"

She turned back to the television. "Few enough people I like in the world. Couldn't very well let one die in the gutter if I could stop it." She rose and walked over to him, sitting next to him on the bed. She took the lit cigarette and put it between his lips. "What happened?"

He inhaled deeply, letting the smoke tingle his lungs before blowing it out in a forceful gust of breath. "Just a shitty day."

"Ain't they all. But what happened today?"

"You are nosey, aren't you?"

"I just saved your life. You'd think you'd be grateful."

He lifted his arm, the pain in his shoulder radiating down to his fingertips, and removed the cigarette. "My daughter tried to kill herself."

She nodded. "I been there. Sometimes life feels like a cruel joke. Like there's some power behind it all just laughin', laughin' that you think you got control. Shit, we ain't got control over nothin'."

"No," he said, and took another drag. "We don't." He looked at her. "Your scar's healing."

"It ain't gonna go away. I don't think I'll be a whore much longer. I'd have to lower my prices so much it wouldn't be worth it."

"People that want work can find work. You'll land on your feet."

"I'm sure I will. So will you. You got that in you, you know. That desire to live. I think you'd live through just about anything and never even think of just offing yourself. Like most normal folk."

"Everybody wants to live."

"No, they don't," she said quietly. "Anyways, we best get you to a hospital. You took a blow to the head and probably have a concussion." She took his cigarette and took a drag before putting it out on the nightstand. "I'll drive."

Baudin had her drive him to the same hospital Heather was in. He got out of the car without goodbyes and turned to her. "Thanks."

"Come see me sometime, when you get better."

Night was already descending, and Baudin wondered exactly how long he'd been out for. He felt out of sorts, as if he'd fallen into a coma and woken up in a different time. Everything had a hazy appearance, and he hoped he wasn't suffering from brain damage.

As he walked into the waiting area before the emergency room, he saw Kyle Dixon lying across four chairs. The man had his suit coat pulled up over his shoulder and was sound asleep. Baudin went over to him and sat down. Dixon stirred and then woke. He inhaled deeply and sat up, twisting his neck.

"You here this whole time?" Baudin asked.

"I figured you'd be back. She's up if you want to see her." He paused. "What the hell happened to you?"

"Long story."

They rose together, and Dixon followed a step behind as Baudin asked to be buzzed back into the actual emergency rooms. Heather's bed was on the right-hand side, up the corridor. When he saw her lying in that bed, bandages around her wrists, the white flesh that seemed sickly, he nearly fell to the floor. She was all he had left, the only glimmer of beauty the world held for him anymore. Even the suggestion that she would rather die than be here with him…

He stopped next to her bed, and she saw him. She closed her eyes and turned away.

"Please go away, Daddy."

"Sweetheart… I'm… I don't even know what to say."

"I'm so embarrassed. I can't even kill myself right. Why am I alive, Daddy? Why am I here if I can't do anything?"

Baudin, tears rolling down his cheeks, pulled a stool next the bed and held her hand. No words were exchanged between them, but he leaned down and rested his forehead against the back of her hand, his tears dripping onto the linoleum.

45

The doctors wanted to keep Heather in the hospital a few days for observation, and Baudin agreed. By eleven, she was asleep for the night, and Baudin sat in the waiting room. Dixon had stayed by him the entire time. He sat in one of the chairs and watched Sports Center on one of the televisions mounted on the wall.

"Her mother killed herself," Baudin said, staring out the windows.

Dixon was silent a long time before saying, "I didn't know that."

"She went to the doctor and got sleeping pills. Two days later she took them with a fifth of Jack. She spent that day after the doctor's visit with us. The whole day. It was a Saturday. I didn't want to do much, just hang out at home. But she insisted. We saw a baseball game, went to a museum, and had a fancy dinner in Malibu at a restaurant that served fresh seafood right on the beach. I can still see her there, the way the sunlight reflected off her eyes… She'd made up her mind she was going to die, but she wanted one last day with us."

"I'm sorry," Dixon said. "I can't even imagine what that would be like."

"I'll tell you what it's like, it feels like you can't know anyone. Not really. There's always caverns in their hearts that they'll never reveal to you, no matter how close you think you are."

"It's still worth it."

"Yeah," he said, exhaling loudly.

Dixon waited a beat before saying, "Well, I'm gonna head home, I guess."

"We're not done, man. We're not done by a long shot."

"Done with what?"

Baudin turned to face him. "You know what."

"Now?"

"Yeah, now."

"We're not cops anymore, man."

"I keep telling you, there is no law. We don't need to be cops. But it's gonna get dirty. If you can't handle that, I'll do it alone."

Dixon rose. "Where do you wanna start?"

46

Baudin smoked while he sat in the driver's seat. Sigma Mu was about fifty feet ahead of him. He and Dixon were parked at the steepest part of the incline and had to fight gravity. Looking up the hill created an odd feeling, like moving through water. Dixon seemed calm, calmer than Baudin had seen him in a while. Making up his mind about a course of action could do that.

"He may not come out tonight," Dixon said.

"He'll come."

"How do you know?"

Baudin tossed the cigarette into the ashtray of the car. "I'll show you."

They left the car and crossed the street to the same side as the frat house. Trudging up the hill, Baudin felt like some grunt in the Spanish Civil War, or some other long forgotten conflict in which blood was spilt and no one remembered why. Or maybe he was the deserter. It didn't matter to him either way.

The red Volvo was parked out front at an angle. Baudin took the gloves out of his pocket and slipped them on as Dixon did the same.

"You sure about this?" Dixon said. "Ain't no going back."

"I crossed that line a long time ago. You sure you ready for it?"

Dixon swallowed and looked at the house. "Let's do it."

Baudin ran at the car, thrust out his foot, and slammed into it, leaving a large dent. The car swayed back and forth, and the alarm sounded: a piercing, shrill cry that broke the night's silence. The two men ducked in front of the Volvo, the alarm so loud Baudin wished he'd thought to bring earplugs.

Orridge ran out of the house. He stood on the lawn, pressing the alarm button on his keychain. He scanned the neighborhood a moment and then slowly examined his car.

Baudin was on him in a second. He tackled him from behind, the impact knocking the breath out of Orridge, who couldn't even get out a cry for help. Dixon wrapped a bag around his head as they duct-taped his wrists and ankles and dragged him into the darkness of the trees next to the house. Dixon sat on his back, pushing his weight into him.

Baudin ran back and got the car, and they threw him into the backseat. As they sped away, Baudin looked into his rearview and didn't see a single frat boy out on the porch checking up on what was happening.

"You see that, Dustin?" Baudin said. "You really see who your friends are when you need 'em."

The car raced up the service streets before getting on the interstate. Orridge tried to get up several times, and every time Dixon would tighten the bag so he couldn't breathe. When he behaved, Dixon would loosen it.

The industrial section of Cheyenne was a mass of manufacturing plants, warehouses, and storage units. Baudin sped up the street at double the speed limit. He hit the brakes hard, Orridge flying into the seats in front of him and the car screeching to a stop, before turning into the parking lot of a warehouse.

The warehouse, something he'd seen on his drives through the city, was abandoned. A "For Sale or Lease" sign was mounted on the side wall, covered in graffiti.

The two of them dragged Orridge while he kicked and swore the entire time. But the boy was too frightened to put up any real resistance. It was more like the fighting of a drowning man, lashing out at anything that was near.

The doors were padlocked, but the windows had been broken out and someone had gone in and opened several of the loading bay doors. Probably bored youths, or the homeless who made these buildings their temporary residences until the owners caught on.

They dragged him in through the loading bay and tossed him on the floor. Baudin went back to the door and slid it down, slamming it shut, more for effect than anything else.

The warehouse was empty except for some abandoned shelves. Cobwebs covered everything, and in the dim light of the moon, it gave the steel walls and the concrete floors an eerie, otherworldly glow.

Baudin removed the bag from Orridge's head. He'd taken his gloves off on the drive over, but now he put them back on, as did Dixon.

"Dustin," Baudin said, "I know you're thinking this is bullshit and that you're not gonna give us anything. You're gonna fight us because you think your daddy will save you. But that's not smart, my friend. It's not smart because no one's coming to save you."

Dustin, drenched in sweat, panting, watched the detectives. "You guys are cops. You guys are cops, you can't do this shit!"

Baudin came close and grabbed him by his hair. "I'm a very special type of cop."

Baudin swung with a left that slammed into the boy's jaw. Before he could recover, Baudin flipped him onto the ground and kicked him in the head, and then the ribs, knocking the wind out of him. Dixon stood by watching.

"I wanna know why you confessed," Baudin said.

"'Cause I did it."

Baudin kicked him again, causing the boy to nearly vomit. He dry heaved, getting up to his hands and knees, and Baudin kicked him again, sending him sprawling onto his back. Before he could do anything else, Dixon came over and stopped him. He put his arm around Baudin's chest and pulled him away.

"We just want to scare him, not kill him." Dixon approached the boy. "Sorry, man. He's… I don't know. He gets all worked up and just loses it. But he's right. You gotta help us. I can only control him for so long."

Orridge spat a gob of blood onto the pavement. "I don't know anything."

The statement was more a plea than anything else, so pathetic and hopeless that Baudin nearly grinned. He turned away from the boy, staring at the cavernous black of the empty warehouse, taking in the scents of dust and mildew.

"Why did you confess, Dustin?" Dixon said. "We both know you didn't do it."

Orridge began to cry. Dixon put his hand on his shoulder and let it go on for a few moments before saying, "Why?"

"They told me they'd take care of it."

"Take care of it how?"

"They said it would be dismissed before it went to a jury. That a lot of judges and lawyers were on our side."

Dixon looked at Baudin.

"The bail," Baudin said. "It was set lower than I've ever seen it for a murder. That's why he's out right now."

"Which judge?" Dixon said. "The one handling your trial?"

"I don't know. My dad told me I had to do it. That they'd take care of me."

Baudin stepped close to the boy, leaning down over him and causing Orridge to recoil. "Your father was a member of Sigma Mu, wasn't he?"

Orridge nodded.

Dixon softly touched the boy's hand. "Dustin, who killed Alli? It wasn't you. Just be honest with us. Please."

"I don't know. I don't know…" he cried. "But people are saying it was probably Casey."

"You know Casey?" Baudin said. "That's his real name?"

"I don't know him. I just know 'bout him. People talk 'bout him. He was, like, a legend at S Mu."

"Where can I find him?" Baudin said.

"I don't know, man. I swear it. He's got this, like, house up in Valley Mills. Some of the brothers been there. But I ain't never been. I ain't important enough. I ain't shit, man. I'm just fuckin'… I do whatever they tell me to."

Baudin looked at Dixon. "You know where Valley Mills is?"

"It's a neighborhood up 200 North. Prime stuff, expensive."

Baudin helped the boy up. "Dustin, I'm gonna find Casey. And if you go running to Daddy or your lawyer about this, I'm gonna tell Casey who sent us to him. You hear me, boy?"

He nodded. "I won't tell anybody."

"Good. Then you're free to leave."

"I need a ride."

The detectives looked at each other. "Fine," Dixon said. "Get in back."

47

Jessop emailed Dixon and told him he was suspended with pay for a week. Baudin thought it was because it would look too odd to fire them over just asking the police chief a question related to a homicide.

Hillary was gone for the day, and Dixon hadn't told her about his suspension. That would be a conversation for tonight when she got home. He'd have today to himself to lounge around, watch sports, and not do a damn thing.

As happened whenever he had days off and wasn't sick, boredom set in after about an hour. He began combing through the fridge for snacks and then went outside and sat in a lawn chair, staring at his backyard and debating whether they should get a dog. Then he checked his cell phone. He told himself he was checking department email so he wouldn't have a stack waiting for him when the suspension ended, but really he was waiting for a text from Baudin. Or maybe from Jessop, if Orridge decided to report their little scuffle the other night. But no texts like that came in.

By midday, Dixon had taken a nap, read several newspapers online, eaten about twenty snacks, and watched two movies on Netflix. He decided the only way to feel like he was being productive was to dress the part, so he showered and changed into slacks and a suit coat.

He left the house and headed for a nearby coffee shop. Ordering a black coffee with milk, he flirted a little with the cashier and felt bad about it. She was young, maybe nineteen, and was only being friendly because he was a customer, but it still made him feel young again and desirable.

The coffee shop had shelves of books, and he scanned them before settling on one: *Of Mice and Men*. It seemed to be the shortest one up there.

Dixon sat at a table by the window and began reading as he sipped his drink. When he was almost through, evening was falling outside, and he was hungry. Hillary should be home and readying dinner. He put the book back on the shelf, used the bathroom, and headed home.

When he walked in the house, he noticed something he wasn't used to upon entering the house later in the day: nothing cooking. He entered the kitchen to find Hillary sitting at the table. Her arms were folded, and she was staring into space. Her eyes lifted and held his in silence.

"What is it?" he said. "What happened?"

"We need to talk, Kyle. Please sit down."

Kyle grinned. "You need a new car again? I told you, when I get bumped up to lieutenant, which shouldn't be too long now, we can—"

"I don't want a new car," she said brusquely. "I need to talk to you."

He pulled out a chair and sat down across from her. "Okay. Here I am."

Her mouth opened, but she didn't get a single word out before a knock at the door stopped her. Hillary's eyes went wide and Dixon, suddenly, wondered who was at the door at this hour. He rose and answered it.

Baudin stood there in a leather jacket with a cigarette dangling from his mouth.

"Ready?"

"One sec," Dixon said.

He ran to the master bedroom and into the walk-in closet. On the top shelf was a gun safe. Dixon input the numerical code—Randy's birthday—and got out his Browning revolver. He tucked it into his waistband and then went back out to the kitchen.

"I'll be back," he said, kissing Hillary on the forehead.

"When?"

"Few hours. We'll talk then. I promise."

The city always looked different at night. Dixon had never lived in any other city, and he wondered if it was the same everywhere. He thought about cavemen and what night was like for them. A disappearing of the life-giving sun without any guarantee it would rise again in the morning.

Orridge had been telling the truth. Baudin had called his father, and he'd clammed up immediately and told them to speak to the family's lawyer. The lawyer and Dustin's father were both alums of Sigma Mu, as were two judges in Laramie County District Court and the District Attorney. Dixon had no doubt that Dustin Orridge never would have gotten anywhere near a jury. It certainly would've halted their investigation, and once a defendant was released—say, for a legal technicality—the detectives assigned to the case were usually reluctant to spend time pursuing him again. Especially if the chief of police told them not to. Or, more likely, gave the case to other detectives who wouldn't care about it as much.

"How's Heather?"

"Good. Not great, but good. She thought she'd be doing me a favor by killing herself. Like my life would be better without her in it. I told her she *was* my life. That nothing else meant anything. She cried for a while… and we talked about her mother. Something we've never done before."

Dixon glanced to him. "What was her mother like?"

"Fiery, man," he said with a smile. "All piss and vinegar. When we were dating, that's what attracted me to her. That confidence and assertiveness, the aggression. But those aren't the qualities you need to be a good mom and wife. You need compassion and forgiveness, and she never learned those. She was angry at us, but it turned inward, into depression." He paused. "I heard once that women marry men hoping they'll change and men marry women hoping they won't. Ain't that the shit."

"Marriage isn't an easy thing for anybody."

"How's Hillary as a wife?"

"The best a guy could ask for. I don't know how a jackoff like me earned her."

Baudin was silent for a second. "That neighbor of yours—Chris. What do you know about him?"

"Chris Hicks? He's a good guy. Bad luck with the ladies, though. Always hoppin' from one woman to the next. We were supposed to go on a double date but that fell through. He probably would've just screwed it up anyway. Why you askin' 'bout him?"

"I don't trust him. And I can read people pretty quick."

"Oh yeah? What was your read on me?"

He grinned. "Naïve, but with a good heart."

"Funny. I thought the same thing of you."

The drive on the interstate was quick, not much traffic. They passed the scene of an accident, a truck that had rammed a sedan from behind. A woman on a stretcher was being loaded into an ambulance.

Valley Mills was about a hundred homes, one of the most exclusive areas in all of Wyoming. The gates entering the development were closed, and a security guard sat in a booth, his feet up on a desk and his face in a magazine. He looked up and was putting the magazine down when Baudin flashed a badge. The guard nodded and opened the gate before going back to his magazine.

"Where'd you get that?" Dixon said.

"You only got one badge?"

"Yeah, I only got one badge."

"So what happens if it gets stolen or you lose it?"

"I put in a request for a new one."

Baudin chuckled. "Man, it is different out here. You lose the gold shield with the LAPD, you better run online and see if you can get a good replica. It's about the worst thing that could happen. The bangers there like them as trophies. They'll wear 'em around their necks as an insult to us. No one puts in for lost badges, man. You won't be respected."

"Well, that's childish. Stuff gets lost. You telling me you never lost your badge?"

"I have. That's why I keep a spare."

Within a hundred yards of the gate, the homes grew from two or three bedrooms to palatial estates with lighted pools in back. Dixon could see a pool party at one, girls in bikinis and boys running after them on the deck.

"You ever get jealous of the rich?"

"No, man. They're as miserable as everybody else. Life is one ridiculous thing after another, and it doesn't matter if you're homeless or a millionaire. You go through the cycle enough times, you start sensing the futility of it. How absurd it is that we take ourselves so seriously."

"Well, you're just a ray of sunshine, aren't you?"

Baudin parked the car at the curb. "Good a place as any, I guess."

"How exactly you plannin' on finding this house?"

He shrugged. "Just thought we'd check every house for furniture with plastic on it."

Dixon chuckled. "Well, we gonna be out here for a while, then." He thought a moment. "There's probably no one living in the house, right? So maybe we look for something that doesn't have lights on. And then it's unlikely they're here right now, so probably something without cars in the driveway."

Baudin opened his door. "Good enough."

48

It was well past midnight by the time Baudin and Dixon stood in front of a home up on the farthest hill in Valley Mills. Dixon scanned the area. The most secluded home was set apart from the others by at least thirty yards, with no lights on and no cars in the driveway.

Dixon approached the house and stepped up onto the porch. He peeked through one of the windows but couldn't see anything. The drapes were thick and black. As he turned to head back down the porch, he noticed the lock on the front door: thick, round, and sturdy, something that should be on a vault, not a home in this neighborhood. The door itself was reinforced, as were the windows.

"Dollars to donuts this is it," Dixon said.

"Well," Baudin said, lighting a cigarette, "only one way to find out."

"It might have an alarm."

"If it's our house, it won't. They wouldn't want the cops coming out here for false trips."

Dixon looked over the area again: nothing but tall grass, weeds, and gravel. Then he hit his elbow against the window. It didn't do anything at first, so he hit it again and again, each strike harder than the last. Finally, it cracked, and he focused the blows on the fracture, making it larger and larger until pieces fell. When the hole was large enough, he reached in, unlatched the window, and opened it. No alarm.

Dixon sneaked through first. Once he got through the drapes, he rose and scanned the front room.

The space was dusty, old, and unused. The furniture had dense plastic covering it, and no decorations hung on the walls. Except one: a painting near the front door of a sigma and mu.

Dixon opened the door, and Baudin came in, blowing out a puff of smoke. He noticed the painting and grinned.

Wordlessly, they began searching the house. The front room was first, but there was practically nothing there. Then they started on the bathrooms and bedrooms. Dixon went into the kitchen. He checked the fridge, which had nothing but an old box of Arm & Hammer, and the dishwasher. A door led out to the garage, and he opened it and froze.

"Ethan, you better come look at this."

Baudin came up behind him and said, "Shit."

A Ford truck was parked in the garage. The tires were dirty, and the scent of exhaust hung in the air. Someone had driven here not too long ago.

"There's someone in the house," Dixon said, pulling out his revolver.

Baudin took out a .40 semiautomatic pistol, and they turned toward the house. Whereas their first search was quick and haphazard, they now moved quietly, scanning the areas they'd already searched for any disturbances.

Neither of them had been upstairs yet. Baudin went up first, his back pressed against the wall, his eyes up, his gun held in front of him. Dixon went up the other side, his heart pounding as he felt the stickiness of sweat on his neck.

On the top floor, they turned two separate directions. Dixon checked the bedroom first: dark, with a large bed and open space and an empty closet. Baudin was coming out of the bedroom he'd searched and shook his head.

Dixon stepped into the bathroom. The shower curtain was drawn, but he didn't think anything of it… until he saw a few drops of water on the sink.

Before he could react, the shower curtain ripped away, and the blade came barreling toward him. Dixon moved, but only enough that the knife caught him in the chest rather than the neck and slid down to his belly, leaving a trail of blood and burning pain.

He tried to lift his gun, but the man swung wildly with the knife, catching him on the cheek. Dixon ducked to try to tackle him. The knife came up, and then Dixon went deaf.

The man collapsed against the bathroom wall, a hole in his cheek the size of a quarter. Blood poured out of it, filling his mouth, and then it began to drain out of his nose. He was choking, but it only lasted a moment. Then he stopped moving.

Dixon leaned against the sink, checking the wound on his chest. A thread of blood stained his clothing. He lifted his shirt; the wound wasn't deep, but it sure as hell hurt.

"You okay?" Baudin said.

"Fucker almost got me in the throat."

They looked at the body on the floor.

"I'm guessing that's Casey," Baudin said.

Dixon moved, and a sharp pain went through him as his abdominal muscles contracted.

"You need a hospital?"

"I don't know. How's my cheek?"

"Just a scrape."

Dixon looked at himself in the mirror. "How exactly am I gonna explain this to my wife?"

Baudin bent down over the body. He searched the pockets and didn't find a wallet, just the keys to the truck in the garage. "I wonder if he lived here."

Dixon took out his phone. "I'll call it in."

"No, man."

"What are you talking about? We got a dead body. It was a clean shoot."

"Yeah? And what are we doing in his house?"

Dixon froze. He was right. They were in the house unlawfully. Since a death occurred, the felony murder rule might apply if some prosecutor got creative and charged them with a felony, and self-defense wasn't applicable to felony murder. Which meant it didn't matter that Casey came at him first.

Felony murder was a capital crime in Wyoming.

"Shit," Dixon shouted. He punched the wall. "Shit!"

"Calm down, man. No one knows we're here."

"We fucking killed someone, Ethan."

"This piece of shit? I hope there is a hell and he burns in it, man. I'd kill him again." Baudin came close to him, resting his hands on Dixon's shoulders. "No one knows we're here, man. All right?"

"All right." He nodded, running his tongue along the inside of his cheek. "All right. Let's go."

"I wanna look in that bedroom really quick."

"Are you nuts?"

"Go downstairs and wait for me. I'll be right there."

Dixon turned. He felt as if he was swimming through milk right now. Everything had a hazy glow to it. His mind was a jumble of thoughts and images, of conversations he'd have to have. As he turned down the hall to head downstairs, a noise made him stop in his tracks. Something from the bedroom. He looked at Baudin, who was staring in there, too.

"You hear that?" Dixon said.

Baudin went in gun first. Dixon followed and noticed for the first time that his hands were trembling. He consciously worked to stop them, forcing them to calm.

The bedroom had one other door, one he assumed led to a bathroom. Baudin slid to the right side of the door, and Dixon stayed on the left. They looked at each other, and Baudin nodded. Dixon flung open the door, and Baudin went in, sweeping left to right.

Inside, hanging from chains that had been bolted to the ceiling, was a nude woman. She had a black mask over her head, something like an executioner's mask. She was young and white, and deep red lashes covered her torso and back.

"Fuck me," Dixon mumbled. He reached for her, and Baudin grabbed his hand.

"She can't see us, man."

"I won't leave her here."

"I'm not sayin' that. I'm just sayin' she can't see us." Baudin turned to her. Her head was bobbing lightly as though she'd been drugged, and every few seconds a soft whine would escape her lips. "I'll drive his truck down and take her to a hospital, then I'll dump the truck. I don't want nobody at the hospital seeing my car."

Dixon reached up to the chains. They were fastened with screws that could be turned with the fingers. Undoing both of them on her wrists, Dixon caught the girl as she fell limply into his arms. Dixon grabbed the sheets off the bed and wrapped her in them. The two men carried her down to the garage and put her in the back of the truck.

Baudin sat in the driver's seat, and Dixon stood outside. They held each other's gaze, some solemn promise or oath between them. Dixon knew that neither one of them would ever tell anyone about this; this was a secret that would die with them. And it gave them a bond they couldn't have formed any other way: the bond of secrecy.

"Get goin'," Baudin said. "I'll pull out when you're gone."

Dixon ran out of the house and up the street. By the time he was at the car, the truck was out and headed down the road. He caught a glimpse of Baudin as he sped out of Valley Mills, and his taillights disappeared into the black.

49

Baudin took the curves back down to the valley quickly and then realized the last thing he needed was to be pulled over by some highway patrolman. So he slowed down to under the speed limit.

The girl was more aware now. She was moving and crying. He glanced back at her. "Can you hear me?" he said. No response. "I'm taking you to a hospital. I'm here to help you."

Baudin thought back to the shot that had killed the man he thought was Casey. A bullet through the cheek that flooded his lungs with blood. Baudin had killed before. The military had seen to that. He'd gotten over the moral repugnance, the aversion that was ingrained in people since they were children. But something about taking a man's life still stuck to his ribs. Then again, he'd erased an entire line of victims that would've existed if that man had lived.

Burn in hell, asshole.

"Please," a meek voice said from behind him. "Please..."

The voice was hardly audible, like the chirp of a bird. Baudin pulled over to the side of the road. He turned back to her.

"Are you awake?" he said through the window.

"Please..."

"I'm not going to hurt you. I'm taking you to a hospital. Do you understand? Hospital?"

"Y—yes."

"What's your name?"

A long silence. "Rebecca."

"Rebecca, I need you to relax. You're safe now. No one's going to hurt you. But I can't take your mask off just yet, okay?"

The girl started crying again, kicking her legs and begging him. All she would say was "Please… please."

He began driving again. The first hospital in his GPS was a ten-minute drive from where he was. Cheyenne Regional.

The hospital had a massive parking structure and consisted of separate buildings. Baudin pulled right up to the emergency room. He removed the girl, holding her in his arms, and debated going inside. Deciding against it, he laid her at the front entrance.

He got into the truck and drove across the street. People already surrounded her. A nurse or orderly ran out, and they helped her inside. One of them pulled off the mask. He couldn't make out her face, but she was young, perhaps no more than eighteen.

He pulled away and took off.

Dixon got home so late that every light in every neighbor's house was off. He had spent some time at the park, sitting on a bench and staring into the pond. After that, he made a quick stop at the ER and, luckily, didn't require any stitches. They cleaned the wound and bandaged it before sending him on his way.

Murders had come across his desk, as had rapes, kidnappings, and every other thing they told you about in Police Officer Standardized Training. But a girl hanging like a doll from the ceiling, to be used and discarded as if she were a piece of trash… that was something he wasn't prepared to see. He hadn't thought humanity's cruelty could surprise him anymore. Even with the death of Alli Tavor, it hadn't affected him like this. She was dead. She was an object to be theorized over. The girl at the house was alive and suffering, and the more she suffered, the more aroused her captors got.

His house was quiet, the only noise the sound of crickets coming through an open window in the front room. He closed the window and decided that they would be getting an alarm tomorrow.

After checking on the baby, he undressed, brushed his teeth as quietly as he could, and climbed into bed. Hillary was rolled onto her side, but he could tell she wasn't sleeping. Only a spouse could tell that about another spouse. Something in the pattern of their breathing, maybe.

"You wanted to tell me something?" he whispered.

She sniffled, as though she'd been crying, and said, "It can wait."

50

The next few days, Baudin didn't do anything. Dixon had called him every day, first checking on Heather and then asking what they planned to do.

"Nothing," he would say. "Not yet."

After five days of what was really an involuntary committal, Heather was released from the hospital's psychiatric ward. Baudin drove her over to Molly's. He would be getting a new house. They were just renting anyway, and breaking the lease here apparently was a minor inconvenience. Talk of lawsuits and lawyers didn't even come up. All the landlord said was, "Well, sorry to see ya go."

The house had an energy to it now. Baudin, someone who considered himself above superstition, was embarrassed that he held on to this minor irrationality: he fully believed that locations could hold the energy of events that occurred there, good or bad. The scenes of murders, no matter how many a detective had worked, always held an eerie feeling that couldn't be shaken. He didn't want the energy of Heather's attempted suicide in their home.

He walked her inside, and Molly hugged her and wept. She took Heather to the kitchen table, insisting she looked thin as bones, and began frying breakfast for her.

Baudin sat on the porch and smoked. His suspension was over today. He could go back to work and get his badge and gun back. Somehow the allure of it wasn't there.

Sometimes the work was all there was, the only reason to get up in the morning. But now he saw that was an illusion. His daughter was why he woke up in the morning, and the work only got in the way of that.

He had one thing he had to finish. After that, whatever came his way came his way.

He walked inside and wrapped his arms around his daughter, planting a big kiss on her forehead. "Back to school tomorrow?"

"Yeah," she said.

"Good." He kissed her again. "I'll be back in a few hours, and then we'll head out to see your counselor."

The sun was bright without any clouds to dim the light. He stopped at a gas station and bought a pair of sunglasses, putting them on awkwardly. He didn't like the feeling of them on his face, but he didn't take them off, either.

The precinct wasn't far—in fact, nothing was really that far. Not LA far. Not sitting-in-three-hours-of-traffic far. It amazed him that people still complained about traffic here.

He got to the precinct and went inside. Dixon was at his desk. When he saw Baudin, he rose and followed him out without a word. They stood on the sidewalk.

"We need to go see her," Baudin said.

"You know where she is?"

Baudin nodded. "She was released from the hospital yesterday. Her name's Rebecca Sapps. She lives in an apartment with her mother. Eighteen." Baudin stopped and exhaled. "You wanna know the thing about freedom, Kyle? It's painful. And people don't want it. If you wanna make someone free, they'll fight you. You break their ideology, and ideology is comfort. You wanna make someone free, you best be prepared to fight them."

"I don't know what any of that means, Ethan."

"I'm saying, we may learn some things about this city and the police that you can never unlearn. You may not be able to ever live here again."

He nodded. "I'll drive."

The Sapps lived in an apartment complex called Green Groves. The apartments were laid out like an H with a row in the middle that was unusually out of place. Anyone driving down would have to go around the row of apartments and enter a blind spot where children playing would probably get hit if they weren't on their toes.

Baudin parked in front of complex X, a flat, square building that housed four separate units. They got out of the car and strolled up to the door. Outside on the pavement, children's toys were thrown around, as were old beer bottles and cigarette butts.

Baudin knocked, and there was no sound from inside. He rang the doorbell and again nothing.

"Maybe she ain't here?" Dixon suggested.

"She's here. She can't leave her comfort zone yet."

He rang the doorbell again and then said, "Ms. Sapps, it's the police. We aren't leaving."

After a while, the locks slid open, and the girl's face appeared at the door. Baudin knew it was her, even though he'd only seen her from across a street and in the hospital's dim lighting.

"Ms. Sapps," Dixon said, "We're detectives with the Cheyenne Police Department. We're following up on your case and had a few questions for you. If you don't mind, that is."

The girl didn't move, didn't speak. She was like an alien who crash-landed on a strange planet and didn't know the customs, Baudin thought. A look of bewilderment. He'd seen it before, in people who had accepted their own deaths and then suddenly, miraculously, had lived. The world was an alien place to them after that.

"How are you, Rebecca?" he said.

Her eyes went wide, and tears welled up inside them. He wasn't sure she'd remember his voice, but there it was. He smiled, and she closed the door, slid the chain off, and opened it.

51

The café had a delightful smell. Melted chocolate, Hillary thought, because of the fondue they sometimes served.

She sat by the window and stared at the passersby. Some of them, the younger couples, seemed so happy. They couldn't keep their hands off each other. She remembered when Kyle and she had been like that. Hell, she thought with a grin, Kyle was still like that. Only she had matured, grown up in a way that didn't seem to affect Kyle. Maybe she'd just grown cynical, and he hadn't.

After waiting ten minutes, she grew impatient. How dare he be late for this? This was her life, her entire life, unraveling. And he had the nerve...

No, it wasn't his fault. He was just as lost in all this as she was. They had committed a great sin together. She didn't mean a sin against God. Though she went to church and played the good wife as Kyle wanted, she didn't believe in it anymore. Her faith had slowly dissipated over time until there weren't even ashes left anymore. Kyle would never accept that, not in the way Chris accepted and understood it.

Chris walked in a good twenty minutes late. He sat across from her without a word and stared into her eyes.

"You're late," she said. "Don't be late again or I'll leave."

He grinned. "You look beautiful. Even when you're sad."

"Don't."

"Don't what? Tell the mother of my child that she looks beautiful?"

She recoiled at the words. "Why do you have to do that? Throw it in my face all the time?"

"I love you, you know that. I just want what's best for you and for my son."

"Then why don't you leave us alone?"

He shook his head. "Do you honestly believe that that boy is better off living a lie? For how long? The rest of his life? You gonna take this to the grave with you, Hillary? Or are you gonna tell him one day? What's he gonna think? Is he gonna thank you?"

"I don't know." She put her face in her hands. "I just wish I knew what to do."

"You need to tell him and end it." He leaned forward. "I'm going to serve him this week."

"No, you can't. I'm not ready."

"Sorry, Hillary. It's for both of us. I'm being strong for both of us."

"Chris, that is the worst possible way he could find out."

"Then tell him."

She averted her eyes from him, staring out the window. "I used to think being married was going to be a dream. Like it just happened, and that was all there was to it. I wouldn't have to worry about it anymore. But it's work. Everything, in the end, is just work." Hillary stood up. "Do whatever the hell you want. I won't be with you, Chris. I'm sorry."

She left, not looking behind her until she was out the door. Chris was staring at her, and smiled. She pushed through the door and hurried to her car.

52

Rebecca's apartment reminded Baudin of his grandmother's house in the best sense: comforting and clean. Lots of quilts and old paintings, the smell of lemonade, carpets so clean you could eat off them.

He sat across from her on the couch. Her eyes looked glossy—a sedative, maybe. Maybe more than that. He couldn't imagine she would be this calm after what she'd gone through.

"Tell me what happened, Rebecca."

She swallowed and looked down at the floor. "They called the police at the hospital. I already told them what I remembered."

"We're not that kind of police. Tell me what happened."

She swallowed again. "I met this guy at a bar. I have a fake ID, and I thought... I met him there. He said his name was Casey and that I was the most beautiful girl in the place." She wiped at tears that had formed. "I'm so stupid."

"No," he said soothingly, "you're not. Please continue."

"We flirted, and he said he would give me a ride home. On the drive back, he convinced me to stop at his place for a drink. We had some drinks, and we talked and laughed. He was so... I don't know. I was used to immature guys. But he talked about what Paris was like and what hunting in Africa was like... he was so... I don't know. And then I started going, like, numb. I couldn't feel anything. And he smiled." She began to cry. "He just smiled at me like I was a piece of meat... and he picked me up and took me upstairs. On the bed... and they... all these men, they..."

"Did you see any of them?" Baudin said softly.

"No," she said, shaking her head and wiping away the tears that were rolling down her cheeks, "no, they wore masks."

"Did they ever take them off?"

"Only one did. He sat in a chair by the bed while the others..."

Baudin wanted to reach out and lay a hand on her to let her know she wasn't alone and no one would hurt her, but she was so medicated, he wasn't certain it would matter. What he was fearful of was when the medication dulled and the true horror of what happened hit her consciousness. He wondered if she would be strong enough to survive.

"Tell me about the one in the chair."

She swallowed again, wiping at tears that were long gone. "He just wanted to watch. He sat in a chair and smoked a cigar. He had to pull his mask up to smoke, and I saw most of his face. I don't think he meant for me to see it, I don't know... and he just looked at me. He would laugh sometimes... he thought what they were doing to me was the funniest thing in the world..."

"A cigar? You're sure of that?"

"Yeah. I remember the smell."

Dixon pulled out his phone and showed something to her. A violent convulsion gripped her, and she nodded, immediately looking away. Dixon showed the phone to Baudin. It was the official photo of Chief of Police Robert Crest on the department website.

"What happened after?" Baudin said.

"When they were done, they put a mask on me, and then I felt myself hanging from somewhere. I don't know how long, maybe just a night, I think. And then you came."

Dixon said, "You're not the first they've done this to, Rebecca. We had another girl a couple weeks ago that the same thing happened to. But they didn't put her in the closet. They drove her somewhere and left her in the street. Do you have any idea why they put you in there?"

She nodded, the tears dribbling down again. "Casey said… he said they were going to kill me. They were… they were going to crucify me. I screamed, and he just laughed."

Baudin felt his heart drop. He couldn't speak, couldn't move. The arrogance of it… the cruelty. He wished he could kill that son of a bitch again.

"Excuse us one sec," Dixon said. He rose and walked out the front door and stood there. Baudin followed him. "This is too big for us," Dixon said. "We gotta take it to the FBI."

"No, man. This is our fight."

"We're not in the Wild West. And I'm not a damn assassin."

"I don't wanna kill him. But answer me honestly: with the connections he's got, is there any chance he's not gonna slide on this? How many people, respectable people, are gonna come forward and say the Chief of Police was with them on the night in question? How many character witnesses are gonna take the stand and call that poor girl a liar?"

"What, then? You wanna take care of it Dodge City style and kick down his office door?"

He shook his head, staring at the girl. "No, man. I wanna force their hand. I want them to make a mistake."

"Like what?"

Baudin looked at him. "You still got that friend in the news, right?"

Dixon was silent a moment. "You wanna use Rebecca as bait?"

"If she goes public, they gotta come after her. They don't have a choice. The allegation, once everybody knows about it, is enough. It'll ruin him. What they'll need is her to commit suicide. Then they can say she was crazy and who knows what else she was making up. They can't do that later, once the story's taken hold. They gotta do it quick. As quick as possible."

"How can you possibly be sure they would do that? They might not do anything. They might just lawyer up."

"No, man. They gotta come after her. It's what I would do."

A long silence passed between them. Dixon looked in on the girl as well. "She'll never agree to it."

Baudin could see the girl's hands trembling, either from anxiety or the medication to treat the anxiety. "No, I think she'd do just about anything to get at them."

53

Baudin sat on the couch in Jessop's office as the five o'clock news played on the television. The letters on the screen and the words coming out of Rebecca's mouth seemed almost comical to him— mostly because he was picturing Chief Crest, his face bright red, a cigar in his mouth, exploding in his office at anyone near him.

Jessop watched the entire broadcast. Rebecca had gone through what she remembered in detail with one fabrication: that she later saw the chief's photo online and that was why she called the news. It helped bolster her story that two police officers had taken her statement at the hospital, verified by a nurse who was there, but had never filed a report. The officers had informed dispatch that the woman was "unreliable" and that they would look into her story, but had never done so.

"Captain?" a female voice said through his phone's intercom.

"What?"

"I have several reporters wanting comments. The chief and assistant chief can't be found."

"Tell the reporters to fuck themselves."

"Um... okay."

"No, Erica. For shit's sake, don't tell them that. Just tell them no comment." He leaned back in his chair, eyeing the two detectives. "You two have anything to do with this?"

Baudin said, "Why would we have anything to do with this?"

"Don't be cute. I'm serious."

"Cap," Dixon said, trying to take the spotlight off of them, "two uniforms took her statement and didn't do shit about it. You know how that's gonna look? Whether the chief is innocent or not, he's already been convicted."

Jessop sighed. "I know. He'll have to resign. There's no other way. He was a friend to the detective division. We needed him."

Baudin folded his arms. "I want to put her in a safe house."

"What? Are you shitting me? She's accusing the chief of police of kidnapping and raping her. You want us to spend funds putting her in a safe house?"

"You don't have to spend anything. My realtor said we can use an abandoned house on Claremont Ave. She doesn't need a detail, I don't think she's in any danger. But the chief has a lot of friends that might try to intimidate her. I think the safe house is a good bet for a while."

Jessop looked to Dixon, incredulous, seemingly searching for anything that would explain what Baudin had just proposed. "She's just a kid, Cap. We'll drive her to the safe house, and that's it. A few days there, and then she's on her own."

He shook his head. "Shit, why not? The whole damn department's goin' to hell. We might as well protect the enemy, too."

Baudin said sternly, "She's not our enemy."

The two men glared at each other. Baudin had done his homework. Jessop was not an alum of Sigma Mu. He'd gotten a two-year degree from a community college in criminal justice when he was in his thirties and never took part in the college life. He was just a blind cog in a big, powerful wheel.

"Few days," Dixon said, "then she's on her own."

Jessop nodded. "Few days. Don't tell anyone. And take a good statement from her so we don't look like we're in on this shit, too."

Claremont Avenue was as middle class as it got. As Baudin stared out the window at the dwindling sunlight, he saw several men driving home from work. Most of the cars here were trucks, large work trucks with mud spattered on the wheels and undercarriage. The men looked tired by the time they got home, trading sweat for money. Sometimes, the thought of working outside all day with his hands sounded more appealing than almost anything else. He wondered how people found what they would enjoy the most. If someone would really love to be a chef but had never cooked, how would they know that was their chosen path in life?

Maybe he had a path, too. Something he was meant to do that never came to fruition. Painter, perhaps, or writer… revolutionary.

More than any other moment in history, he would've liked to have seen the French Revolution with its upending of society and replacement with something else. The upending wouldn't have been beautiful. It had been bloody and vicious: some of the proletariat ate the bourgeoisie in the streets. Cannibalism, the ultimate act of conquest. The streets must've been coated in blood so thick it would've soaked the shoes… and Baudin always returned to the same question when he thought these thoughts: could it happen here?

The door opened, and Dixon hurried in, carrying a thick canvas bag that looked as though it contained a cello. He put the bag down in the center of the empty living room and unzipped it. Inside were two M4A1 assault rifles.

Dixon picked one up. "Smaller and lighter than the M16. Thirty round mags, high fire rate." He tossed it to Baudin, who caught it, running his hands along the smooth surface.

"Where'd you get military assault rifles on such short notice?"

Dixon grinned. "Shit, man. This is Wyoming."

Baudin lifted the weapon and looked down the barrel. It felt light, much lighter than he'd expected. He swept back and forth with it and then leaned it against the wall. Also inside the bag were two pistols, several boxes of ammunition, and two Kevlar vests. He took one of the vests and put it on over his shirt as Dixon did the same. CPD was written in bold print across the back.

The men looked at each other. Baudin felt like asking if Dixon was certain he wanted to be here but thought he already knew the answer. And somehow, just the asking seemed insulting. Instead, he grinned.

"Now what?" Dixon said.

"Now we sit on our asses until they get here."

54

Folding chairs next to a window wasn't exactly the most comfortable position Dixon had ever sat in for a long period of time. But it probably wasn't the worst, either. As he ate a Hershey bar, the M4 between his legs, a cap turned backward on his head, and his eyes out the window, he somehow felt more like a real cop than ever before. That was in spite of the fact that what he was doing would not only cost him his job but probably his freedom as well.

He didn't expect the chief to show up. Neither one of them did. But if they were right, someone would have to come down. Jessop was loyal to the chief and would tell him what they were doing.

If someone did come, then Baudin and Dixon were correct, and the chief of police of Cheyenne was a monster. Once he had that certainty, Dixon would do anything to stop him. Right now, he didn't feel that. They had to be certain.

Outside was pure black with only the porch light illuminating the lawn. Most of the neighbors had gone to bed, and the street didn't have much traffic. Dixon took another bite of chocolate and scratched his scalp underneath the cap.

"There's someone out there," Baudin whispered.

Dixon froze. Slowly, he put the chocolate bar down. He pulled the curtain back just slightly, peering farther onto the lawn.

At first, he didn't see anything. Just an empty blackness that fought any visual penetration. Then, slowly, he could see movement. Just on the outskirts of the blackness, a figure moved across the lawn. It skimmed along the edge, around the house, and disappeared in back.

"On it," Baudin said, before rising and silently disappearing to the back of the house.

Dixon's heart was in his throat, and he wished he hadn't eaten anything. Nausea was clawing at him, and he fought it the best he could.

On the other side of the house, he saw the same movement. A dark figure scurrying through the blackness. It didn't go around back. It came right to the porch.

A man, tall and lean, dressed all in black, with a black mask. He tried the doorknob, and when it didn't open, he took out a small kit. He inserted something into the lock and began jiggling it. Baudin had been right; Jessop wasn't Sigma Mu, but he was in on this. At the very least, he was reckless.

Dixon took the M4 and duck-walked to the front door. He perched on the stairs leading to the second floor and aimed the weapon. Sweat stung his eyes, and his heart was so loud he thought the intruder could hear it.

The lock clicked open, and the door creaked. Nothing happened at first, no one came in. Then the figure in black casually stepped inside and shut the door behind him. He scanned the space, starting on the right, the direction opposite where Dixon was.

Dixon stood up. "Put your damn hands on your head."

The man's head whipped around. Dixon expected him to run, or surrender, or scream, but not to attack. But that was exactly what he did. He ran at Dixon and jumped on him like a cat. Dixon squeezed the trigger, and the rifle shot along the wall and up into the ceiling as he was knocked back onto the stairs.

The figure struck him in the face with a fist so hard his head bounced off the step behind him. He struck again and again, and finally Dixon rolled to the side and then swung wildly, impacting against the man's jaw just enough to stun him. Dixon wrapped his fingers around the man's throat and squeezed. The man did the same. The air was cut off. He felt his eyes bulging, and his head felt as if it were being blown up with air like a balloon about to explode.

Dixon let go and slammed his fist into the man's face in a succession of blows that loosened his grip. He kicked out with his legs, and the man tumbled back. He hit his head on the hardwood floor, and Dixon was on him.

Now on top, he was pummeling him with his fists as he heard rounds fired in the back. But he didn't stop until the man wasn't moving anymore. Not until his hands screamed, and he felt as though he'd broken his knuckles. With every blow, the fear left him a little. He didn't stop until it was nearly gone.

Out of breath and bleeding, Dixon rolled off the man and lay next to him on the floor. He felt as though he'd been drowning and had just been rescued. Every muscle cried for relief, but no matter how deeply he breathed, it didn't come.

The figure was breathing, too. A shallow, dry breath. But he wasn't moving.

With the last ounce of strength he had, Dixon got to his knees. He crawled up the stairs and retrieved the M4. Before he could turn around, the figure had him again. His arm was wrapped around Dixon's throat, squeezing the life out of him.

Within moments, Dixon felt himself passing out. In a Hail Mary, he flung himself off the stairs, landing with the man still on his back. The grip around his throat loosened, and he rolled over. He wrapped his fingers around the figure's throat again and pressed.

The man's windpipe crushed under his grip like dry cereal, and a gasping, hacking sound came from the figure. Dixon moved away as the man thrashed violently, his hands at his throat in the universal sign of a lack of air. Dixon didn't move. He probably didn't have the stamina to help even if he wanted to. But he'd also never killed before and didn't want to. He pulled out his cell phone to call an ambulance, and it was ripped out of his hand.

Baudin flung the cell phone across the room.

"What the hell!" Dixon shouted.

Baudin ripped off the man's mask. The man was young, and his eyes were wide with terror. He was sucking breath like a fish that'd been thrown from a lake onto dry land.

"I know him," Dixon said. "That's Josh Everett. He's a uniform with the city."

Baudin lit a cigarette. "Not no more."

Dixon watched him. He had a flicker in his eye, the terrible calmness of someone in his element. "We can't let him die."

"Why not?"

"Because we ain't murderers."

He shrugged. "I don't think calling anybody's gonna help. He'll be unconscious in about thirty seconds and dead in three minutes. Brain death will happen two minutes after that. He's already gone."

Dixon rushed over to his phone. He called it in and gave the address, requesting an ambulance. When he'd hung up, Baudin was still smoking over the now unconscious man.

"One in back's still alive," Baudin said.

They headed to the kitchen. A man was lying on the linoleum with blood pooling around his legs. Baudin had shot out both knees. Baudin bent down over the man and stuck a finger in one of the holes the M4 had torn. The man screamed.

Dixon recognized him, too, another uniform. The two who'd taken Rebecca's statement at the hospital.

"Tell him what you told me," Baudin said. "Go on now."

"The chief..." the man said in a quivering voice, "the chief said we had to get rid of her."

"Rid of her how?" Baudin said, taking a drag.

"Su—suicide."

Baudin grinned. "I do amaze myself sometimes."

"This isn't funny," Dixon said, staring down at the man.

Baudin stood up. "I told you, freedom is painful. Well, you're free now. And you can see the horror behind appearances. It's a rare gift, Kyle. Not everyone can survive it, but some people can grow stronger from it, and use it to their advantage."

"Like you?"

He put his cigarette out on the wall and shoved the butt in his pocket. "I don't think we should be here when the ambulance arrives."

"No, we're doin' this part my way. We are gonna be here, and we're giving statements about what happened. Then I'm going to go over to Chief Crest's house and put those damn handcuffs on him myself."

Baudin chuckled. "It's good to see you passionate about something for once."

55

The uniformed officers and detectives on scene at Claremont Avenue looked like the survivors of a civil war. The man Baudin had injured repeated what he'd told them to several officers, paramedics, and a detective. The chief of police had ordered a hit. Baudin made sure he understood that he wouldn't survive the night if he didn't stick to the truth. "The truth shall set you free," he whispered to him as the police were rushing into the house.

Everyone was walking around the scene as though they were lost. No one seemed quite sure what to do or where to go. They weren't even going to take statements from Baudin or Dixon until Dixon requested it.

The statements were given and the two would-be hitmen taken to a hospital. The man with a fractured windpipe had survived, despite Baudin's pessimism. Dixon wondered whether he had actually wanted the man to die and so hadn't wanted to get him help.

One detective even said, "What the hell do we do now?"

Dixon replied, "I'm goin' to arrest our boss."

Chief Crest's home was ritzy, ritzier than Baudin had ever seen for a police officer, chief or no. It had a long driveway and a barn in back with at least three horses. A black Mercedes sat in the driveway, and the lights to the house were off.

"Any kids in the house?" Baudin asked as Dixon parked in front of the home.

"No. He's married, though."

They stepped out of the car. Several police units pulled up behind them. The district attorney had been informed of the situation and, rather than protecting him, had realized Chief Crest was a lost cause. Better to make him look bad now in case he pointed the finger at others. He'd met with a judge, and a warrant for the arrest of Chief Robert Crest was issued by the Laramie County District Court. Dixon had the arrest warrant in his back pocket.

Dixon hurried to the door and pounded on it with the side of his fist, but Baudin took his time. He lit a cigarette and smoked while staring at the house. He threw the cigarette on the gravel after only a few puffs and withdrew his firearm.

"He's not answering."

Baudin kicked at the door several times until it cracked enough that they could break it down. It flung open, splinters of wood raining over the atrium.

The house was dark and quiet. The only sounds were sirens as officers sped up the hill to assist in the arrest.

"I'll check upstairs," Dixon said.

Baudin stood still. The home was immaculately decorated. The chief either came from money or had found a way to exploit the police department to get his money. Baudin walked over to the fireplace and touched several expensive-looking vases on the mantle. He was heading to the kitchen when he heard Dixon shout, "Shit. Fuck me!"

"What?"

"His wife. He fucking shot her. She's gone."

Baudin froze. These were the actions of a man cutting his losses. He either wasn't here and was already on a plane to another country, or he was lying in wait. Baudin lifted his weapon and searched the kitchen then the bathrooms. By that time, Dixon was back downstairs. They searched the rest of the home together. Nothing.

"He's long gone," Dixon said. "Shit! We shoulda had someone here."

Baudin spit on the floor. His mouth had a sticky dryness to it that seemed disgusting. He looked down at the linoleum of the kitchen floor where he'd spit and then scanned the entire room. Underneath the dining room table was a slight misalignment of the linoleum. He moved the table aside and bent over it. Reaching into the alignment with his fingertips, the linoleum rolled up, revealing a door. He lifted the latch, and the door came open on a set of steps going down.

The sirens had stopped, and officers were coming into the home. He looked at Dixon and then climbed down.

The darkness was consuming. Dixon fumbled with his keychain, which had a small flashlight on it, but it was hardly more than a glimmer.

They got to the bottom of the stairs, and Baudin couldn't see anything. The light from the kitchen upstairs was completely gone. They were at least thirty feet below the home.

"Search the walls," he said.

He ran his fingers over the walls, hoping for a light switch. He came across something thick and smooth and tried to wiggle it but couldn't. "Bring your light, would you?"

Dixon came over and shone his flashlight on Baudin's hand. A plastic case covered a light switch. The case had a lock on it. Baudin bashed it with the handle of his gun, breaking the plastic rather than the lock. He broke enough away that he could reach in and flip the switch.

The basement wasn't a basement. It was a torture chamber.

Chains hung from the ceiling, a board with nails and straps sat in the corner, and various cutting utensils like cleavers and knives hung on a wooden beam. Several small chainsaws hung on another wall, along with tools like blowtorches and pliers.

"Who the hell were we working for?" Dixon whispered.

A voice bellowed, "Glad you came."

Baudin swung around with his gun just in time to see the figure of the chief flip another light switch. The darkness overtook them, and the last image he had was the chief dashing away.

Baudin fired several times, lighting up the basement with each round. But he knew he hadn't hit anything.

"You're the damn chief of police," Dixon shouted. "I fucking trusted you."

A voice, hardly a whisper, said, "Why do you think I wanted to be chief of police?"

"Fuck you!" Dixon began firing now, randomly spraying blasts in every direction.

"Stop firing," Baudin shouted. "Kyle, stop—"

Dixon squealed, a mixture of scream and grunt. His weapon tumbled out of his hand. Baudin could tell because he heard it clatter against the floor. Baudin fired into the wall so he could see what was happening. The chief was behind Dixon, a knife plunged into his back. Dixon's wide eyes stared at the ceiling.

Baudin rushed to him, feeling the burning pain of a slice across his chest. He jumped back and pointed his weapon as the blade entered his arm. He screamed as the sheer bulk of Crest hit him like a freight train and knocked him onto his back.

He was on the floor, and the gun had dropped out of his hand. He searched the floor with hands and feet but couldn't find it. A searing pain entered his calf, and he screamed as Crest laughed.

"You boys gonna die with me here. This is our tomb."

"You gonna die alone," Dixon said.

Crest swung around. Baudin was up and tackled him. Baudin swung wildly with punches, hitting wall, bone, and flesh. Crest was grunting and fighting back, getting cuts in with the knife.

"Shoot him!" Baudin shouted. "Shoot!"

Dixon fired in the dark. The first round illuminated them, and the second entered Crest's skull. He stopped fighting. Blood seeped out of him. Baudin could feel its warmth on every part of his body, soaking his shirt, his pants, his soul.

He saw Dixon, or the outline of Dixon, standing over him as the chief's body collapsed in a heap on top of him. He rolled it off and got to his knees.

They heard footfalls on the stairs, the basement lighting up as someone flipped the switch.

Before them, Crest lay on his back, staring up at the ceiling, his eyes like marbles. Dixon's jaw clenched, anger coursing through him, but Baudin reached down and closed his eyes. The two of them stole a quick glance to each other and then headed up the stairs.

56

Baudin had never minded bandages. But the amount he was now wearing made him feel like a mummy. Nothing serious, nothing permanent other than scars, but cuts deep enough that he was given intravenous antibiotics to be safe. Several of them required stitches, the one in his calf being the worst.

When they were through with him, he rose from his bed and hobbled straight to Dixon's room without checking out. A line of reporters and cameras were in the waiting room of the ER. He didn't say anything as he passed.

Dixon had been stabbed in the back between the ribs. He'd be going in for surgery because the tip of the blade had nicked a kidney. Dixon's wife sat next to his bed, her eyes red rimmed from crying, and they spoke softly.

Baudin stood next to the bed. He didn't say anything, and neither did his partner. He thought the two of them must've looked like grinning idiots. Baudin reached out and squeezed his shoulder before he turned and limped out of the room.

EPILOGUE

Baudin smoked as Dixon drove.

Several weeks had passed since Dixon got out of the hospital, and he seemed better than ever. Baudin even thought he'd lost weight. He seemed happy and would talk frequently about his "near-death experience" and the peace it brought him, the comfort.

Baudin wished he felt that way. He knew real life wasn't ideal, and taking down Crest had only done so much. Without any proof, Jessop was still captain. The DA was still the DA, and everyone else involved was still out there, still breathing, still hunting. The very acts of their breathing insulted Baudin. But he didn't give up easily. He'd get them, every single one of them. One by one by one. He'd use each one he caught to turn on the others, and then they would start turning on themselves.

But that was a long-term plan.

The car stopped in Dixon's driveway. Inside, all his friends were waiting for them to get there with the beer. The University of Wyoming was playing some other school that was deemed a rival. Baudin hadn't really paid attention when he was invited. But he was glad he was.

Dixon turned the car off in the driveway. "I never said thanks."

"For what?"

"For my freedom."

He snorted. "Shit, man. We just beginning. Before you know it, you'll be talking about explosives planted in the Twin Towers."

"I said freedom, not insanity."

They stepped out of the car. "I don't know how much of a difference this all made. Hey, who's that?"

Dixon looked up and saw where Baudin was looking. He turned and saw the man who was walking quickly toward them. A man in jeans and a baseball cap with something in his hand.

"You Kyle Dixon?"

"Yeah?"

He shoved the papers forward, and Dixon took them. "Consider yourself served." Dixon hesitated a moment and then opened the papers.

"What is it? Court subpoena?"

Dixon was quiet a long time. He looked up suddenly, and his eyes were different, wide and full of fury and tears. He growled like an animal and bounded across the street, the papers fluttering in the road behind him.

"Kyle, what the hell, man? Kyle!"

Baudin jogged after him. As he ran across the street, he saw the caption of one of the documents: LARAMIE COUNTY DISTRICT COURT, MOTION AND ORDER FOR PATERNITY TEST.

"Shit," Baudin said, breaking into a full sprint. "Kyle, stop!"

Dixon had entered the apartment. Baudin rushed after him.

What he saw when he ran inside sent an icy chill up his back.

Chris was on his knees. Dixon had his weapon out, the muzzle pressed firmly against the man's head. Tears rolled down Dixon's cheeks, and his hand was trembling.

"Kyle," Baudin said gently, "give me the gun."

"You motherfucker. You motherfucker!"

"Kyle, wait. Look at me. Look at me!"

"No," he said, shaking his head, "no. Tell me this is a fucking lie. Tell me it's a lie!"

Chris had his eyes closed tightly, his hands behind his head. Baudin took a step forward. The house was quiet, and Baudin wished there was noise somewhere, banging pipes, a dishwasher, anything other than the silence.

"Kyle, don't ever let a man pull you down so low you hate him. Do you hear me? Give me the gun, Kyle. Kyle! Give me the fucking gun!"

Dixon, his hand shaking, wouldn't lower the weapon.

"There's darkness that runs this city, Kyle. It thinks it's invincible. We gonna get 'em, buddy. Me and you. Every last one of 'em. But right now, you need to go home to your wife. Go home, Kyle."

"She loves me," Chris said. "It's my son, Kyle. What would you do, just leave him? He's my son."

"Shut the fuck up," Baudin said.

"He's my son, and she loves me. That's my family."

"Chris, shut up."

"You wouldn't leave them, either," Chris said. "I just did what anyone would do." He looked at Dixon. "He's my so—"

In an instant, the house wasn't quiet.

The pop echoed through the room, through Baudin's head. It seemed to go into his bones and shake him. The blood spattered over the carpet and the couch, and bits of brain matter scattered over the rug, a few droplets of black blood even hitting the wall across the room.

The corpse hit the floor, what seemed like gallons of blood streaming out of the head. Dixon put his hands to his face and wept.

"I fucking shot him, Ethan. I fucking killed him. He said… he said she didn't love me. He said—"

Baudin slowly came up to him and took the weapon. They stared at the body as Dixon continued to cry. Baudin said, "Go home, Kyle."

"What?" he said, looking up. "I have to… I have to talk to her, and… we have to call it in. I… we have to call it in."

"We're not calling shit in. Go home."

The two men glared at each other. Dixon looked to the body and then back to Baudin. "What're you gonna do?"

Baudin said softly, "Go home."

Dixon didn't have sense or reason left. His eyes were vacant. At that moment, Baudin knew he would do anything he told him to do.

"Go home."

Hesitantly, Dixon crossed the living room and left the house.

Baudin ran around quickly and closed all the blinds. Then he searched the house. In the garage, he found tools. He grabbed a hacksaw, a hammer, a chisel, a hatchet and one of the thick metal pipes that lay in a pile on the ground. He brought them inside and then locked all the doors.

Baudin stripped nude, laying his clothes in the kitchen before he grabbed the corpse and wrapped a towel from the bathroom around the wound in the head, trying to prevent any more blood from seeping out. He dragged the corpse into the bathroom and lifted it into the tub. It looked almost like a doll, now, with no appearance of once having been human. The instant the bullet hit the brain, that part of him was gone.

He would cut up the body and then leave at night and bury it somewhere in the desert. All the parts in different locations. He would clean this house with hydrogen peroxide and salt water—bleach wasn't as effective as hydrogen peroxide—and then he would go check on Dixon.

He picked up the hammer and chisel, bent down over the body, and slammed the chisel into the shinbone, breaking it in half. A loud crack echoed in the bathroom.

He inhaled deeply, staring at the blank eyes that gazed up at him from the bathtub, and then pulled the other leg nearer to him.

AUTHOR'S REQUEST

If you enjoyed this book, please leave a review on Amazon. I love hearing from my readers and reviews are great feedback as to what you want to see in future books.

So please leave a review and know that I appreciate each and every one of you!

If you haven't left a review before, simply scroll down to the end of the reviews and find the "Write a customer review" button.

Copyright 2015 Victor Methos

Print Edition

License Statement

This book is licensed for your personal enjoyment only. This book may not be re-sold or given away to other people. If you would like to share this book with another person, please purchase an additional copy for each recipient. If you're reading this book and did not purchase it, or it was not purchased for your use only, then please return to Amazon.com and purchase your own copy.

Please note that this is a work of fiction. Any similarity to persons, living or dead, is purely coincidental. All events in this work are purely from the imagination of the author and are not intended to signify, represent, or reenact any event in actual fact.

Made in United States
Troutdale, OR
11/19/2023

14739626R00179